MANHATTAN TRIPTYCH

Catherine Butterfield

This book is a work of fiction. Names, characters, businesses, organizations, places, events and incidents either are the product of the author's imagination or are used fictitiously. Any resemblance to actual persons, living or dead, events, or locales is entirely coincidental.

Printed in the United States of America.

For more information, or to book an event, contact :

Westerfield Press : 310-612-3516

ISBN - Paperback: 979-8-9992911-0-3

ISBN - Ebook : 979-8-9992911-1-0

First Edition: October 2025

FOR MARILYNN

2025

Ashy white flakes fell softly from the California sky, landing on the redwood deck outside Diane Daly's over-leveraged Craftsman style bungalow. She stared at the slowly accumulating patches of fluffiness, which looked progressively less pristine as they piled up. Other people's memories. Their things. Their lives. From inside her house, she could smell the gaseous cocktail of noxious chemicals from exploding Teslas, decimated office buildings, incinerated household products, mixed in with the cleaner smell of burning wood. It caused her to think of a film she had seen recently about people living next to a Nazi death camp, their home so pleasant and clean, while next to them was unthinkable horror. She turned away from the window.

How to proceed? It seemed wrong to kill oneself under the circumstances. Indeed, the thought, so alluring yesterday, had now taken on the aspect of the absurd. Today, her sluggish blood quickened by the adrenaline of near-disaster, (the fires had come within a block of her home; she had lost power and been evacuated for three days) she felt the need to re-examine the situation. How selfish to take oneself out of the picture when the picture had changed so dramatically.

She thought to present herself at one of the many relief centers cropping up around the city to lend a hand, but when she drove by the one on Sepulveda, there were so many people milling about that she couldn't tell the afflicted from the helpers, and this disturbed her. Surely, with that many people there, they didn't need her. Anyway, she didn't see a parking space.

She went home, and instantly became ashamed of her cowardice. Rummaging through her closets, she pulled out everything that didn't "spark joy," as the lady said, and put the clothing into a couple of bankers boxes she still had left from her move there some thirty years ago. Loading them into her car, she drove down the trendy retail street adjacent to her house, filled with the kind of shops that label a neighborhood "desirable," and saw an empty storefront with a "Fire Relief" sign in the window. A slim young woman in a blonde ponytail and leggings that drew attention to – in fact demanded that you look at -- her ass and vulva seemed to be directing activities in front of the building, before which were stacked some new looking luggage and a rack of ski jackets with their price tags still on them. Through the windows she could see makeshift racks of colorful clothing and items like toasters, hair dryers, and Cuisinarts on shelves, many still in their boxes.

The young woman lifted the top of Diane's banker's box and fingered an item, a lightweight lavender cardigan, hesitantly.

"Is everything in 'Like New' condition? No stains or missing buttons?"

"I — I don't know. No, probably not. You're only taking new items?"

"Or items in perfect condition."

"Why, because some of these people were rich? They have nothing now. I don't think a sweater with a missing button will offend them."

Startled by Diane's bluntness, the young woman smiled a bright, fakey LA smile. "Sorry! We're only taking pristine items," she chirped. "There's a Goodwill on Fifth street, though!" Insulted, Diane decided that on non-cataclysmic days this Barbie was a development girl at a studio, the kind whose sole business was to make sure a script was never seen by anyone else. More abruptly than she intended, Diane snatched the box from her and marched back to her fourteen-year-old Prius C, suddenly ashamed of the scrape on the driver's side and glad that, from her angle, the girl couldn't see it.

Instead of the Goodwill, Diane found herself going down the California incline and onto the Pacific Coast Highway. She was determined not to be a character from that upsetting film, she had to see the disaster for herself. On the short stretch of untouched coastline before the burn area, Diane was newly stunned — it happened every time - by the grandeur of the ocean, so far-reaching and seemingly impervious to civilization's influence (the Texas-sized floating island of plastic between this coast and Hawaii notwithstanding.) The wind had shifted; now the sky and ocean collaborated to produce a vibrant sapphire blue, as if ashamed of their earlier color and trying to atone for it. Or perhaps the lingering chemicals in the air made the blue even more radiant. Or it might have been the microdosing with which Diane had been recently experimenting, which made colors so vivid. At any rate, hard to believe the angry mud-red skies of only yesterday. She turned onto Temescal Canyon Road and soon found herself faced with a police barricade, before which were clustered some fifty people. A dozen uniformed men and women were posted behind the barricade. Some wore the dark navy blue of the LAPD, others the camouflage of the National Guard.

"I have to get in! My dog is still in there!" a young man in coveralls and bandana wailed. "She got away from me, but I know she's there. PLEASE!" The policewoman he had collared drew out her phone. "Give me a description, sir. We will keep an eye out."

"Roxie won't trust you! She has to hear my voice!"

"Sir, I'm sorry. No one gets behind these barricades until we have determined that it is safe." The dog owner crumpled to the ground, dissolving theatrically into loud hiccupping sobs. Diane was embarrassed for him, then felt ashamed that she was embarrassed and tried with some success to convert her embarrassment to compassion.

Nearer to her were two diminutive females, most likely mother and daughter although they looked more like sisters, as mothers and daughters tend to do in Los Angeles. The mother's dermal fillers were not recent, however, and the growth at her scalp revealed a grayish contrast to her honey-streaked hair. She looked exhausted.

"Are you trying to get to your home?" Diane asked gently.

"It's impossible," said the girl in the unfortunate vocal fry of her age group. The flower, bird, and angel tattoos on her baby skin placed her in the 18-25 range. "They said if we came back today, they would let us in for five minutes, but they lied."

"The day's not over," said her mother.

"Mom, wake up. They're not going to let us in. Let's go back to the motel.'

The woman shook off her daughter's words and turned to the presumably more sympathetic Diane. "It's just things, I know. But I have a collection of antique glass figurines that are so beautiful. They belonged to my great-grandmother. If just one of them survived - "

"They melted, Mom. Everything melted."

"Maya, will you PLEASE – " The woman stopped herself, pressed her lips together for patience, shivered. A cool breeze had come up from the ocean. Diane brightened.

"Would you like a sweater? I have a sweater, lots of them, in the car."

"Oh, I don't –"

"Mom, take the sweater, the sun is going down."

Before the woman could respond, Diane ran back to her car and got the box. The woman and girl drifted toward her and Diane proudly displayed the box. "Take whichever one you want!" she declared, then watched as the woman rummaged around and came up with a rose-colored sweater embroidered with flowers at the neckline, which Diane instantly regretted having contributed; it went so well with her gray slacks.

"You sure this is all right?"

"Of course! It's yours!" exclaimed Diane, enjoying the feeling of sudden martyrdom. The woman smiled at her, meeting Diane's gaze in an honest, direct way atypical in Los Angeles. "Thank you. You're very kind."

Trapped in the woman's eyes, Diane suddenly felt like crying. She never cried; she had developed an ability to process emotion years earlier in such a way that crying was not part of the process. Unpleasantly surprised, Diane mumbled something in reply, put the box down on the ground and dashed back to her car.

She drove home quickly, a burgeoning headache beginning to demand her attention, and lay on the first piece of furniture that would receive her recumbent form, her living room sofa. Far too much breathing had gone on down there. She could feel the chemicals circulating through her body.

"I need a Great Escape," she said aloud to the empty room. And the room agreed.

In Boulder, Colorado, Nikki Barone was taking a Yoga class. The view of the leafless aspen trees out the picture windows reminded her of a Chekhov play, which was pleasant to think about during warm up, but as the class went on – it was a Level B, her usual - Nikki thought less of "The Three Sisters" and more of her aching muscles. Looking around, she noticed the relative youth of the other women (and one man) in the class. They didn't seem to be exerting at all, yet she was definitely breathing hard. How puzzling. She hadn't put on any weight, she was still her slim self, so why was it suddenly so hard? Child's pose, the one that is supposed to be the rest position before you do the next thing, was killing her knees. It can't have been that long since she took a class. Doing a mental calculation, Nikki reckoned the last time she had taken this class to be …oh my God, ten years ago. Where had those ten years gone? She looked at the clock. Seeing that there were twenty minutes left, she made the embarrassing decision to roll up her mat and leave the class, before they had to carry her out.

"How was it?" asked the girl at the front desk. "Would you like to sign up for a package? We have a great introductory offer--"

"Oh cool, let me think about it!" Nikki enthused as she escaped the building in shame. Maybe she'd try Zumba.

Sitting in her car in the parking lot, Nikki was reluctant to begin driving. Her dentist appointment wasn't until two, and she didn't feel like wandering through a grocery store when she didn't really need anything. How to kill the time? She gazed at her reflection in the rearview mirror. Her long hair was more than fifty percent gray now, and had gone from straight to frizzy. Did she look frumpy, or cool like Andy MacDowell? Such a thin line.

Lowering the windows for fresh air, she got out her phone and scrolled through Facebook. Apparently, the world was coming to an end. A number of her "friends" who used to be completely oblivious to politics were suddenly in panic mode and urging everyone else to go out and demonstrate. Nikki wondered if they were demonstrating themselves, or just telling everyone else to go. She scrolled down her feed. Orla hadn't posted in a long time, maybe she'd gotten off the site? Nikki missed her old friend Orla, and thought about giving her a call. Instead, she scrolled further. Many of these people were friends for reasons she couldn't remember. Some she hadn't seen since high school. Many came from the world of theatre, which meant they were very good at dramatizing events on stage and less able to grapple with real world events. The only person Nikki knew who was truly political from a young age was Diane, an early feminist, and hadn't she been involved in protests early on? Something about the demolition of theatres in New York? Nikki seemed to remember Diane being very fervent on that subject, and even arguing with Gordon about it one day long ago. Gordon. Where had they been? Nikki dimly remembered cypress trees. She wished she had a clearer memory of her youth which, though filled with volatile incident and floods of tears, in retrospect seemed like one big lark.

Being single again was such a strange thing for Nikki to process. In a way, she supposed she had almost always been single, so the fact that Gordon wasn't around now didn't dramatically change Nikki's life. On the other hand, Nikki had taken great comfort in being part of a couple; it made her feel stronger as she went about everyday life, part of the status quo. She struggled not to be bitter or angry at Gordon for leaving her to her own devices. She certainly wasn't going to date again. This whole world of cyber dating was entirely alien to her. She knew it was how most people met these days, but the idea of putting out personal information about oneself, hoping it appealed to someone who wasn't a serial killer, and then meeting them in some darkened bar (she assumed it would be a darkened bar) was beyond creepy to her. Whatever happened to the good old days, where you saw someone across a crowded room, dialed up your sex appeal and willed them to come to you? Nikki used to be good at that. She looked in the rearview mirror again. Maybe the light had shifted, but her reflection definitely now trended closer to frumpy than Andy MacDowell. And she couldn't quite remember where she had put that sex appeal dial.

The worst part was that no one needed her anymore. Not her husband, obviously. Not her child, who lived in Oregon now. Diane and Orla lived in cities on opposite ends of the country. Diane checked in pretty regularly, but she barely ever heard from Orla anymore. Nikki used to have other friends when they lived in Westchester; PTA moms, a few actresses and neighbors, but moving to Colorado after a traumatic event didn't get her off to a good start in the friendship department. It wasn't until she came out of her haze of depression that she realized she had never wanted to move in the first place, and now all these years later she was the only one there. She didn't even ski, for God's sake. This wasn't how she thought things would go. She thought there would at least be grandchildren. What do I have to show for it all? She wondered. When all is said and done, what did it all add up to?

Oh, well. Maybe it didn't matter what it added up to. Maybe you just put one foot in front of the other. 1:42. Nikki started the car and drove slowly to her dentist's office.

Six months earlier, Orla Nevins negotiated her rather cumbersome body around the stacks of paper on the floor of her New York apartment and wandered into the bathroom, humming a tuneless tune. She urinated to the tune of the non-tune, pulled up her puppy imprinted flannel pajama pants, and stood to face her morning reflection in the ornate gilt mirror, which had always been and would always be a bit too high.

The first thing she noticed, rather than her own face, was the water pipe behind her, which seemed to have an enormous horsefly upon it. Orla froze. She had never seen a horsefly that large, and was too unnerved to turn and look at it directly. As an evasion, she finally focused on her own face, which seemed this morning to have rearranged its features in a rather frightening way, like a Picasso painting. Was her right eye, the blue one, always this much lower? Unsure of the answer, she gathered her courage and turned to examine the water pipe directly.

It was a splotch of black paint. Nothing demonic, just paint. Orla sighed in relief. And now, she remembered that the splotch had been there yesterday as well, and most likely every day for the forty-one years that she had lived in the apartment. Feeling more confident, she again took up the mirror and was relieved to see that her features had resolved themselves into a more symmetrical pattern. Orla smiled. Another beautiful day had begun.

"Harvey!" she called out. "Better get up, it's almost nine!"

Harvey mumbled something. Or maybe he just groaned? She went to her fridge and pulled out a tin of dog food for Homer, her Maltese, the dearest and nearest creature to her heart, the center of her universe now that poor Trixie had left this earthly plane. Orla watched Homer eat, taking delight in his delicate little bites. Swamy Deshpande was right; she had needed to bring a new living thing into her apartment. How prescient he was! Homer's life force kept Orla alert; it gave her purpose. She rummaged through the tall stack of the Sunjay's writings beside her bed and came up with the prediction for this week. "You will find happiness and fulfillment in the act of giving, a joy unlike any you have ever known."

Wow! That was incredibly insightful, and reminded her a bit of the prediction she received from him last week, which turned out to be absolutely true. The man could see into her heart in the most miraculous way. And such a warm and lovely voice he had.

Orla rummaged through her desk, found her stacks of checkbooks from various banks, and wrote him a donation. She slipped it into an envelope and changed into her all-black work attire.

Black is a good color. You can spill on it and people won't notice. It makes you look thinner, that's what Nikki says. Orla felt less vulnerable in black. What was it Diane had said that time at Bloomingdales? "I could rule the world in this little black dress!" Looking fabulous, she struck a pose before all three mirrors and in that moment, Orla believed it. Diane was so strong. Well, she seemed strong, sometimes. Other times…

There was something she meant to do, something Swamy Sunjay had told her was important, and he was quite emphatic about it. Oh golly, what was it? Yesterday had been such a strange day that she was having a hard time accessing the memory. It was about money. She was supposed to call someone, who was it? It was annoying to Orla when little things slipped her mind, but she didn't worry about it because she still did the New York Times crossword puzzle. Maybe not Sunday anymore - who has the time for that? But definitely the earlier days. Monday, for sure.

"Harvey! I'm going to work. Don't sleep all day, please!" Yes, definitely a stir from the bed. Or -- *was* that Harvey? No, it was Homer, finished with his meal now and wanting attention, his little pleading paws up in the air, manipulating the air like he was nursing it, hoping to draw milk. Oh, that's right, Harvey didn't spend the night. Harvey was uptown. He was safely uptown. He was fine in his own apartment, although he was very touchy lately. It was good Harvey wasn't here, actually. She didn't want to get into an early morning argument with him, she had so much to do and people relied on her. It was good. All was good.

Orla packed Homer into his little travelling case, grabbed her big leather bag, and left the apartment.

Two days after her yoga class, Nikki was still trying to recover. Lying on her couch watching a Hallmark Christmas movie (even though Christmas was a month past) took her mind off her aches, as did vodka tonics. She wouldn't mind if they ran Christmas movies all year long; they were so comforting with their identical plots, generic dialogue, and optimistic endings. She was pouring herself another glass when her phone rang, and an unflattering version of Diane's face popped up. Nikki always wondered at the pictures people chose to use as their ID's. She assumed they reflected how they wanted to be seen by others. Apparently, Diane wanted to be seen as severe and slightly depressed. Or maybe she didn't realize this huge picture of her is what everyone saw when they answered her calls. Somewhat regretfully, Nikki paused the film.

"Are the fires out?"

In Santa Monica, Diane was examining the moldy contents of her refrigerator, which had lost power for two days. "Just about. I know twelve people so far who have lost their homes."

"Damn! And it came so close to you. Are you still in the motel?"

"No, home now. Place is okay, but the neighborhood smells like a dry cleaner. I would have been so screwed if this place went down. It's mortgaged to the hilt."

"I should have called earlier, but I've been so busy," responded Nikki. What a lie. She wasn't busy. She was nothing.

"Do I hear the tinkle of ice?"

"Uh, yeah. I'm drinking iced tea." "Iced tea" came out kind of slurry, though.

"Go easy on that stuff, will you?"

"I reserve the right to drink myself in a stupor if I want to. As is your right as well."

"Thanks."

"Wasn't Gordon's memorial beautiful?"

"Yes, it was." The memorial was almost a year ago. Nikki was definitely drunk.

"Better late than never, right? I wish there had been more people. He knew a lot of people, but you know, lag time. People have other things to do, other people to grieve."

Diane simply could not go down this road again. "Yeah, but it was great. Listen, have you heard from Orla?"

"Oh God, no, I really should call her, too. It's been forever, but I've just had so many other things on my mind." What things? Nikki thought. Name a thing.

"I've been trying to get hold of her. I'm in need of a Great Escape."

"She's running the travel agency by herself now, you know. Her creepy partner Isaac finally quit and left the whole thing in her hands."

"Really? When was this?"

"I think she told me at the memorial. Or maybe before, I don't know. Time just blends together, doesn't it? I do remember she sounded pretty overwhelmed."

Diane remembered now that Orla's trip to Colorado had been very short, and that she and Diane hadn't talked much at Gordon's memorial, which was odd for Orla but a self-defense tactic for Diane. Orla was so deeply empathic that just looking into her eyes could make a person burst into tears, and Diane didn't want to do that.

"Shit. I didn't know. Isaac was a jerk, but at least he did the books."

Nikki could hear the weary edge in her friend's voice. "You know, Di, if you need an escape why don't you come here? We can take long beautiful trail walks, star-gaze, maybe go to a museum."

"Oh honey. A red state is really not what I need right now."

"Colorado's not red, we're blue."

"Oh. Why did I think you were red?"

Nikki felt a sudden surge of guilt. Did Diane suspect how she had voted recently? She did it out of loyalty to Gordon, and because she thought it could do no harm. No one would ever know, right? Ballots were secret. But then why was she suddenly being inundated by email from the Republican party?

Eager to change the subject, she said, "You know what? I just realized the other day it's forty years now since we did "Fiddler." Can you believe that?"

Diane sighed. "Sometimes it feels like eighty."

Nikki was not accustomed to the resigned tone of Diane's voice and suddenly felt like the stronger of the two, which was an unusual and pleasant feeling. "You okay, honey? Tell me what I can do for you."

"Nothing. This is one of those times when you just have to put one foot in front of another." Nikki deeply understood this sentiment and, buoyed by Diane's depression, was newly filled with a sense of purpose.

"I'll get hold of Orla today, I promise. How did you reach out? Email?"

"Emailed, texted, called. Nothing. And I never had any contact information for Harvey, did you?"

"No. I'm amazed that relationship has lasted this long."

"Orly probably lost her phone. You know how she can be."

"I'm sure it's nothing to worry about. Why don't you go get a massage or something? Leave this to me."

After she hung up, Nikki toyed with the idea of putting the Christmas movie back on, but her sudden sense of mission stayed her hand on both the remote and the Vodka bottle. Orla and she had had their ups and downs, but she was one of Nikki's oldest and dearest friends, and had been there for her during some very tough times. If something bad was going on, Nikki wanted to know about it.

She put the Vodka back in the freezer and got her laptop out to do some investigating.

1985 – Forty Years Earlier

The three young actresses playing Tevye's daughters in "Fiddler on the Roof" were sharing a getting-to-know-you joint outside the actors' housing. It was a large greyish-white clapboard house with a pleasant front yard that faced a wide street, quite a change from New York City. A maple tree dappled dancing patches of sunlight onto the three lovelies as they sat companionably on the steps leading to the house. Diane, the tallest of the three, was not normally a pot smoker, but sensed it was an important communal act and so took a couple of rather deep inhalations, one of which ended in a coughing fit.

"You don't have to inhale that deeply," said Orla. "Just take sips, and you won't hurt your voice."

"Yeah, I know," replied Diane, who didn't.

"I think this is gonna be fun, don't you?" said Nikki. "The music is so beautiful."

"The way you sing your ballad, Nikki," said Orla. "It makes me want to cry."

"Thanks! You're both from the city, right? Where do you live?"

"Upper West Side," said Orla, who Diane was starting to see as a kind of pixie or Peter Pan type, with her little body and spiky hair. She envisioned Orla levitating right in front of her, and laughed aloud. Orla interpreted this as Diane thinking the Upper West Side was a funny place to live, and giggled with her.

Nikki, who was pulling her shiny, bone-straight black hair into a ponytail, reminded Diane of Barbara Hershey. Or rather Barbara Seagull. Diane remembered that actress announcing that she'd taken a new name because she saw a seagull die on the set of a film she was making and absorbed its spirit. How did that happen? Was she high at the time? Was she still a seagull now that filming was over, or had she gone back to being human?

"How about you, Diane?"

"Huh?"

"Where do you live?"

"Oh. The Village. But I'm getting kicked out soon. It's a sublet."

"Oh, too bad! I love the Village," cooed Orla.

"I'm on the East side," volunteered Nikki. "Which is weird for an actor, I know, but my parents want me there, they say it's safer."

"Where does your family live?"

"Jersey," replied Nikki, who had the accent to prove it.

"They're probably hoping you'll meet a lawyer. Or a doctor."

"Or a security guard," offered Diane.

Nikki laughed. "A security guard! You are so funny, Diane!" Diane felt confused, as she did not mean this as a joke. "This show came up at the perfect time for me, I was running out of money and my parents were like 'Give it up, Nikki. Come home.' But I want to do this! I believe I can."

"Me, too," said Diane, running her hands through her thick wavy auburn locks and wishing it was straight like Nikki's. Why was hair so important? What is it about hair, anyway, why does it just keep coming out and out of your body? Is it true that it keeps growing after you die?

"This is good weed," commented Nikki. "Where did you get it, Orla?"

"A guy I met in Turkey. He was so sweet. Everyone told me you couldn't get to Turkey from Greece, but he heard I was looking and offered a lift on his sailboat."

"Cool. Turkey and Greece." Nikki turned to look at Diane, who was examining a strand of her hair with interest. "You look so familiar, Diane. Were you at the open call for "Grease?"

"Greece?"

"Grease. The musical."

"Oh!" Diane laughed. "Yeah. I got a callback for Marty."

"No kidding!"

"But I didn't get it, obviously. Summer stock in Indiana, or Broadway. Which shall I choose?"

"At least we're working."

"True." In fact, this was Diane's first paid acting job, and though she desperately wanted to keep that fact from the others, another (stoned) part of her wanted to blurt it out. A "late bloomer," was the way her mother had described Diane, to make her feel better about being the last of her friends to menstruate. She was also late to college due to financial reversals after her father's untimely death, and the last in her class to start earning money as an actress, although she did plenty of unpaid showcases in the city. This job had been a big surprise for her, as her main goal in life was to perform in the classics. But she could sing, and singers were what they seemed to need these days. Thus, 'Fiddler.'

A spring breeze sent pollen whirling through the beams of sunlight, mesmerizing the three of them for a moment, or perhaps an hour. Orla finally stood up and stretched. There wasn't much to stretch, but her limberness was impressive.

"I was on Broadway once," she said casually.

The other two looked at her with new respect. "You were?"

"I played Pepper, one of the orphans in 'Annie,' for six weeks."

"Why only six weeks?"

"I was the understudy. The girl they cast had to have her tonsils out."

"Was it totally great?"

"I guess so. My mom was really happy."

"Tell us! That must have been a huge audience. What was your biggest memory of the whole thing?"

"Well, um…. One of the men in the ensemble showed me his penis."

"WHAT?"

"We were just standing in the wings, and he said, 'Hey, look at this."

"That's horrible!" gasped Nikki. "What did you do?"

"I looked at it. Then we went on stage."

"Did you tell your mother?"

"After the second or third time, yeah."

"Omigod. What did she do?"

"She said, 'The next time he does that, ask why it's so small."

"That was her response?"

"Uh-huh. So, I asked him why his penis was so small, and he quickly put it away and never did it again. I saw my mother on the other side of the stage - she had snuck out from the green room to watch - and she was laughing so hard."

"She thought it was *funny*?"

"Yeah. It is kind of funny, I guess. I mean, thinking about it now, it's funny, right?"

"No! It's horrible!" But Nikki exploded into a laugh, and Orla laughed with her, and Diane really wished she hadn't smoked that joint.

"But… You must have been, what? Ten? Twelve?"

"Fourteen. I was small for my age, that's why they cast me."

Diane, searching for a way into their hilarity, finally came up with, "Well, at least your mother had a good time." Which caused an outburst of laughter from Orla and, in a strange way, cemented their friendship.

Will, the athletically handsome actor playing Perchik, threw the front door of the house open dramatically. "God! The provinces. Have you ever had such terrible food?" They admitted it was pretty bad, and Orla told him about a pizzeria on 3rd. He shouted into the house. "Michael! There's a pizzeria on 3rd, I'm going!" The girls watched him stride across the yard in his cut-off shorts and tight tank top, open the gate of the white picket fence, turn and shout again at the house, "Michael!" A voice from within the house responded, "I'm coming!" There was a pause, then Michael, the angel-faced boy playing Fyedke, burst out of the house and sprinted over to join Will. He stopped at the gate and turned to the girls.

"You all want us to bring you back pizza?"

"Yes! We're starving!" said Diane. "Thanks Michael." He gave them a salute and ran to catch up with Will. "Michael's so sweet and polite. Home town boy, right?"

"Yep, said Orla. "Local hire."

"I think Will might be gay. Those shorts."

"He is definitely gay. He kisses like I'm his mother," replied Nikki.

"Is Michael gay?"

"They're all gay," said Orla with authority. "The rabbi, Lazar Wolf. Even Tevye."

"Paul is gay? Oh no!" wailed Nikki. "He was going to be my showmance."

"Paul? He's got to be forty! "

"Uh-huh, he's just thirty-seven, I heard him say."

"Which means he's forty! And he's playing our father!"

"Well, and he's gay, according to Orla. I would say that's the biggest obstacle."

"At least no one will be showing us their penises," commented Diane.

"But we want penises now!" wailed Nikki, which caused a woman walking her dog to turn and look at them, and doubled their hilarity. They were at the age where anything regarding sex caused them to dissolve into fits of overstimulated laughter.

Nikki wondered which one of the other two girls she should befriend. She came from a family of three girls, which led her to believe that they couldn't all be friends. In her experience as the youngest child, one girl was always the outsider and it was often her. Therefore, she knew she must choose one and do it quickly. Diane was tall and carried herself with some elegance, which Nikki respected. She seemed smart and said funny things, always a plus in a friend. On the other hand, the combination of Orla's diminutive size and apparent feistiness made her very appealing. She also seemed a bit worldly and obviously had a leg up on both Nikki and Diane professionally. Nikki's ambitions included meeting people who could introduce her to other more important people in the business. The clock was ticking, as her parents had told Nikki that if she didn't "make it" by the time she was thirty, they would stop supporting her and insist she come home. Therefore, possibly Orla. Then again, there was something disconcerting about Orla. One blue eye and one brown eye, for one thing; was she wrong to let that throw her off balance?

Diane considered the other two and thought about the acting training at her "highly accredited drama school." She firmly believed that in order to play the role of a sister to two other girls on stage she must believe in them as sisters offstage. She didn't need to like them, but she wanted to find a way to love them the way sisters loved each other, which always involved a little hate. She was playing Tzeitel, the oldest sister, so she knew she had to be the dominant force in their friendship, which felt comfortable to her. She towered over Orla, so presumably no problem there. Nikki might be a bit more of a challenge as she seemed to possess an air of entitlement alien to Diane, who felt like she had to fight for everything she got. It would be interesting to see how the dynamic unfolded, and she intended to write Helene, her drama teacher, about her progress. Yes, it was a musical and it was not Chekhov, for which Helene thought she was more suited. But it was work, and Diane was determined to take it seriously. This meant it would be in her best interests to form a relationship with each of them.

As for Orla, she thought Diane and Nikki were both wonderful and couldn't wait for them all to become friends.

Rehearsals were whirlwind and done in broad strokes. Basically, the director was just following the template for the Broadway production, so there wasn't much innovation required. The Matchmaker scene was fun to rehearse, because the girls had to slide their mops toward one another during the course of the song and catch them on time. It was a little tricky, but soon they managed to do it with relative ease.

Diane, however, took these things very seriously. Before rehearsals started, she had read Sholom Aleichem's book, "Tevye's Daughters," upon which the musical was based, and found she had some opinions which needed to be expressed.

"I've been thinking about Tzeitel and her place in society," she announced to the director, bringing rehearsal to a screeching halt. Frank Collins was a fifty-year-old drama teacher at the local college who supplemented his income by directing summer stock. He was overwhelmed by his rambunctious, largely New York cast and seriously concerned the show would be a disaster. All he wanted was for rehearsals to move forward quickly.

"Okay," Frank replied cautiously.

"Women were so oppressed in the *shtetl*, even if they themselves didn't realize it. But I think Tzeitel does realize it. I mean, she's the first to break with the societal rules, right? By refusing to marry Lazar Wolf. And Motel isn't even part of their *meshuggah*."

"Their *what*?" Paul, the actor playing Tevye, almost spit out his coffee. He was stretched out in his seat in the audience along with a few other actors waiting for their scenes.

"*Meshuggah*? Family network."

"Darling. *Mishpacha*. *Meshuggha* means crazy. Are you not Jewish?"

"Uh, no."

"Well, let's give the girl a hand for learning a little Yiddish!" The others laughed and applauded.

Diane blushed and, to cover her embarrassment, gave a little curtsey, and soldiered on. "What I'm saying is, I think Tzeitel was an early feminist in some ways. So in this song, I think there's a bit of anarchy there. I mean, think about it. She's been in love with Motel ever since she was a child, but here she is singing a song hoping the Matchmaker will put her with someone else."

"I'm not sure that's what she's doing," said Nikki. "She's probably hoping Yente knows she's in love with Motel, and will designate him as her perfect match."

"Maybe," said Diane. "But I think there's every chance she'd sing this song ironically. Maybe Hodel and Chava would, too. Maybe we understand on some level that we are victims of the patriarchy, and the three of us are rebelling in our own little way by sliding our mops back and forth to each other. It's like, who cares which guy we get, or if we both get the same guy? They're interchangeable."

"Okay," Nikki shrugged.

"So shall we try it?"

"Try what?"

"Doing it that way."

"Sliding our mops ironically?"

"Why not?"

"Sure!" said Orla, always game.

Frank tried to disguise the almost desperate impatience he was feeling. "Okay, let's take it again!" The music started. The girls started sliding their mops more and more forcefully, with strange little flourishes. Nikki wiggled her eyebrows, which caused Orla to laugh and drop her mop, but she made an emergency rescue and tossed it back. Then Diane started to laugh and pretty soon they were all giggle-singing. The director signaled the music to stop.

"What seems to be the problem?" sighed Frank.

"Sorry!" they said in unison.

"I wasn't being ironic enough," offered Orla.

"Yeah, that was more like sarcastic mop throwing, Orla," Diane teased.

"I thought the whole thing was *meshuga*," Nikki said, which triggered a new wave of laughter from Paul and the cast. Diane was a bit miffed that Nikki got that payoff line; after all, Nikki wasn't Jewish, either. Frank, sensing yet again that he was losing control, decided to move on to the next number, which was Tevye's.

As it turned out, Paul was not entirely gay. At any rate, he was susceptible to the flirtations of women. His full name was Paul Parnes. He was handsome in a Leonard Bernstein kind of way and, much like Bernstein, he had charisma to burn. Largely due to the dearth of other options, by the end of a couple of weeks both Diane and Nikki were in love with him. (They were in their twenties, and it was summer stock; they had to be in love with *someone*.) Diane didn't think they had a shot because, even offstage, Paul treated them with a kind of lofty parental indulgence. "My goyish daughters!" he would exclaim at the bar, which maybe wasn't true because Orla said her mother told her once she could be half-Jewish. Then he would gather them into a hug (weighted equally amongst the three of them,) release them with a kiss atop each head and move toward the largest table to hold court, because the men loved him, too. Paul told hilarious tales of previous productions he had been in, theatre luminaries he had worked with, even a film he had shot but had been largely edited out of. Every night, the girls would grab their drinks, drift over to the table and be as much in thrall to his stories as anyone else. A Jewish pied piper.

One night, Nikki came into the bar a bit later than Diane and Orla, and Paul said, "Ah, here she is, my beautiful Greek Hodel. Golde, who have you been *schtupping* to produce such a child?"

Doris Schmidt, the actress playing Golde, struck a coy pose. "Wouldn't you like to know, Tevye, dear?" Everyone laughed, but Diane frowned at the "beautiful."

All of Paul's stories were amusing and, though often at his own expense, still managed to bolster his image in their eyes. His laugh was huge and infectious, he exuded bonhomie wherever he went. As a result, rehearsals were a joy. It was Paul who formed the cast into a cohesive whole, which was needed because Frank was definitely not a people person. Paul seemed to do best in groups;

he needed an audience. After rehearsal, he often tended to slip away and head straight for his rooms, ostensibly to learn his lines but, as he'd done the show before, this seemed unlikely. Diane desperately wished he weren't so elusive.

Opening night was a huge success. It was Indiana; no one cared (or even noticed) that so many of the cast weren't Jewish, or that some of the singing wasn't of the highest caliber. This heartwarming story of a Jewish shtetl in 1905 Russia, shorn of much of the hatred and brutality of the time but with just enough to raise a tear, appealed deeply to the local audience. The love stories were eternal and beautiful, the music stirred the soul, and anyway it had been a Broadway hit. Everyone was anxious to have a ticket to the Broadway hit they would never get to New York to see. So, the audience went home happy, and the cast retired to the bar to celebrate a job well done.

Diane was wearing a black spangly off-the-shoulder number she had bought expressly for opening night, which made her feel like Liza Minelli in Cabaret. She danced with Orla, Will, Young Michael (they all called him that even though he was only two years younger than the youngest of them) and Stewart, the actor playing Motel who didn't interest her at all but at least was straight. Young Michael was in high spirits. With the encouragement of Will and

Paul, he had made the big decision to move to New York. They all cheered and toasted the home town boy.

"To Young Michael! Next stop, Broadway!" Young Michael beamed with delight. Diane flirted with the bartender, got a little tipsy and then announced she was going back to her room.

"So soon?"

"We have a show tomorrow."

"Oh, don't be a party poop!" shouted Will, tugging her hand.

"I am a party poop! I'm old, old, old!" Diane shouted back.

"You're a Dianasaur!" laughed Orla, and they all giddily hugged her goodnight.

The next morning Diane woke up and discovered that Nikki was not in her bed, that she had not been all night. She got up and knocked on the door of the room next to hers, which Orla shared with Doris. Orla opened the door, looking bleary-eyed and spiky-haired. "Nikki didn't come home last night!" Diane stage-whispered in alarm.

Orla raised her eyebrows. "Really?"

"Ahh," said Doris, nodding knowingly. She was sitting at the open window filing her nails.

"What does that mean?" demanded Diane.

"Just Ahh," responded Doris. This wasn't her first time doing Fiddler, either.

A few minutes later, the screen door downstairs could be heard to squeak open and closed, followed by the very light footfall of someone trying to sneak upstairs as quietly as possible. Nikki rounded the corner and stopped short, confronted by the sight of Diane and Orla standing in the hallway. Nikki's hair was rumpled, and her make-up smeared. Her feet were bare and she was holding her boots, one of which was missing a heel.

"What are you guys doing up?"

"Oh. My. God. You were with Paul, weren't you?" said Orla, which shocked Diane; she never would have guessed such a thing.

Nikki blushed brightly. "Please, don't tell anyone!" Her face was red with shame and — was that victory? Nikki rushed past them and into her room. Orla giggled and started to sing.

"Matchmaker, Matchmaker, make me a--"

"Shut up, Orla!" snapped Diane, stunning Orla into silence. Diane followed Nikki back into their room and stood with folded arms as Nikki grabbed up things to take a shower.

"Really? You were with Paul?"

"Shh, Diane, not so loud!" Nikki looked both embarrassed and pleased with herself, which enraged Diane further. "I don't know how it happened. We stayed late at the bar, and I got awfully drunk. Paul and Young Michael and I were the only ones left, and Paul said let's go upstairs. Did you know he's got a whole apartment over the bar? It's kind of amazing. It has a pinball machine."

"So? Then what happened?"

"So, the three of us went up, and one thing led to another-"

"Wait. The three of you? What did you do?"

"I'm not sure. At one point it was Paul and me, and then it was Paul and Michael. I think it was mostly Paul and Michael."

"Oh my God!"

"Don't! I feel gross enough. Look, I broke my new boot." As if this were the ultimate punishment, Nikki grabbed her shower things and ran down to the shared bathroom.

Diane suddenly hated Nikki violently. It was bad enough that Nikki seemed to have independent means and didn't have to take any of the shitty jobs Diane was forced to take in the city. It was bad enough Nikki was so beautiful. But to be the favorite of Paul? Diane knew she was being irrational. She knew that, in any other circumstance, she would have easily been drawn to someone younger and more hetero for her summer romance. But in the rarified atmosphere of this particular production Paul was the holy grail.

The next night, when they did their Matchmaker number on stage, Diane slid her mop in an off-target way so that Nikki could barely catch it. The next night, Diane missed her entirely, and Nikki had to scurry to the floor to pick it up.

"Diane, what the hell? You did it again tonight."

"Sorry."

Orla was on Nikki's side. "Stop being so bitchy, Diane. You're totally over-reacting." This rebuke from Orla stung, but did nothing to diminish Diane's anger. Walking back to her room after the show, she saw Doris up ahead and caught up with her.

"Hey, girlie," said Doris. "Calling it an early night, huh?"

"Yeah. You too?"

"Believe me, I used to be able to party all night and still do two shows the next day. But yeah. These days, I need my beauty sleep."

"Doris, if Orla says it's okay, can I move in with you?"

Doris glanced at her sideways. "You kids still fighting, huh?"

"I just don't feel comfortable with Nikki anymore."

"You snore?"

"I don't think so."

"Then okay. But you girls should make it up. Paul's a charmer but take it from me, fighting over him is not where you should put your energy."

So, Diane moved in with Doris and, though she was deeply uncomfortable with all this conflict, Orla acquiesced and moved in with Nikki.

The company became aware of the tension amongst "the sisters," and although a number of them laughed it off as just another cat fight, it turned out to be a bit contagious. Before long, a certain bitchy element had seeped into the cast dynamic. The younger actors started to find fault with the actor playing Lazar Wolf's personal hygiene, and one of them left a bar of Mum's deodorant on his dressing room table. Lazar Wolf, (whose real name was Doug, but no one ever seemed to remember that,) sabotaged one of the bottle dancers by hiding his bottle just before he went on stage. The poor guy had to do his dance with nothing on his head, leading to many accusations later in that dressing room.

Paul, the team leader, could see this was getting out of hand. The following night as the bar was getting ready to close, Paul made his way over to Diane and placed his hand on her shoulder.

"Darling, come upstairs with me, won't you?" Surprised and thrilled, Diane followed him up the spiral staircase, breathlessly expecting some kind of Valhalla to reveal itself.

He had the entire floor above the bar, but it looked more like a storage room than an apartment, filled with furniture from past productions. The walls were covered with programs from previous shows – "Barefoot in the Park," "Man of La Mancha," "The Music Man," etc. There was a white bear rug thrown over a Cleopatra chaise, and a Bally pinball machine offering a game called "Delta Queen" in one corner of the room, but on the whole, it was nowhere near as impressive as Diane expected. In the other corner of the room was a bed, where Diane supposed the nefarious activities amongst Paul and Nikki (and Young Michael) took place, but disappointingly Paul led Diane over to the large stained sofa by the pinball machine and pulled her down to sit next to him.

"You're a bit of a dark horse, aren't you, darling? I didn't know what to make of you at first, but it's becoming clear to me that you are one of those people who tends to affect the direction of things without seeming to do anything. Perhaps you don't even know you're doing it."

If this was a form of seduction, it was new to Diane, but she was ready to go with it. Paul ran his fingers through her hair and Diane shivered slightly in anticipation.

"God, you have beautiful hair. What I wouldn't give to have thick, wavy hair like this." As he said this, Diane noticed for the first time the bald spot forming on the top of his head. "I love doing this show. I've done it five times and I will probably keep doing it five or six more. It's a story of love, of community, of suffering, of following your heart. It's the Jewish experience, darling, which I know you are doing your best to approximate, and kudos to you method actors, you're very sweet, but some things are beyond your ken. What's more, when this show is over, none of this will mean anything to you. You will move onto the next thing, as you should, and you will never see me again." Diane started to protest. "No, darling, it's true, I will go out of your lives. But you three sisters, you're going to be friends from now on."

This was not the direction Diane was hoping the conversation would take and she pouted. "I seriously doubt it."

"Oh, you will," he said, pushing a tendril of hair away from her face. "You, Hodel, Chava." Diane wondered if he'd forgotten Nikki and Orla's names — how embarrassing for Nikki! — followed by the thought that he might not even know hers. "Darling, in all the productions of Fiddler I've done, it's always the same. When it's over, the men go their separate ways, but the women bond. I really wouldn't want to get in the way of that beautiful experience for you three; it's hard on the rest of us. Do you understand what I'm saying?" Diane nodded, not entirely sure that she did. "Good. You're a lovely girl, darling. That hair! May I kiss you?" Diane nodded again, and Paul kissed her on the lips. It wasn't much of a kiss; in fact, it was rather terrible as his breath reeked of the Marlboros that he chain-smoked. He drew back and looked at her meaningfully.

"Go, darling," he said. "Live your beautiful *shiksa* life."

The next morning, Diane went to Nikki and apologized. They kept the rooming situation the way it was, but the crisis of friendship was over.

2023

Sunjay Despande took a cold hard look at his website. "I provide predictions in astrology and management of your astral future. My services include scientific analysis, diagnosis, and permanent solutions for your problems."

What was missing? Sunjay scrolled through the websites of some of the other astrologers in Mumbai and found one he admired from a man who called himself Dr. Harif. It had great pictures! Pictures of the planets, astrological symbols, leather bound books, a Victorian looking compass, gemstones, even a shot of the good doctor himself, in sunglasses and a pink Nehru jacket, smiling broadly and looking a bit like Ringo Starr. Clearly, Dr. Harif had paid someone to make this website. He offered not only astrology but numerology, palmistry and the reading of gems, with compelling pictures to depict each discipline. What a successful man he must be! Sunjay briefly considered attaching the title "Dr." to his own name. Doctor Sunjay Deshpande. No. It sounded too intimidating. A man like Dr. Harif would appeal to, say, a businessman wanting to know where to put his money. Sunjay suspected his success would lie with women. Swamy? Swamy sounded nice.

He scrolled to another website. This fellow claimed to be "the only man to have perfected the art of Manopravesha, a form of telepathy." Sunjay googled Manopravesha and found the word existed nowhere else on the internet. The man had made it up, but what a compelling word! Sunjay didn't judge him for it. "A kind soul full of compassion and good will." This sounded like the sort of man a woman could trust. He stole the phrase for his own website.

Now about the picture. Sunjay was sure that any photo taken of him, from whatever angle, would not win him any customers. He stood to look at himself in the mirror, banging his head on the dormered ceiling of his rooftop apartment for the umpteenth time. Though he possessed a full head of hair, he was the unfortunate bearer of an enormous pockmarked nose, yellowed teeth and small, deeply set eyes. His biggest asset, a mellifluous voice, was not something that translated well on a webpage.

Sunjay rummaged through his mementos and came up with a photo he had saved for many years, that of his high school teacher Mr. Bhandari. Sunjay had ripped it from the school album that was sitting on the principal's desk while the principal was out of the room. Mr. Bhandari was the only teacher who had ever been kind to him. Sunjay remembers vividly the day Mr. Bhandari placed his hand on Sunjay's head and said, "Well done, boy." The thrill that ran through him at that moment! He wanted - he *needed* to have the photo to remember him. No one would notice he'd ripped out a page, and even if they did there would be no repercussions; he was about to be expelled, anyway.

Sunjay examined the photo closely. Straight white teeth that gleamed perfection. Large lucid eyes, an intelligent gaze. A prominent but unblemished nose. Yes. This is a face women would admire. Sunjay remembered seeing Mr. Bhandari with his wife, a delicate woman in a powder blue sari, at a school assembly honoring Mr. Bhandari as Teacher of the Year. She stood beside her husband shyly, holding his hand. When they said Mr. Bhandari's name, she gazed up at him adoringly and released his hand as if releasing a dove to glory, a gesture which seemed to propel him up to the podium. She clapped fervently as he received his award, an embossed piece of paper, and laughed when he made a not very good joke. Sunjay envisioned her carefully placing that piece of paper in a frame, a frame she had bought – or no, perhaps she had made the frame especially the moment she heard about the honor. Such was the power of Mr. Bhandari to inspire love.

Sunjay scanned the photo and placed it onto his website. There was nothing to suggest that the picture was twenty-five years old except that it was in black and white, but the man who knew Manopravesha had a black and white picture, so Sunjay found it acceptable. Gazing at Mr. Bhandari's picture on his page, Sunjay was charged with feelings of hope and purpose. A man like this deserved a better website, and Sunjay would do everything he could to provide it for him . With a website that was as excellent as Mr. Bhandari, he knew he could attract the kind of women who could change his miserable life forever.

2025

Email from Trevor Guildford to Nikki Barone.

"Hi, Nikki.

Sorry, your email went to spam for a few days but thankfully I just came across it. Of course I remember you! Sounds like you didn't know, the Great Escape travel agency closed this past July. The business had been losing steam since before Isaac Ford left. The pandemic hit us very hard, even with the PPP loans from the government. Post-pandemic there was really no way for Orla to get it back on its feet, especially after Isaac left her holding the bag. Additionally, I hate to say this but there were some irregularities about Orla that came to light. I believe she was the victim of fraud, for one thing, she was giving away a great deal of personal money to dubious causes. She also stopped paying her employees, which was the final straw for the others, who all quit on the same day. It was just Orla and me toward the end, and finally there was no alternative but to shutter the agency.

I hate to be the bearer of bad news. I'm sorry to say I don't know where Orla is now. I called some of the other former employees and they don't know, either. If you do make contact with her, please give her my best. She's such a sweet lady."

Nikki forwarded this email to Diane, who immediately called her.

"Fraud? Okay, this is weird. I don't have a number for Harvey, do you?"

"No. He's the kind of guy who wouldn't have a number. You probably have to put a note in a bottle and throw it into the sea. Anyway, didn't they break up again?"

"No, he was back in her life. I think."

"Funny that with all her fabulous lovers, she ended up with Harvey."

"I think one of us needs to go to New York."

"What? It's brutally cold there right now."

"Nikki, Orla is missing, and there's no one else we can ask about it. She has no other family that I know about. You and I haven't been much good to her lately."

There was a pause while they both felt a bit guilty.

"Yeah, one of us should go to New York. We've got to figure out what's going on."

1985

Diane, Orla and Nikki got off the subway at 42nd Street on a brisk October day. They'd been back from Indiana for two months, and Diane was indeed being kicked out of her sublet. Orla, who Diane discovered to be a very resourceful person, had found this listing in the paper. But the closer the three of them got to Eighth Avenue, the slower they walked.

"I don't know about this, Orly," said Diane. "Pretty sleazy area."

"It's not so bad. They say midtown is coming up."

"My mother would kill me if I lived in this neighborhood," offered Nikki unhelpfully.

They passed the huge marquis for Show World, ("Live Sex Acts!") with its peep booths and sex toys and God knows what all that went on there. They passed Ultima Cigars and a few porn theatres ("The Filthiest Show in Town!") They saw a number of drug deals taking place. And the trash! Didn't Mayor Koch promise to do something about all this? But Diane was desperate, and two-hundred and fifty a month was a seductively low price.

They turned the corner and walked toward 45th street. Though it was a frigid day, a bare-legged young Latina girl in a furry tube top, red crushed velvet hot pants and platform heels strolled the block. "Hi!" smiled Orla, and the girl cut her eyes at her. Diane consulted the piece of paper and pointed. "It's that one."

Across the street from a gay porn theatre currently featuring the film "Rear Deliveries" was a nondescript gray building nestled between an adult book shop and a rundown looking bar with windows so dirty you couldn't see inside.

"Hey, Jimmy Ray's!" crowed Orla. "It's a total actors bar. I hear Al Pacino hangs out here." This rumor provided the girls with some reassurance, springing from their hitherto untested conviction that actors were safe people. Nevertheless, they approached the forbidding looking massively locked door of the apartment building with trepidation. Then they looked down.

In the exact middle of the black and white tiles at the foot of the door was a large coil of feces.

"Oh my God!" recoiled Nikki.

"I don't think that's dog shit," said Diane.

"Yeah. How do we know that?" responded Orla.

"I don't want to think about it. Is this an omen?"

Orla considered this. "I don't think we'll know until we see the apartment."

"You're not seriously thinking of going in this building?" Nikki was horrified. "We should turn around right now and go back, this is insane!"

Nikki's abject horror strengthened the will of Diane and Orla to see the place. Orla produced the key she had gotten from the landlord, handed it to Diane, and with a great deal of effort Diane unlocked the door and threw the bolt. In front of them lay a steep ancient looking cracked marble stairway flanked by pitch black walls.

"Okay! Here we go."

"I can't. Guys, I can't!" Nikki looked pale with dread. "Look, I'll stay out here. No, I'll go into Jimmy Ray's and wait for you, and if you're not back in ten minutes I'll call the police."

Diane and Orla stepped over the ordure and into the smokily dark entranceway. There was no vestibule to speak of; the stairs just started. What used to be wall sconces flanking the filthy grey marble stairway were now just bare lightbulbs, reflected spookily in the shiny jet-black walls.

The two girls stood there uncertainly for a moment, trying to gather their courage to ascend. At the top of the first flight of stairs a door opened, and a black woman in a tight red dress, turban, and sparkly Wizard of Oz heels stepped out.

"Hi!" chirped Orla brightly. "We're here to see the apartment."

"Honey, I got no idea what you're talking about," responded the woman, who they now realized was a man. He locked his door and came tottering down the stairs toward them.

"3B," said Diane to the others, looking at the paper. "I guess it's on the third floor."

"Oh, okay. He dead now. Yeah. 3B is up there." Slipping past them, s/he opened the door. "God damn! Who keeps lettin' that old woman squat here? Where's the po-lice when you need 'em?"

Diane and Orla climbed the steps. It got better as you went up. The walls continued to be black, but there was a skylight that gave you something to hope for. They arrived on the 3rd floor and saw that there were only two apartments on that level. 3b was the one that faced 8th Avenue. Diane fit the key in the lock and opened the door.

Suddenly, there was sunlight and air. What a contrast! The apartment was huge. Though the oak floor had suspicious gouges in it and half-peeled flocked silver wallpaper from the '50's in the living room, it had high ceilings and large windows that let in buckets of light. And the best thing - it was partially furnished! The landlady hadn't told Orla that. The living room looked like something out of a 1940's movie, with an ornate mahogany chaise covered in green velvet, a bamboo throne chair that Sidney Greenstreet would have looked good in, and a massive dark walnut breakfront on one wall. Several paintings of dubious merit hung from the moldings, suspended by wires. An ell off the living room comprised the kitchen, which had a red vintage oven and a skinny battered refrigerator. Diane drifted to the bedroom. In the center of the room was a large, ornately carved mahogany four poster bedframe.

"Wow," she whispered.

"This place is incredible!" called Orla from the living room. "And there's a fireplace!"

"I'll bet it doesn't work."

"Who cares?"

Diane rejoined Orla in the living room. "Someone died in here?"

"Maybe not, maybe he went to a hospital. Come on, is this place not amazing?"

"Either that or amazingly creepy. The bedroom has a four-poster bed."

"No way!"

"But I tried the windows, and they're stuck closed."

"So, we'll unstick them."

"Think they'll give this place a paint job?"

"It's a pocket listing. You take it warts and all. I mean come on! It's great, right?"

"It is. You should take it, Orla. Your place is so tiny, and you found the listing."

"No, no, no. My place is perfect for me, it's right over my favorite restaurant so I'll always have somewhere to eat. But this apartment – it's you, Diane! You'll feel like Greta Garbo living here!

Diane had to admit the place had theatricality.

They burst into Jimmy Ray's and looked around in the sudden gloom at all the tables covered with red and white checked tablecloths, the smattering of desultory customers at the bar. At first, they thought Nikki wasn't there, but as their eyes adjusted, they spotted her at a corner table hunkered down into her coat as if for camouflage, clutching a bottle of Coca-Cola like a weapon.

"Omigod, what took you guys so long?"

"Nikki, this place is amazing, you've got to come up and see!"

"No thanks. This is an actors' bar like Show World is a ballet school. Tell me those girls aren't hookers."

In a booth by the bar, three semi-naked women were sitting with their pimp, who was better dressed for the weather than they in a wide brimmed hat and fur collared corduroy jacket.

"Cool," said Diane. "Great character study."

"You've got to be kidding, these are lowlifes! That creepy guy at the bar was totally hitting on me when I went to get my Coke." Nikki nodded dismissively toward the tall dark-haired man whose back was to them, nursing a drink at the bar.

Orla turned to look. "Omigod, I think that's Frank Langella!"

"What?" Nikki's jaw dropped in amazement. "I saw him in "Dracula," he was incredible! Oh no! And I was so rude!" Nikki jumped up and dashed toward the bar.

Orla turned to Diane. "I think you should take the apartment, Di. Places like this don't come along that often, and they get snatched up fast."

"Okay, but Nikki will never visit."

They turned to look at Nikki, now engaged in genial conversation with Frank Langella. She had shed her coat, and looked as if she'd never felt more at home than in this seedy dump of an establishment.

"I don't know," replied Orla. "Nikki's more adaptable than she appears sometimes. Girl knows how to pivot."

The 'Seventies

Orla spent her early childhood in the Bay area of San Francisco, in a little town called Los Gatos. Orla's mother, Janita, was what you might call a hippie although she hated that word. She preferred the term "free spirit." She had large brown eyes which she outlined to a Cleopatra effect, blunt dark bangs, full lips, and a graceful way of waving her lithe body at music events. When Orla was very little, they lived in a commune in Sonoma County, but Orla had only brief memories of that time in their lives. Some of it she remembered as fun, with singing, dancing, and much laughter. But Orla also remembers her mother crying hysterically upon occasion and getting into heated fights with others. By the time Orla was seven, life had stabilized a bit, because by then Janita had met and settled down in Los Gatos with a man named Jack, who had something to do with computers. Though he didn't feel like a father to Orla, he was still very nice to her in his distant way. Jack told her that the future lay in something called the microprocessor, and that she could "take that to the bank." He also taught her how to type. They always had food to eat, and when Orla outgrew her clothes, she got new ones. This was a nice change.

One day toward the end of the school year when Orla was thirteen, the principal came to her classroom and said that her mother was waiting for her outside and that she should gather all her things. Puzzled, Orla went outside to find Janita perched in her shorts and flipflops atop the hood of their yellow Volkswagen hatchback, which was packed to the rafters.

"C'mon, honey, get in! We're going to New York!"

"When?"

"Now!"

"Jack, too?"

"No, Jack's staying here but we'll call him when we get there!"

What followed was a highly entertaining road trip, with Janita and Orla singing all of their favorite songs (The Grateful Dead, Buffalo Springfield, some tunes from "Oliver" and "Mary Poppins,") staying in Howard Johnson's roadside inns some days and sleeping in the car on others, stopping at parks and meeting small town folk in diners. Janita told a waitress in Bakersfield that they were going to visit her mother who was ailing, so now Orla had three more pieces of information: that she had a grandmother, that she lived in New York City, and that she was sick.

Janita talked excitedly about how wonderful New York was going to be, painting it as a wonderland of magic and possibility. They passed through Arizona, New Mexico, Texas, Oklahoma,

Kansas, Missouri, Illinois, and it was when they hit Ohio that Janita revealed the real reason they were going to New York.

"Honey, you're going become a Broadway star!"

"I am?"

"Sure! With your beautiful voice and your big soulful eyes, you are a cinch, like a baby Linda Ronstadt! I thought for a while that it might be better to go to Los Angeles and try the movies, but my friend Simon says that singers go either to Nashville or New York, and I don't like country music, do you? Blegh!"

Orla was surprised and a little frightened. She had never heard the name Simon before, and had no ambitions to be a Broadway star. Theatre was a completely alien creature to her, and Orla wondered why her mother was suddenly so fixated on the idea. But this was Janita's way; she would get an idea into her head and then just run with it, until something took her in a new direction. Orla hoped a new direction would happen soon.

They were on the road for five wonderful days, singing in the car, stopping often to "take in the sights," passing through bucolic farmland and quaint little towns. They picked apples and Orla learned how to milk a cow, and soon she forgot her mother's plans. When they started seeing the signs for New York City, however, Orla's stomach started to tighten. And when they emerged from the Lincoln Tunnel and found themselves suddenly thrust directly into the turbulent maelstrom that is Manhattan, she was unprepared for the shock. The enormity of the place! The masses of people! The noise! Orla turned to look at her mother, who seemed similarly stunned. She watched Janita's face lose color at the honks of horns protesting her shitty driving, and was alarmed to see her start to hyperventilate.

"Mommy, why don't you pull over for a moment?"

Janita cast her eyes about frantically. "Where? WHERE!?" It was true; there were no parking spaces. Every single one of them for blocks and blocks was taken and Janita's emotional state seemed to fray further and further with every block they circled. Whimpering as she drove, Janita suddenly switched lanes, and a large truck blasted its airhorn at her.

"Leave me alone! Leave me alone!" Janita shrieked. She yanked the wheel and drove up onto the sidewalk in front of a corner bodega, scattering pedestrians and knocking over a mailbox. Then she put her head on the wheel, and fell asleep.

Orla sat there beside her mother, unsure of what to do next. She decided staring ahead neutrally was her best option. Outside the car, she could hear the protests of passing pedestrians. Someone knocked on the window.

"Little girl! Who hit you? Is the lady okay? What happened?"

"Call an ambulance! Somebody call 911!"

A few minutes later a red-headed policeman opened the driver's side door and addressed Janita, still slumped over the wheel.

"Lady? You okay? What happened, little girl? Can you tell me?"

Orla smiled at him politely. "We couldn't find a parking space." At that moment, Janita rose her head from the steering wheel, yawned, and noticed the cop.

"Oh, hello, officer. What can I do for you?"

Janita was taken to a hospital for observation. Orla was taken to Child Services. Orla knew her mother would come and get her soon, because she always did. What the hospital people didn't understand, Orla felt, was that Janita was a sensitive woman, and when stimulus got to be too much for her, Janita's body just shut down for a while and she fell asleep. When she woke up, she was always just fine.

In fact, the stay in the hospital did seem to rejuvenate Janita, and when they were reunited (under the gaze of a disapproving social services lady,) Janita decided to reveal to Orla the genesis of her idea for this road trip.

"Remember that Be-In we went to four years ago, honey? Do you remember my friend Simon?"

"No."

"Oh, sure you do, we had so much fun! Simon and I dropped a little acid and he just became mesmerized by your eyes, remember?" Orla did have a dim memory of a strange grownup staring for a long period of time into her two-colored eyes, until she threw up to discourage him.

"Simon predicted that very day that you had an inner power that none of us understood, and that one day you would be a star. Remember that?"

For purposes of self-preservation, Orla had developed a selective memory, which meant she had very little recollection of the Be-In, or indeed of so many of the "meaningful events" in her childhood. For Janita, however, the notion of her daughter's imminent stardom stuck in her mind as an inevitability. In the months that followed the Be-In, Simon and Janita had kept up with one another on the phone, at first because Janita owed Simon money, but after Janita mailed Simon a check, their friendship deepened. Simon subsequently moved to New York to become an actor and they resumed their semi-flirtatious phone calls.

"Simon knows everyone, Orly! He's connected to the business and will help us find an agent and get auditions and all that stuff actors do."

They were sitting in a coffee shop at Grand Central Station. The car had been impounded and Janita couldn't afford to get it out, so they were reduced to the things Orla had grabbed before they took her to child services; her mother's purse and a duffel bag.

"We don't need that car, anyway, do we? We're in New York now!" Janita chirped. She reached into her purse and drew out her little address book. Simon lived in a place called Greenwich Village, on Bank Street. The lady at child services had given Orla a map of all the subway and bus stops in the city, so Orla plotted the course to Bank Street.

"See, Mommy? We're going to walk over to Times Square and get the bus to –"

"I believe you, honey, don't weigh me down with details. Let's go!"

They got off the bus in front of a bar called the White Horse Tavern and walked down Bank Street to the address in Janita's address book, a banana yellow townhouse. Janita grabbed a mirror out of her bag, applied her bright red lipstick, fluffed her hair, and rang the buzzer. A crackly voice came over the loudspeaker, saying something indecipherable.

"Simon, it's Janita!"

"Who?" Orla's heart sunk. Such a fine line between things going well and utter disaster.

"Janita, and Orla! We're here from California!"

There was a pause, and then the buzzer sounded releasing the door. Sighing in relief, Orla followed her mother up the stairs.

At the top of the second flight of stairs a door was thrown open and a young man in a torn t-shirt, studded pants and a headband encircling his long, golden-brown hair padded out onto the landing in his bare feet. He looked like the picture of Jesus Christ Orla had seen at her friend Pam's house.

"'Nita! I can't believe you actually came!"

"Sure, I did! You told me to, didn't you?"

"But I never thought you'd do it! You look fabulous, and oh my God – this is Orla! How old are you now, sweetheart? Eight?"

"She was eight when you first met her. She thirteen now."

"Thirteen!" Simon reached out and gave her a hug. "She's so small!"

"Yeah," responded Janita. "Her father, I think, was small." This statement confused Orla. It was the first time she had heard anything definitive about her father, and yet the "I think" threw her. Wouldn't you know if a person was small or not?

"That's good that she's small. They're always looking for kids who can play younger. And those eyes! David Bowie has eyes like hers, you know. Come in! Come in!"

The apartment was a dingy one room affair cluttered with fast food wrappers, dirty dishes, cigarette butts and discarded clothing. Album covers and Simon's photos and resumes were strewn on the floor and Broadway show posters were tacked to the walls, but there was very little furniture other than a bed and a crate to sit on. Security bars crisscrossed the windows.

Simon started practicing dance moves as he talked to them. "I've got an audition for a new musical called 'Annie' tomorrow, so I have to stay limber. Oh hey, Orla should audition for that! There's a ton of kids in it. You can sleep here tonight if you want, but it will have to be on the floor. Do you have sleeping bags?... Oh shit, impounded, huh? That's gonna take a lot of money."

That night they placed a call to Jack. Janita coached Orla on what to say when she got on the phone; that she was having a good time but that grandma was "not doing so well."

"When do we see my grandma?" Orla asked after they hung up.

"Soon, honey, soon. We've got stuff to do first."

The next day, Janita took Orla to Bloomingdales to buy some "cute New York clothes." The following week, Orla and Janita were in the midtown office of Simon's talent agent, a tiny gnarled looking old guy named Stan Fleisch, who told Janita to leave the room so he could interview Orla personally and "see what she's got." Janita complied, and Stan reached into his desk, pulling out a yellow, dog-eared piece of paper.

"This is casting right now," he barked. "It's a commercial. Read the copy."

Orla looked down at the mimeographed sheet of paper. Some of the words were smeared from previous fingers, but she could make out most of it.

"It's panties! No, it's hosiery! Believe it or not, it's both of those things! Gentlemen Prefer Hanes pantyhose, now with padding in the derriere! Feel a little insufficient in your hind quarters? Gentlemen Prefer Hanes padded pantyhose will address your needs and give the man in your life a little extra something to admire. Put a little curve into your life. Treat yourself to leg luxury!" Orla looked up expectantly to Stan, who was watching her avidly.

"That was very good, young lady, that was very good. Do it again, and this time run your hand along your leg like this." He demonstrated.

By the fourth time Orla had read the copy she was getting bored, plus she suspected Stan was no longer paying attention because he was doing something with his hands under the desk that she couldn't see. Her eyes drifted to a picture on the shelf behind his desk.

"Is that your wife?" Orla asked. "Is she a talent agent, too?"

Stan's hand stopped moving. "Uh, no. She's a housewife. She doesn't need to work."

"She looks really nice."

Stan cleared his throat. "Okay, little lady, I can tell you've got talent. I'll probably send you out on a few things, but if you don't hear from me don't call, I'm very busy."

"Can I be in "Annie?"

"Huh?"

"Annie. They're making a musical out of the comic strip."

"I know that, how do you know that?"

"A good friend of ours is going to be in it." Orla meant Simon, who was Stan's client. No offer had come in for Simon yet, but Orla had faith.

"Can you sing?"

"I think so."

"Lemme hear you."

Orla cleared her throat, then sang one of the songs she and Janita sang in the car, "I'll do Anything" from "Oliver." They had sung it about fifteen times over the past week, so Orla's voice was nice and strong, and she knew she was hitting the notes right. Stan had put a cigar in his mouth, but when she started to sing, he forgot to light it, and when she was done, he put it in the ashtray and started rummaging around for paperwork.

"Okay, I'll get you in on 'Annie.' Go out and get your mom, I need her to sign a few things."

That was the beginning of Orla's career as a child actress. She was cast as an understudy, and soon after that Janita decided the time had come for Orla to meet her grandmother.

"She can't call me a loser now!" crowed Janita. "I've got a daughter's gonna be on Broadway."

"I'm just an understudy, Mommy."

"So what? You're making money. It's just the beginning!"

Janita and Orla took the subway all the way uptown to the Bronx, where her mother lived in a big building on a street called the Grand Concourse. It didn't look very grand to Orla. The lobby of the building was enormous, but there was no furniture in it. Orla wouldn't have noticed this if her mother hadn't asked the doorman, "Where's all the furniture? There used to be some really nice stuff down here."

"Stolen," was the doorman's reply. Stolen? Orla tried to imagine burglars coming in and stealing an entire lobby of furniture. They got in the elevator and went up to the ninth floor, then walked down a long dirty hallway. Orla's grandmother, a white-haired woman with sky blue eyes in a matching blue dress, was waiting by her door. She cast a glance around as they approached.

"Hurry up, come in," were her curt welcoming words, and once they got in, she double locked the door behind them.

"So, this is our little Orla, look how she's grown!" She exclaimed, and even though she had an accent that made Orla want to laugh, she saw the affection in her grandmother's eyes and thought better of it. "Gimme a hug, sweethot," she said, and when Orla entered into her embrace it smelled like talcum powder and roses. Her arms were soft and white. "You don't remember meetin' me when you were little, do you, honey? That was before your mother decided she didn't need me in her life anymore."

"Ma! Don't be that way. I'm here now, right?" Orla noticed that Janita seemed to have suddenly acquired the same accent. The older woman nodded, eyeing her daughter thoughtfully.

"So why are you?"

"Can't I bring my kid to see her grandmother? You said you wanted to see her."

Janita's mother pursed her lips, then decided to drop this line of inquiry. "C'mere, honey, I'm gonna show you sumthin," she said, and led Orla down a floral wallpapered hall to a small room with shelves on three walls loaded with bolts of fabric and boxes of buttons. In the middle of the room was a Singer sewing machine and an ironing board. "My sewin' room!" she declared proudly. "I make all sorts of stuff here. I'll make you a dress you want me to, a pretty one. And I'll bet your mother didn't tell you I could do magic with this sewin' machine."

Janita rolled her eyes. "Ma, she's thirteen." Her mother waved her hands over the sewing machine in a mysterious way. "Abra-cadabra!" She pronounced, and suddenly she had a stick of Dentyne gum in her hand, which she handed to Orla, who thanked her politely.

"Manners! That's nice to see. So. you finally named her, huh? Why'ja name her Orla?"

"It means Golden Princess."

"In what language?"

"I forget."

"That's nice, Golden Princess. You could do worse, right? My mother named me Desdemona. Know what that means?" She asked Orla.

"Unlucky," parroted Janita.

"Unlucky! What kind of mother names her kid Unlucky? That's why I ended up here, I guess, on the Grand Concourse where nobody lives anymore and crime is through the roof. She couldn't of named me Felicity, right?"

"That's why I named my girl Orla, Ma. I wanted to give her a good start."

"Okay, you did something right," said her mother, kind of grudgingly, Orla thought.

"And now guess what? Orla's gonna be on Broadway!"

Janita then launched into the story of how they left California (she didn't mention Jack) and drove to New York (she didn't mention the impounded car or her stint in the hospital) and how Orla right away got an agent (enough about him) and landed a Broadway show (she didn't mention the shelters they slept in until Jack agreed to send more money.) Grandmother, or Mona as it turned out she preferred Orla call her, kept watching her daughter suspiciously, like she was waiting for the other shoe to drop. Occasionally she would turn to Orla for verification of Janita's somewhat embroidered story, and Orla had no choice but to nod and smile.

"Broadway, huh? Who you playin'?"

"One of the orphans," said Orla.

"Which one? Molly? Kate? Tessie? Pepper? Duffy?" Orla and Janita looked at one another in surprise.

"Um, all of them. Actually, I'm understudying, so if one of them gets sick I go on." Janita winced, but Mona nodded, impressed.

"Okay. That's good. That ups your chances, right?"

"Ma, how do you know all their names?"

"I read the papers!" Mona looked insulted. "You think I don't read?"

"No, I just… I'm surprised, is all."

"Well, don't be so surprised. Now, where you stayin'?"

"50th and Ninth."

"Hell's Kitchen? No. No way any granddaughter of mine who's gonna be on Broadway is staying in Hell's Kitchen."

"Ma, it's right near the theatre. They said we need to be nearby."

"Okay, so you go to Hoboken. It's right across the river and you can get into town lickety-split."

Turned out, Mona was a pretty shrewd woman. She knew, for instance, that that very year Hoboken had decided they needed to stem the tide of a twenty-years-long exodus from the city by instituting rent controlled housing. Within days, she had found Janita and Orla half a duplex in Hoboken that was only a little bit more than what they were paying in Hell's Kitchen. The place was run down, the roof leaked and the plumbing was unreliable, but it was a far sight better than the fourth story walkup where they had been staying, which Janita had been paying for by the week.

"Holy hell, I never thought I'd be living in Hoboken," was Janita's constant refrain, but Orla could tell that she was pleased her mother was taking an active interest in their welfare.

It hadn't always been this way. When Janita had gotten pregnant with Orla and wouldn't (or couldn't) say who the father was, Janita's father Patrick had been enraged and kicked her out of the house. Janita had expected that of her father, who was a strict and distant parent, but she was broken-hearted when her mother took Patrick's side and wouldn't even take Janita's phone calls. She went to California because she had heard about the peace-love movement there, and it seemed to her peace and love were very much in short supply in her own life. For some time, San Francisco and its embrace of good vibrations seemed to heal the hurt within Janita's soul. Orla was born, and was the kind of baby who stopped traffic on the sidewalk as Janita wheeled her through the Haight-Ashbury district, where she lived. She sent pictures of Orla to Mona, not expecting to hear back, and was astonished when her mother announced her intentions to visit. Mona took the train from New York to San Francisco, defying her husband's wishes because she had been entranced by the photos of Orla, with her mesmerizing multicolored eyes and serious, soulful little baby face. It seemed to her that this beautiful baby would patch over all their differences.

It didn't work out that way, however. Mona's immediate adoration of Orla caused her to judge Janita in an even harsher light. She didn't understand why Janita hadn't even named the baby yet, rolled her eyes when Janita explained that she was waiting for the baby's name to present itself. She didn't understand how she could raise the child in this filthy district, with all of its grubby hippies and drugs and the smell of pot constantly in the air. She didn't understand how Janita could go to her waitressing job and leave Orla in the care of the spaced-out flower children in the next apartment, who let Orla play on their filthy floor with their dog. She distrusted the concerts and the singing and dancing everywhere and the glazed expression in so many eyes. The whole thing was a horror show to Mona, and one night when Janita got home late from work, Mona unloaded her frustrations on her.

"What if I wasn't here? You really woulda left the baby this long with those hopeless drug addicts next door? You have a child, Janita! A precious child you haven't even named yet! And you play with her life as if it means nothing to you! Why can't you take some responsibility for once in your life?"

Janita was taken aback by her mother's anger, and as usual when she was confronted by something that upset her deeply, she started to yawn. This only made Mona angrier.

"Fine! Don't listen to me! Ya never listened to me before, no reason to start now. But I can't stay here any longer and watch what you are doing to this sweet, sweet child!"

Dazed, Janita walked into the room where Orla was curled up fast asleep holding her teddy, and fell instantly asleep beside her. Mona took the train home the next morning.

Janita's father Patrick died five years after that incident. Janita sent flowers but did not come back for the funeral. Mona wrote thanking her for the flowers, and then wrote again, and again, but Janita didn't write back. There seemed to be no question of anyone picking up a phone. Mona assumed it meant that Janita had not forgiven her, and in a way she'd hadn't, but in another,

Mona's words had gone deep. Janita loved her baby deeply, and suddenly saw through her mother's eyes that she was not doing right by her, so she gave the baby a name — Orla, which in Irish means "Golden Princess." And when a nice young man showed up at the restaurant one day and Janita saw the expensive watch on his wrist, she started flirting with him. Four months later, she was married to Jack and she and Orla were living in Los Gatos.

But married life in the suburbs was never going to be a long-term solution for Janita; the people were too "straight." She missed her old friends, and couldn't resist bringing Orla into the city for concerts and Happenings, always telling herself that, because she was a married lady, it was okay now. Even after the Manson murders, when everything started to go to hell and her friends either drifted out of the city, died, or went straight themselves, Janita still believed in flower power.

She didn't need to work anymore, so she mostly stayed at home with Orla and watched a lot of TV. One boring rainy afternoon while Jack was at work and Orla at school, Janita munched on some psilocybin mushrooms and sat down to watch Millon Dollar Movie. They were showing an old musical called "Golddiggers of 1933," and it was fantastic! Ginger Rogers was in a Broadway play, and she was singing "We're in the Money," and then dancing with a bunch of girls dressed up as dollar coins! And then suddenly, there Ginger was in extreme closeup singing the whole song in Pig Latin! This sequence really blew Janita's mind, and she started to think about the time she and Simon did acid together and he saw inside Orla's spirit. Suddenly, Janita saw the path that lay before her. She was going to make Orla, her Golden Princess, a Broadway star, just like Ginger Rogers!

2025

Diane arrived in New York and made her way from JFK to the Empire hotel near Lincoln Center. It was old, it was a bit battered, and that's what she liked about it. Old and battered, like her, she thought with a laugh. She hadn't been in New York since before the pandemic, and it was taking a little time for her to adjust. Everything that she had loved on the west side when she lived there — Coliseum Books, Shakespeare and Company, the Thalia movie theatre, the Russian Tea Room, O'Neal's, the Silver Palate restaurant — all were long gone, and in their place, more often than not, was a bank.

This was the first time Diane had come to New York without making plans to see some theatre, but this wasn't that kind of trip. Anyway, Diane had seen quite a lot of New York theatre in previous years. It was all very splashy and musical and much like going to Las Vegas. The great theatre empresario Joe Papp had been correct in his dire prediction; there wasn't much theatre left that explored the human condition. The Broadway plays she did see frequently had something to do with computers; robots falling in love, people texting one another on big screens, the advent of AI had introduced lots of dazzling technological stage shenanigans. It was fine; some of it was even good, but it was a bit depressing for someone who had made her living focusing on the intricacies of being human. Diane thought of all the days she picketed in the freezing cold those many years ago, sure that she was saving Broadway theatre for the day when she would be a part of it. She had never been a part of it. Her life had taken a different path. Maybe that was okay.

Diane walked up Broadway talking to Nikki on her phone as she took stock of her surroundings.

"Hey! Gray's Papaya is still here."

In her bathroom, Nikki had Diane on speakerphone as she painted her toenails. "Well, that's good. Once Gray's Papaya is gone, the city's done."

"Truly. I will say, everything looks a lot cleaner."

"What they're charging for rent these days, it sure better look clean! Thank God Orly's place is under rent control." Nikki gazed around her bathroom, which was fully the size of Orla's whole apartment. Through her shower window, there was a commanding view of the mountains surrounding Boulder. Beautiful. Yet somehow, all Nikki wanted at this moment was to be eating a hotdog with Diane at Gray's Papaya.

"I'm on my way to Orla's now," continued Diane. "If she's not there, I'll see what I can find out from the doorman."

"Maybe she's off having an exotic holiday."

"I think those days may be over, Nick," Diane said sadly.

"God, I hope not. Is Café Monaco still there?"

"I think so."

Nikki put her nail polish down and started to Google it on her phone. "I loved that place. I can't remember the last time we all hung out upstairs in her apartment, though, can you?"

"Not really. She had that Murphy bed that took up half the apartment."

"It didn't even have a kitchen."

"I think Café Monaco was her kitchen. She never let us pay the bill, remember?"

"You had to get there early and slap a credit card down." Back when you could afford to eat out all the time."

"I don't think I could ever afford to do that," said Diane.

"I just Googled Café Monaco. It's still open, but holy hell! Those prices!"

"It's kind of remarkable that Orly still lives here. The way everything has changed, I think I'd go crazy." They stopped talking, both thinking the same thing.

"Fraud. Giving away money. I mean, she was always generous, but -- Do you think she's okay?"

"I don't know, Nick. I guess we'll find out."

1986

Diane and Orla were hanging out in Orla's tiny 13th floor studio apartment (though it was labeled the 14th floor on the elevator, like all the other pre-war high rises in New York, for superstitious reasons.) They were waiting for Nikki so Orla could show her pictures of her latest trip hitchhiking around Peru, then they planned to go downstairs to lunch at Café Monaco. Diane was playing catch with Zina, Orla's very game Yorkie, but the room was so small, retrieval of the ball was no great accomplishment. Plus, Diane's arm was getting tired.

"I'm starving, where is Nikki?"

"She's always late."

"Not usually this late. Let's go down to the restaurant, we can leave a note on the door." But at that moment the buzzer sounded and the doorman, Jesus, announced that Nikki was on her way up.

When Orla opened the door to Nikki, she was shocked at her appearance. Her face was swollen from crying, mascara ran down her face and she had a desperate look in her eye, as if she were on the run from something. She slumped down on Orla's couch without even first brushing the crumbs off of it, a sign that something was truly wrong.

"Nikki, what is it? What's the matter?"

"Paul Cohen has the gay cancer." Diane and Orla stared at her in shock.

"What? We just saw him a few months ago."

"He has it. Will told me, I just saw him at an open call. And he's not sure, but he thinks Young Michael might have it, too."

"Oh, no! Sweet Michael?"

"They're not calling it the gay cancer anymore," offered Orla. "They're calling it AIDS."

"AIDS? That's gonna put the diet candy right out of business."

"Diane, this isn't funny!"

"I'm serious. Isn't it kind of irresponsible to name a disease after a product that is currently on the shelves?"

"I can't believe you!"

"What? I'm upset! I love Paul. Can't I be upset about Paul and think about how nobody's going to buy Ayds anymore?"

"NO!" shouted Nikki, who never shouted. "Do you understand what this means? Paul and Michael. This disease is contagious. You get it through sex."

Suddenly they got it.

"Oh Nikki."

"I'm gonna die."

"No, you're not. It was months and months ago."

"Seven months ago, and we don't know how long this thing incubates. We don't know a thing about it." Nikki started to sob. The two other girls surrounded her on the sofa making comforting sounds, but Nikki was inconsolable.

"Is there a… I don't know. A test or something?" asked Orla.

"I don't know."

"I'll find out."

Diane, stroking her hair. "We're here for you, Nikki. We're *mishpachah,* remember?"

"Crazy?"

"Family! Whatever happens, we'll be by your side."

Suddenly, Nikki sat bolt upright. "Oh my God! What if I gave it to Frank?"

"Who?"

"Frank Langella!"

"Oh!" Diane and Orla looked at one another, processing this information.

You, and Frank Langella —?"

"It was only a couple of times, then he had to go to Los Angeles. Oh my God, what if I've got it? That means I have to call him and tell him he might have it, too!"

"Can that happen?" asked Diane.

"Of course it can," said Orla. "It goes from sexual partner to sexual partner. Remember that play La Ronde? That play's about syphilis, but a prostitute picks up a soldier, the soldier has sex with a chambermaid, and on and on. It ends up with some nobleman getting it."

"Oh my God. I'll kill myself. I'll kill myself!"

"Nikki, calm down! It's all right, I'm sure of it." Soothed Orla. "We'll just call your doctor and ask how to get a test —"

"Are you out of your mind? I can't call my doctor about this. He'd tell my parents!"

"He can't. The Hippocratic oath."

"Dr. Reynolds and my father play golf together at Pennbrook. There is absolutely no way I'm calling him and telling him about my contaminated blood!"

"Okay, Nikki, take deep breaths," counselled Diane.

Since Nikki was too hysterical to think straight, Orla and Diane did a little research and found a clinic in the city that would test for antibodies. Three days later, the three of them sat in the avocado green hallway of a clinic with about fifteen others, mostly men, some of whom looked visibly unwell. Holding her hand, Diane worried that Nikki was going to pass out from fear, she was shaking so much. In the folding chairs across from them were two young men, obviously a couple as one of them would periodically caress the other's hand as if hoping to impart strength. The strength-provider wore a pin on his jacket lapel, a pink triangle and the words SILENCE = DEATH. It was the first time Diane had seen such a pin. She was to see it many, many more times in the years to come.

Orla started a conversation with the young man sitting on the other side of her and found out that he was a Broadway dancer. They compared notes on people they knew, and Orla got him laughing a little even though he, too, looked deathly afraid. When Nikki's name was called, she jumped up like a gun had gone off. Diane offered to go in with her, but she shook her head and went in alone. Minutes later, she came out, pale as a ghost.

"They gave me an ID number. I have to come back in ten days for the results."

"Ten days! So long!"

"Can't they tell you on the phone?"

"I guess not."

They left the building and walked silently for a long time.

"I think it will be okay," Orla finally said, and neither of the others responded. They walked a while longer.

"So many people," said Diane. "Some of them just boys. What's going on here?"

Nikki walked grimly, her mouth moving slightly.

"What did you say, Nikki?"

"Nothing. I'm praying."

"Look, when all this is over and it turns out you are fine, I have a brilliant idea. Let's go to Italy." The other two looked at her dubiously. "I've started a temp job at a travel agency, and I'm learning about all the cool places you can go for not that much money. Italy is cheap, it's recovered from the oil crisis, and it has great food! Let's say we're going to do that, okay? When you test negative. We can celebrate."

"Sure," responded Nikki dully. "Why not." Nothing more was said for the rest of the walk to the subway.

Nikki went home to her parents' house in New Jersey for the ten-day waiting period. She told her mother she had the flu and locked herself in her room. Diane and Orla tried to call her, but always one of Nikki's parents would answer and say she was napping. The third time Diane called, Nikki's mother was starting to sound worried. "Did something happen in the city? She's so lethargic." Diane said she was sure Nikki would be fine soon.

At the end of ten days, Nikki came back into town and went to the clinic alone. She waited again in the sad green hallway, and finally her number was called. She went into a small room with nothing but a desk in it, behind which was sitting what she guessed was an orderly in green scrubs that matched the walls. What made them decide that vomit green was a good color? He gestured for her to sit down, and consulted a file with a long line of numbers containing their test results. Her number was 86.

"Let's see, 86… I don't want to get this wrong, we had an incident the other day….Yes, here it is. 86. Negative."

Her first thought when she heard "Negative" was that the news was negative and she had AIDS. When the orderly clarified what it meant, Nikki collapsed with relief and for the first time since this whole event began, started to cry. "Thank you, God! Thank you!" She jumped up. "And to you, too, sir," she said to the man. "Thank you!" She started for the door.

"One moment." Nikki turned. It was of the utmost importance that she vacate the clinic immediately, but she didn't want to be rude. "State law requires that we offer you counselling, miss. Would you be interested in that?"

"Counselling? I'm negative."

"Yes, but you have self-identified as being at risk."

Nikki was horrified. "I'm not at risk! It was a mistake, a horrible mistake that will never happen again. I'm not one of these people."

The orderly put down his folder. "One of which people?"

"I'm not homosexual. I'm not a drug user. I'm not hemophiliac. I just came here --- out of an abundance of caution."

"I see." He stared at her intently. "Well then, aren't you the lucky one?"

Nikki was suddenly flooded with guilt. "I'm sorry," she murmured, and fled the room.

Diane and Orla were thrilled for Nikki when she called them with the news, and Orla proposed they meet at a bar in midtown to celebrate, but Nikki had recently returned to her apartment and said she had much to do. She also had much to do the next time a reunion was suggested, and the next time.

Months went by. Diane started to worry that Nikki associated her and Orla with the whole frightening event, that she possibly wanted to forget she had ever met them.

Then, one day Nikki called each of them with big news. She had been cast in the role of Agnes in "Agnes of God" at a theater in New Jersey, and would love to meet the two of them for lunch before she went into rehearsals. "Pick somewhere nice!" she instructed ebulliently. "My treat!"

They met at Café La Fortuna on the Upper West Side, because Orla had heard that David Bowie got coffee there sometimes. There was no Bowie sighting, but there was a very excited Nikki, who sailed into the café a bit late in a lovely camel hair coat, beaming radiantly at the other two. The contrast between this Nikki and the one of three months ago was striking.

"Oh, how I've missed you both!" she exclaimed, and pulled them into a three-way hug. "How have you been? What's going on?"

Diane had shot a Tide commercial, which was very exciting for a while because of all the money everyone on set told her she was going to make. She had bought a new stereo and a color TV in anticipation of her largesse, but so far, the commercial had not aired. As a result, she was back to checking coats at the Jockey Club on Central Park South. She hated it. She hated the little closet they stuck her in, hated the spoiled rich women who thrust their fur coats at her without acknowledging her humanity, and most of all she hated the dripping umbrellas and galoshes she had to store on rainy days. The one upside was that she got a lot of reading done, and was currently in the middle of Dostoyevsky's "The Idiot," the tale of innocence tainted by human greed. It felt somehow appropriate.

Orla was still recovering from the infamy of having been involved in the biggest Broadway disaster of all time, "Moose Murders." She had been the understudy for the role of Gay Holloway, the crazed tap-dancing daughter who keeps demanding a martini and is finally poisoned by her mother. Unfortunately, she never got the chance to go on, because it closed after opening night. Frank Rich described it as "the season's most stupefying flop — a show so preposterous that it made minor celebrities out of everyone who witnessed it, whether from the stage or in the audience." Orla was shocked by the terrible reviews; she thought the show was fun and loved the cast even though, after Eve Arden couldn't remember her lines and quit the show, some had a presentiment they might be on the Titanic. Audience members might have gone on to minor celebrity, but unfortunately the show's notoriety did nothing for Orla's resume; she had been auditioning unsuccessfully for some time since.

Nikki was therefore currently on the highest rung of the Ladder to Success, and her delight oozed from every pore of her body. She told them how her audition had wowed the producers, springing as it did from Nikki's newfound passion for God.

"Really? Which God? Jesus?" marveled Orla.

"Or whoever. His name definitely came up. I prayed for ten days straight."

"Uh-oh. Better not tell Tevye his Hodel is born again," quipped Diane.

Nikki shot her a murderous glare. "I have been given a second chance at life, thanks to divine intervention. Don't make jokes."

So, they didn't. It was clear that free-spirited Nikki had been scared straight, and as a result had done another pivot to a new course in life. In rehearsals, she poured her heart and soul into the role of Agnes, losing her accent and speaking her dialog with such fervency and conviction that the director actually asked her to tone it down a notch. On the phone with Orla, she spoke of the joys of the spiritual life, feeling that Orla would understand her need to renounce alcohol, smoking, and sex.

"Wait. Sex?"

"A celibate life is the only one worth living, Orla. It clears the head. It gets you closer to the Godhead."

Orla felt that was debatable, but was impressed by this miraculous conversion. On opening night, Nikki's extremely moving performance led to rave reviews in all the local papers, and an uptick of auditions for other plays.

But then came the next bit of surprising information. A week before closing, Nikki announced that she was getting married to a guy named Gordon Barone.

"What? Married?" Protested Orla. "But we said we'd go to Italy!"

"I know, and I totally want to, but first I want to marry Gordon!" she declared. "He's amazing, you guys, it's like he was delivered to me out of the blue and I'm so happy! We don't want to wait around. He's not into a long engagement, and I guess I'm not either."

"What happened to the celibate life?"

"Clearly, I was saving myself for Gordon." Saving herself. It had been all of six weeks.

"So, how did you meet this guy?" asked Diane.

"He came to see me in 'Agnes of God' and just fell in love. That's what he told me. He's seen the show three times."

"But Agnes is a total whack job."

"No, she's not! She's pure and innocent and suffers from stigmatas. Come on, you saw it."

"Do your parents know about this?" Asked Orla.

"Not yet, but they'll be thrilled. They've been wanting me to settle down for ages. Gordon knows I'm not really that character, he just loved my essence. And he's totally supportive of my career."

Diane and Orla were deeply skeptical of men who mistook you for the character you played on stage. Diane had played Gwen in "Fifth of July," and her date at the time showed up with a packet of meth, assuming she'd want to smoke it with him. Orla played Baby June in "Gypsy," and still got fan mail from pedophiles.

There was nothing to do but to meet this Gordon Barone. The following week, Nikki brought him to lunch at Marvin Gardens, leading him to the table as if the girls were about to meet Marlon Brando. He seemed nice enough. Good looking in a rough sort of way, with unruly hair that he kept raking back from his face like Kenickie from "Grease." He laughed at Diane's jokes, displayed interest in pictures of Orla's dog, and did seem very much into Nikki. (Diane could tell he was caressing her leg under the table.) Yet there was something kind of ... well, "elsewhere" about him. It was hard to put her finger on why Diane had the impression that, while he was being perfectly engaging with them, he was thinking about other things. Perhaps it was because she caught him glancing at his watch a couple of times. The third time, he saw her watching him and winked collusively, which made her feel as if she was in on something she didn't really want to be in on. At length he picked up the bill, which was of course very nice of him, then rose to excuse himself for a "pressing business appointment." He reasserted his delight at meeting them, kissed Nikki, and departed. They all sipped their cappuccinos for a moment.

"So?" prompted Nikki.

"He's handsome," said Orla. "Is he Italian?"

"On his father's side. Jewish on his mother's."

"Good combo."

"He's very into you," commented Diane. "And he has good hair."

"But?" Nikki eyed the other two warily.

"No 'but'."

"Come on. I totally hear a 'but' from both of you."

There was a pause.

"Is it a little too soon?" ventured Diane. "So much has happened to you in the past few months, Nick. The AIDS scare – "

"I don't want to talk about that."

"And your Jesus conversion," said Orla.

"Stop calling it that."

"—and this show. It seems like you just met him."

"What does that matter, if we're in love?" Nikki snapped peevishly.

"No, you're right." The girls backed off instantly. Nikki could be prickly sometimes.

"He's got a very steady job in real estate. He's gonna make a lot of money this year."

"Well, there you go," said Diane lamely. Orla sipped her tea and said nothing.

Diane's apartment may have been in a dicey neighborhood, but it was only half a block away from magic. Any evening Diane wished, she could see a Broadway play for around $30, slightly more if it was a musical. If she didn't have the money, she could just have a little dinner, wait until intermission, mingle with the crowd outside and then slip into the theatre with them, finding herself an empty seat. It was heaven.

Early morning on a brutally cold winter day a few weeks later, Diane awoke up to the sound of a persistent chant taking place in the distance outside her window. Against her will, (the bed was warm; the room was cold) she opened her window, brushed the snow off the window sill and leaned out as far as she could to see what was going on. Below, she saw people streaming in the direction of 44th street, but couldn't make out what was going on. She had planned to stay inside and write, as lately she was toying with the idea that she might be able to write a play if she put her mind to it. But the chants grew louder and louder, and finally she couldn't resist. She threw on her coat and boots and trudged over to see what all the excitement was about.

A clutch of about fifty people, young and old, were marching in circles midway down the block carrying signs that said, "SAVE OUR THEATRES!" "THE MOROSCO IS A PRECIOUS LANDMARK!" and "SAVE THE HELEN HAYES!" Across the street was a gigantic hole where the Picadilly Hotel had once been, and a demolition vehicle with Cuyahoga Wrecking Company labelled on its side was doing even more damage. A platform was being hammered together by a couple of young men and placed on the sidewalk across the street from the Morosco Theatre, which was the wreckers' next intended victim. A short, intense looking middle-aged man supervised the activity as he clutched his coat around his body for warmth. Diane recognized him instantly from pictures she had seen in the trade papers — it was Joseph Papp, the founder of the Public Theatre. For an actor, this was like getting a close-hand look at a president.

Excited, Diane raced home to her apartment and called Orla.

"Diana," whispered Orla. "Do you know what time it is?"

"Sorry. Why are you whispering?"

"Eduardo is in town."

"Oh!" Eduardo was an archaeology student Orla had met in Peru. "Sorry, but listen! There's a big rally taking place to save the theatres on 44th street, and guess who's out there right now? JOE PAPP!"

"Omigod, really?"

"They're putting up a platform, I think he's going to speak. And if he's going to speak, you can bet a lot of other people are, too! You've got to come uptown."

"Honey. Eduardo."

"Bring him!"

'Well, he's asleep but when he wakes up, I'll ask if he wants to."

"They're going to destroy these two theatres to put up a big ugly mall, you know about that, right? This is a travesty!"

"Okay, yeah, I'll see what I can do. 'Bye!"

Diane made a quick coffee, put on her gloves and went back out. The crowd had gained in size. Four girls were handing out ready-made picketing signs. Diane recognized some actors from auditions she had been on, and others from plays she had seen.

Everyone was charged with an angry enthusiasm that Diane found very attractive. She grabbed up a picket sign and joined the circle of marchers.

"SAVE OUR THEATRES! SAVE OUR THEATRES!" It felt so good to yell in solidarity with others. She had never worked in a Broadway theatre, but she felt that someday she would, and this personal investment stoked her indignation. The crowd grew, and now some really famous faces started to arrive: Jason Robards, Colleen Dewhurst, Christopher Reeve, Liza Minelli. Camera crews had been milling around for some time; now they rushed toward the platform as they heard a microphone test. Joseph Papp stepped onto the platform and took the mic.

"Look across the street there and you are looking at a huge disgrace in the city of New York. Look at that destruction!" he yelled, pointing at the cavernous hole in the ground. The wrecking ball had already taken the Bijou, the Astor and the Gaiety theatres, but the Morosco and the Helen Hayes were perhaps the most beloved. "Look at the price that they expect us to pay for the price of this monolithic monster they're calling the Broadway mall. By striking this blow, they are striking a blow against the spirit of this city! The importance of these houses has to do with plays. They say they're going to reconstruct in their plans another musical house. Well, musicals are fine, we have a couple on Broadway ourselves. But there has to be room for serious writing on Broadway!"

Diane fervently believed in this sentiment. She liked musicals, but in her heart, it was drama that appealed to her most. When Jason Robards spoke of how theatre reveals the human condition, she cheered. When Christopher Reeve said, "This is one time I wish I WERE Superman!" she laughed. Tears came to her eyes when Colleen Dewhurst said, "The heart of New York is the theatre. To tear out these two theatres is to tear out the heart of the city." Jules Feiffer spoke, the reviewer Brendan Gill, Celeste Holm, Alfred Drake. It went on and on, and pretty soon Diane's hunger set in. Additionally, the temperature had dropped and she couldn't feel her feet. She was going to put her sign back on the table, then decided not to. After all, she would be back there tomorrow and the next day, and every day until those beautiful theatres were saved from destruction.

Two weeks later, Diane was still picketing. When Diane threw herself into something she went all the way, so she had called in sick at her temp agency and dedicated all her time to walking the picket line and yelling her support. Orla came by a few days into the protest (after Eduardo had gone back to Peru.) She carried a picket sign with Diane for a while and yelled all the right slogans, then went home. The whole thing made Orla sad; Diane's passion for the fight was admirable, but Orla could see already that it was a losing battle.

Weeks later, Nikki's fiancé Gordon was on his way to his office in mid-town when he spotted Diane on 45th street, circling the block with what was now a diminishing core group of dispirited protestors. Joe Papp was nowhere to be seen, nor any celebrities. It was a bitterly cold day and Diane didn't even have gloves on, which seemed absurd to him. He considered going over and giving her his but realized that, working for a real estate development firm, he represented the enemy. Gordon shook his head at Diane's naivete and continued on.

On March 22, the protest came to an end. Diane stood with a small group of other actors who clutched one another and sobbed audibly as the wrecking crew got on with its heartbreaking work. Mayor Koch had not come to the rescue. No one had. It was Diane's first lesson in the inexorable force that is capitalism.

In May, there was a bridal shower for Nikki at Tavern on the Green. Nikki had asked Diane to be the maid of honor, which Diane learned meant she held Nikki's hand when she freaked out, chose the restaurant, and did most of the work of organizing the shower. It took some time and effort and Diane was still playing catchup on all the money she had lost demonstrating, but she did her best, and Tavern on the Green turned out to be a wonderful choice. Nestled just inside Central Park, the décor of the restaurant picked up the colors of the greenery carefully planted outside, giving the delightful impression that the restaurant was part of a blooming garden. The strings of Tivoli lights, which flashed on as the day progressed toward dusk, heightened the ambiance. It was pretty magical.

In addition to Diane and Orla, Nikki had chosen her cousin, Cindy, and a friend from high school, Beth, as bridesmaids. Cindy was kind of chunky and laughed a lot at nothing. Beth was wispy, homespun in appearance, and seemed dazzled just to be in the city. They were all dressed in their garden party finest; floral spring dresses, pearls and kitten heels. It was a festive afternoon; there had already been a couple of celebrity sightings (Bianca Jagger, Emilio Estevez) which titillated all. There was hilarious laughter (especially from Cindy) over the gag gifts, and the girls were feeling agreeably tipsy on the bottomless champagne that Diane had ordered. Diane could see that Nikki was enjoying every moment of being in the spotlight. As the afternoon wore on and Diane felt the energy flag, she signaled the waiter that it was time to wrap it up and call it a job well done. It was then that Orla said,

"What an amazing day. Diane, you did such a beautiful job organizing this, thank you!" Everyone concurred. 'And Nikki, you are so beautiful! Look at these lights that have just come on, the way they play over your face, isn't that just magic! Before we go, I feel that I must say out loud what we're all feeling today. Is that okay?"

"Of course!" said Nikki.

"Okay, it's this. You shouldn't marry Gordon, Nikki. You really shouldn't."

Cindy had activated her trigger laugh, which now turned into a choke. There was a ghastly vacuum where their peals of laughter had once been, though the hubbub of the restaurant continued in the background. Nikki stared at Orla in horror.

"What?"

"He's just not good enough for you. You don't have his full attention, and I worry that you never will. I think we all worry about that."

Nikki turned to look at the others, who were too stunned to speak. "I think what Orla means -- " started Diane. Orla cut her off.

"I just don't think you will be as happy as you deserve if you marry Gordon, that's all. And I love you, we all love you, Nikki. You deserve such happiness. There's still time to change your mind, so just reflect on it a little, okay?" Orla smiled warmly at Nikki, whose eyes filled with furious tears. She turned and ran out of the room, and Diane whirled on Orla.

"What the hell, Orla!"

"What? Don't we all feel that way?"

"Not really. I think he's handsome," said cousin Cindy.

"And he's got money," offered high school friend Beth.

"Yes, but is that all that matters? Isn't it more important to feel that you are with a man who has your full attention? A man who makes you the center of his world?"

Diane wanted to wring Orla's neck. "For God's sake! You just ruined Nikki's bridal shower, doesn't that mean anything to you?"

Orla shrugged. "I think it's a sacrifice worth making for a friend who's about to make a terrible mistake. I'm surprised that you don't."

Nikki married Gordon. And she didn't speak to Orla again for the next three years.

2023

Sunjay opened his email and saw this message:

"Dear Swamy Deshpande,

I clicked on your website today, which I found to be very interesting. I have encountered some sadness in my life involving the loss of someone I love, and feel I need help in processing my thoughts and deciding what to do next. I have never consulted an astrologer before, and am not familiar with Whats App or Venmo, but if you can talk me through it, I would be eager to converse with you.

Yours sincerely,
Orla Nevins"

A customer! Sunjay was very excited; he knew this newly redesigned website would be compelling. And a female, as he predicted. Sunjay wrote her back immediately.

"Dear Orla Nevins,

I am delighted to make your acquaintance. As you know, I am well versed in all things astrological, and would be *happy to assist you in discovering your astral positioning in the universe. My charge is minimal: just $100 for a one-hour natal chart reading, which I will do by phone with you. First, you must share with me the time, location and date of your birth. I also advise you to get WhatsApp; you can find it easily in your App Store if you have an iPhone, and this too is where you can find Venmo, which I accept as a form of payment. I am excited to begin this journey with you!*

> *Respectfully,*
> *Swamy Sunjay Deshpande"*

In anticipation of her response, Sunjay ran to his bookcase and pulled out the book that he had found in a rumble sale the previous year, the book that had sent him on this journey and made all of this possible: "Astrology for Dummies," by Rae Orion. At first, he was a bit put off by the title — why would someone direct a book toward stupid people? - but he did find it easy to understand, and when he went to Amazon to read the reviews, he was very much reassured that this was the book he needed. One American reviewer wrote, "*This book is not for dummies! It is simple to understand and doesn't confuse you with complicted (sic) words that aren't helpful. I have been a student of astrology for years, and I always come back to this book for a general grounding in astrology.*" Sunjay had been at a crossroads at his life when he found this book, and he dove into it as a parched man struggling across a desert will dive into the cool waters of a pond in an oasis. (He liked this analogy, which he thought of himself, and used it on his website.) Reading the reviews on Amazon, he realized how many people (particularly Americans) were drawn to astrology and willing to pay for it, and then on Reddit there was a discussion of what people were paying astrologers, who always seemed to have Indian names: One hundred dollars an hour, minimum! This is where he had his "Aha!" moment. Sunjay had an Indian name and it was his real name! He could easily become an astrologer, too. Once this woman Orla gave him her birth information, he knew enough now to make up a chart for her and help her find her way back to a happy life. Additionally, he will make more money than he has ever dreamed.

It wasn't until the following week that Sunjay received his response. It was tonally quite different from the first one.

Dear Swamy Deshpande,

Namaste, as they say on your side of the world! You're probably wondering how I found you! I was actually looking up, or thought I was looking up, Australia (I'm a travel agent) but I spelled it wrong and suddenly astrology came up and I thought, well this must be a sign, lol no pun intended. So, I clicked on a few links and then I saw your picture. You look like such a kind, thoughtful man that I just had to reach out to you.

People are so beautiful, aren't they? They start to talk, and you can just see all the little things happening inside them that they can't do anything about, and it makes your heart just fill with love. Like Apollo. He would like people to think he is angry when they ask him too often about things. But he cares. Deep down, he's worried about your package himself, the same way he's worried about his mother's cancer. Or look at Homer. He needs everyone to think he's ferocious and could possibly kill you if you got too close, but what a beautiful soul! Sometimes, though, people will show a side of themselves that is not so beautiful, and that is troubling, isn't it? And maybe that is what has led me to you.

You asked for my birthday. It is May 23rd. I hope that helps.

Sunjay felt confused. Was she writing to him about the ancient Greeks? He did a quick google search on the Greek god Apollo, and didn't find much about his anger, or his mother's cancer. Sunjay didn't think gods got cancer. Homer was of course a poet, the author of the Iliad, but Sunjay had never read that book even though it was required reading in two of his high schools. He decided to ignore all the Greek references and keep it simple.

Dearest Orla,

Your email meant so much to me. I am more familiar with Hindu gods, but I can tell that you are a beautiful spirit, and your birthdate tells me much about you. It would help if you also told me the year and exact time you were born. That would enable me to find your anchor, the Ascendant. Also known as the rising sign, the Ascendant is the furthest left point of the central horizon line and quite literally reveals which zodiac sign was emerging from the eastern horizon at the exact moment of your birth. This will reveal the gifts and obstacles you will encounter in this lifetime. Once we have established that, I would love to talk to you in person about what I have learned because it is clear to me you are a very special person with unique gifts. Does this sound agreeable to you?

A few days later he received this response.

Sorry, sorry! I've been so busy with the Schauffhausens, who thought they wanted to go to Puerto Vallarta but at the last minute changed it to Dubai. Some people, right?

As for what time I was born — Gosh, I don't know. My mother burned down our house and my father died when I was very young, at least that's what my mother said, so I can't ask either of them. I don't even know what hospital I was born in, isn't that funny? So maybe you don't want to talk to me, I totally understand if that's the case but let me send a little check to support you in your valuable mission. I'm sorry to have wasted your time. Can you provide me with your address, please?

His address? Sunjay started to panic. Was this a real person? Or was this some kind of sting operation to weed out fraud? That would be so unfair, he had barely even started yet! Sunjay closed his laptop in a panic.

In New York, Orla closed her laptop, too. Then she picked up the squirming Homer, her new Maltese puppy who so beautifully filled the void after the tragic loss of Trixie. Homer was dying for a walk although he had already peed on the carpet, so Orla decided to take him downstairs for sidewalk training. She also needed to again ask Apollo, her doorman, about that missing package.

1986-88

The marriage between Nikki and Gordon thrived in its first years. Gordon was impressed by the fact that Nikki was an actress, and Nikki was impressed by Gordon's income-earning abilities, so that ticked off the box that asked, *"Do you respect one another?"* in the Good Housekeeping quiz. They were also quite attracted to one another's looks, so Nikki decided that gave a positive answer to the question, *"Is your sex life satisfying?"* Her family liked him and his liked her, so that was two more points. They seldom argued and when they did, it was usually settled amicably, because Nikki remembered her mother's good advice; never go to bed angry. This generally involved Nikki conceding whatever point was under dispute.

The only problem was, every time Nikki thought of Orla's outrageous behavior at her bridal shower, she became enraged all over again, so in the interests of not going to bed angry she decided to just block Orla from her mind. When she and Diane spoke on the phone (she and Gordon had bought a big house in Westchester, so it was harder to get into town for lunch,) Diane would sometimes offer tidbits about Orla, hoping to engender a little interest and possibly broker a reconciliation. Orla was doing summer stock in the Berkshires this summer. Orla had a new romantic adventure, this time in Prague. Orla got a new puppy, its name is Schatzi and it's so cute. All of these comments would be met with "Mmm," from Nikki, who would then redirect the conversation. She was very good at compartmentalizing, and thus Orla was locked away.

To Nikki's surprise, she herself was cast in a production of "Otherwise Engaged" at a theatre in Connecticut. Nikki had gone to the audition on something of a lark; her field was really musicals, but the play was British and Nikki's mother had moved to America from England when she was fourteen, so Nikki was fairly sure she could come up with a passable British accent. The casting people liked her immediately, and sent her to the director. The director asked her if she knew that the role required partial nudity. Nikki did, but hadn't thought she'd get so far in the audition process as to be asked about it. The director eyed her in her tight cashmere sweater and decided she'd be right for the role.

Gordon was delighted. He loved having an actress wife, and he wasn't the least concerned about the nudity, in fact he praised her bravery for taking it on. Nikki, however, was in something of a torment about it. The bra under the tight cashmere sweater had had a fair amount of padding in it, and she was terrified of being a disappointment. In the interests of full disclosure, she arrived at the first rehearsal wearing an unpadded bra. If the director was disappointed, he said nothing about it. The play was a fairly depressing piece filled with sardonic humor that Nikki guessed was meant to take the sting out of its nastiness. She was playing an aspiring writer who disrobes in front of a publisher in order to get a book deal. Nikki had never known anyone who would even contemplate such a thing, but then again, these people were British, so who knew? The rest of the cast had assumed the miserable disaffected attitude of the characters, and as a possible result none of them bonded with one another. Nikki wasn't even able to form a friendship with the actress playing the lead's wife, which was a surprise to her, having made so many friends in musical theatre. Everyone stayed in their dressing rooms until it was their turn to rehearse, and when it wasn't their scene, they wandered off and called their significant others.

This was fine with Nikki. She was terribly nervous about her nude scene; the fewer people around the better. She decided that, as they got closer to tech rehearsal where all the visual aspects had to be in place, she would shed one item of clothing each day until it didn't seem like such a big deal to be naked. She decided, too, to invest her little silver chain with magical shielding powers so that, even nude, she would feel somehow dressed. (She would never admit it, but she was channeling Orla with this idea.) And so, on a day carefully predetermined by her, Nikki removed the sweater she had been wearing to all the rehearsals and did the scene in a tee shirt and bra. The next day, she removed both the sweater and the tee shirt, and played the scene in her bra.

On the third day, it appeared that all the actors who normally hid themselves in the dressing room suddenly found business that needed to be attended to in the audience of the theatre. So did all the tech staff, the stage manager, the costume designer, the front of house guy and the janitor. The director did nothing about the sudden audience. After all it was the 'eighties; an actress wasn't supposed to have feelings about this kind of stuff or she'd be considered "uptight." And anyway, he was just as curious as the others.

When the moment came, Nikki closed her eyes, removed her bra, and played the scene as convincingly as she felt possible, given the incredibly vulnerable way she was feeling. Somehow, she got through it, though she suspected not very well. When she got off stage, she threw her sweater back on and ran for her dressing room. "Nice tits," commented the lighting designer, who had been watching from the wings.

"How did it go?" asked the other actress, who until then had taken almost no interest in her.

"Brutal," responded Nikki.

"You'll get used to it."

Nikki did get used to it, but it was never the liberating experience Diane had predicted for her; she just felt sleazy. At notes on tech night, the director said, "Nikki. What did I write here about your little strip scene?" Nikki waited, her heart in her throat. "Oh, right, crucifix! Is that a crucifix you had on?"

The costume designer spoke for her. "That wasn't our choice, it's the actress's personal property, she wanted to wear it."

"No kidding." He looked at Nikki, whose eyes implored him. "I like it, it's kinky. But honestly, I thought you were Jewish. Didn't I see 'Fiddler on the Roof' on your resume?"

"It was summer stock," said Nikki lamely, and the rest of the cast laughed. Suddenly she hated them all.

Gordon loved the show; he saw it three times. He tried to get Nikki to use her British accent in bed, but it made Nikki feel like her mother, and anyway she didn't go for that "silly stuff." Still, she recognized that when she was doing a play, Gordon was more attentive toward her than at any other time. She resolved to do as many plays as possible, if only for that reason.

Then she got pregnant with Mimi.

The birth of Mimi changed Nikki's outlook on life entirely; she simply could not believe that she had brought this exquisite child into the world, with her inquisitive saucer blue eyes and serious demeanor. From the very beginning, she sensed that Mimi was extraordinary. Changing her diaper when Mimi was only an infant, she would watch the expression on her face, a listening expression, as if she were taking last minute instructions from God. Yes. This child was blessed.

As Mimi grew, Nikki's passion for her child only increased, and her protectiveness along with it. Letting Mimi out of her sight was physically painful for her; she was sure the child would fall prey to pederasts and kidnappers (or both.) One day, when Mimi was three, Nikki needed to do some laundry. Since Gordon happened to be home (for a change) and was downstairs working on a spreadsheet, Nikki asked him to watch over Mimi for a few moments. When she came down a few minutes later, the front door was ajar and Gordon was scowling at his spreadsheet, oblivious. "Where's Mimi?" Gordon looked up at her blankly. Nikki's stomach lurched and her brain was suddenly flooded with a piercing white light, as if a florescent bulb had been turned on that would never go off, the florescent light of hell. She threw the door open and raced out the door to the busy street. No Mimi. She ran to the alley and found the child wandering near the trash bins.

"Mimi!" she screamed, and swept the child up into her arms. Carefully, so as not to betray the fact that she was on the verge of hysteria (although that was probably quite clear already,) she instructed the child never to go outside without Mommy or

Daddy. "Oh," the child said, digesting this information seriously. Nikki never forgot that, "Oh."

And she never forgave Gordon for his dereliction of duty. She used it as a weapon against him whenever they had an argument, and the "never go to bed angry" mantra somehow fell by the wayside. She still went into town for auditions, but she only did a play if she could get back to Westchester after rehearsals, and the idea of "making it" receded from her list of priorities. All she really wanted was to be safe at home with her perfect little girl.

Since Nikki and Orla weren't speaking, Diane became the connecting rod for communication. She went to see Orla in "Little Shop of Horrors" downtown, the fourth Audrey in that long running show, and she was terrific, very quirky and appealing. Nikki did "Pump Boys and Dinettes" in New Jersey, but she only invited Diane to come see it, which hurt Orla's feelings. Diane found the show corny but fun, and was glad to be asked by Nikki, who had been somewhat less communicative since the wedding. (She also saw "Otherwise Engaged," and could understand why Nikki hated being in it.) As for her own acting career, Diane was having a bit of a dry spell, and had returned to her loathed job checking coats in high end restaurants. She got a lot of reading done sitting in that little coat-stuffed cubby with book and flashlight, but as she always chose tomes like "Crime and Punishment, it hardly lightened her mood.

Then, it all changed. Her agent, who hardly ever sent her out on anything good, managed to get her an audition for a Shakespeare festival in Connecticut. She brought in a monologue from "Much Ado About Nothing," Beatrice's emotional and powerful speech about women's unfair role in society. She performed it with conviction, and was offered a season at the festival. She could hardly believe her good fortune.

"Shakespeare? La dee dah!" crooned Orla.

"Shakespeare? Why?" was Nikki's response. But classical theatre suited Diane well. She had trained in the classics in college, and had never had much confidence in her singing voice. She found much happier refuge in words. That season, she was cast as Olivia in "Twelfth Night," and in spite of the fact that the actor playing Orsino was quite handsome, the person who captivated her most was the lanky silken-voiced director, Tony Asquith. He was British, and incredibly smart about Shakespeare. He could quote line and verse from other plays at the drop of a hat and in giving notes said the thing that caused her to see Olivia with fresh eyes.

"She's in mourning, Diane. Never forget she's in mourning for her brother, whom she deeply loved."

God. How could she have missed that? From then on, even when Olivia was deliriously in love with Cesario/Viola, Diane always played it through the lens of grief. It earned her outstanding reviews and the respect of the rest of the company.

It seemed to Diane that, with Tony, she could realize her full potential as an actress. She set herself toward winning his favor, and it didn't really require much effort on her part. Before long, he was waiting for her after rehearsal and they would take long walks around the pond discussing their craft. It was all a bit secretive at first, as actor-director romances were somewhat frowned upon by the establishment, but after a certain length of time it became clear to all Tony and Diane were a thing and there wasn't much anyone could do about it. They were both tall, looked beautiful arriving together at parties, and everyone seemed to want to know them. When the season was over, the actresses in the company were hoping the romance would end, too, but Tony was still smitten with Diane. Though he had a nice apartment in the Village, he spent more and more time in midtown at Diane's "Heavenly Hellhole," as he called it.

When the Shakespeare festival started to gear up again, Diane was of course invited back, and this time she was offered the roles of Beatrice in "Much Ado About Nothing" and Isabella in "Measure for Measure," extraordinary casting for an actress in her second year who had seemingly come out of nowhere. Tony and she went out to a Spanish restaurant he knew and she ordered paella, a dish she had never had before, to celebrate the enormous promise of the upcoming season.

And that's where it all started to go south for Diane.

2023

Sunjay was trying not to panic. Orla sounded like a very nice, perhaps slightly idiosyncratic person, not the kind of person he would guess the FBI would hire to do a sting. On the other hand, what did he know about the FBI? He reread the email Orla had sent, and decided to respond in a way that would place in him an honest and favorable light to any officials who might be monitoring.

My dear Orla,

Please don't send me any money as I haven't performed any service for you yet! That would be unethical, which is not my way. I do astrological readings primarily for the love of sharing my knowledge with others. If, after a phone conversation between the two of us on WhatsApp (which is absolutely free!) it is your decision to pursue a reading, I would be happy to arrange that for a nominal donation, but for the moment let us just speak as new acquaintances who would like to know one another better. Your mother and father's untimely death does provide an obstacle, but one that I'm sure can be overcome.

By the way, my website may have given you the impression that I live in Mumbai, India. I was born there, but we moved to the US when I was thirteen, and I now live in Houston, Texas. I want to be absolutely clear about that and upstanding in our communications.

Yours most professionally,
Sunjay Deshpande

2025

Diane walked briskly on a snow-dusted sidewalk on the Upper West Side, gripping her insufficient jacket closed. She was only a block away from Orla's building when Nikki called again.

"I think I've found this horoscope guy. Wasn't his name Sunjay? That's the name I remember her saying all the time. Swamy Sunjay."

"Yeah, that sounds right."

Nikki was in Gordon's office sitting at his desk, which she had only recently summoned the courage to co-opt as her own. "He's right here online, advertising his services. Totally smarmy guy grinning into the camera like he thinks he's hot shit. 'A kind soul full of compassion and good will.' Yeah, right!"

"Did you contact him?"

"I clicked the link, yeah, and left a message. Posed as someone who's dying to know what the future holds for me."

"Good. Hope he gets back to you."

"Oh, he will. I know how these guys work. He'll ask me to talk to him on WhatsApp and then he'll start to smooth-talk me."

"Are you going to ask him about Orla?"

"No, that would be too obvious! I'll tell him Orla recommended him, and see what I can get him to spill about her."

"You sound kind of excited."

"I am! I feel like a detective!"

"Be careful, Nick."

"What, you think I'm going to give him my credit card number?"

"No. But these guys can be wily. Just talking to him on WhatsApp could compromise you."

"How?"

"I don't know. I didn't even know what WhatsApp was until recently. The future is leaving me behind."

"You gotta keep up with these things, Di. The singularity is near!"

"I don't even know what that means."

"It means —"

"I'm almost at Orla's. Call you back later."

1988

It was a clear, chilly September day in the city. Looking out the window of her room at the Plaza hotel, Nikki was dazzled by the vivid ice cream cones of color that comprised the tree tops of Central Park. The view could have existed a hundred years ago if it weren't for that taxi going by, and those old guys in in World War II bomber jackets playing chess. Nikki knew the park had become dangerous; she read about all the drug addicts and criminals and how the infrastructure was falling apart, but it certainly didn't look it from 59th Street. It looked idyllic. She flopped happily onto the luxurious queen-sized bed. What a difference experience being in the city was when you had money! Why don't we move back to the city, Nikki thought for the umpteenth time, but she knew Gordon thought of Manhattan as only a place to do business. He preferred the suburbs and his golf course and if she was honest, Nikki wasn't sure she had the stamina anymore for life in the city. Still, wasn't it exciting to be here!

She and Orla had recently made up. When her marriage with Gordon reached the three-year mark, Orla called to wish Nikki a happy anniversary and they talked it out. Orla explained she had just wanted the best for Nikki, and acknowledged that she had clearly made a mistake about Gordon. She was delighted for Nikki's happiness and the birth of her daughter, and she hoped they could still be friends. Of course they could. Now that Orla had fallen on her sword, Nikki realized she had hated every moment of being estranged from her; it was truly like losing a sister. She was so happy that the three of them could do things together again.

Gordon came out of the bathroom, his still-athletic body flushed from his hot shower and wrapped in a fluffy oversized towel, his black hair spiky. Nikki watched his reflection in the mirror as he donned underwear and reached into the closet, where Nikki had already unpacked his things.

"I spoke to the nanny. She picked Mimi up at school and now they're home having a snack."

"Okay."

"She said Mimi was fine with our being away. Didn't cry once."

"Great!"

"I gave her the Goldstein's number, just in case."

"Honey, we're an hour away."

"I know, but you never know when something might–" The hotel phone rang and Nikki dashed to pick it up. "Hello?.... Hi, Orly! Yes! We're here!"

At the Triple A Travel Agency in Chelsea, Orla sat at a small metal desk covered with itineraries, booking information, contracts, brochures, and a framed picture of her current pooch, a French bulldog named Popeye. Surrounding her were four other young people at desks, also on phones. All the buttons on Orla's phone were blinking, signifying customers on hold.

"Fabulous! I can only talk a minute because I'm at my temp job and the boss is on the prowl. Guess what? I got us tickets for Dreamgirls tomorrow night!"

"Oh my God! I'm dying to see that! Gordon, too?"

"Of course, Gordon too!"

"Gordon, Orly got us tickets for Dreamgirls!"

"When?"

"Tomorrow night."

"Honey, I told you, I have a big meeting with investors tomorrow night."

"Oh right! Orly, I'm so sorry, Gordon can't make it!"

Orla assured her it was fine, that she'd be able to resell the ticket easily (although she wasn't exactly sure how. Stand at the entrance to the theatre and hawk it, she supposed.) At that moment Isaac, Orla's boss, came out of his office. He was a weedy looking guy with a Fu Manchu mustache that Orla found repulsive.

"Gotta run, bye!" Orla hung up and pushed one of the buttons on her phone. "Triple A, this is Orla, how may I help you?" Isaac came over and lingered by her desk, ostensibly looking at a travel folder but she knew he was listening to her. Orla put her finger on the disconnect button and talked into her phone.

"Did he really say that about me? That is so kind, I'm happy to hear from a satisfied customer!....... Florida? Yes, Florida is very nice this time of year, but have you thought of going international? Bali is absolute heaven this time of year … Great! Come to our office in Chelsea and I would be happy to book that personally."

Isaac moved away from her desk and went to the coffee room. Watching him exit, Orla took her finger off the button and dialed a number.

"Dianasaur! Guess what I got us tickets to?"

The next night, three young women dressed in their cosmopolitan finest burst out of the Imperial theatre into the brisk night air, joining the throng of others being released from their respective plays. It was a well-calculated few moments of pandemonium under the bright lights of Broadway as people jumped into taxis, dashed into restaurants, or ran for the subway.

"AND I AM TELLING YOU!" belted Orla.

Diane joined in. "I'M NOT GOING! YOU ARE THE BEST MAN I'LL EVER KNOW! AND YOU, AND YOU, AND YOU —"

"YOU'RE GONNA LOVE ME!" they all sang at the top of their lungs.

"Amazing!"

"Incredible!"

"But! Is it as good as 'Matchmaker, Matchmaker, make me a match –" deadpanned Diane, and they all laughed, because life was hilarious at the moment.

"Don't mock 'Fiddler,' we wouldn't even know each other."

"True! Long live 'Fiddler!'"

They linked arms (as best they could with such a crush of people) and proceeded toward Joe Allen on 46th. Handing their coats to the young Indian man in his little cubby, Diane prayed she'd never have to become a coat check girl again herself. She looked at Nikki and Orla, arms linked and chattering happily as they went to their table, and it seemed to her that the three of them had never been apart. Yet much had happened in the intervening years; Nikki's marriage, the birth of Mimi, the ups and downs of Diane's own life, and as for Orla:

"Girls, Santorini is magical!" Diane and Nikki sat back comfortably in the warm restaurant, its walls amusingly covered with posters from failed Broadway shows, ready for her latest story.

It was Orla's habit to suddenly vanish from the scene and reappear in some exotic location, staying there sometimes as long as a month. It was unclear how she managed to finance this. Nikki's theory was that she was a trust fund baby, but when queried, Orla was always vague. Generally, a check of some kind had just arrived, and she felt she must spend it. It meant that Orla's acting career, such as it was, frequently took a back seat to her wanderlust.

"I arrived in Crete on the ferry from Brindisi, with no clear idea of what I was going to do or where to stay, but that's always the way to travel, don't you think? If worse came to worst, I was prepared to sleep on the beach. But then I ran into the loveliest man –"

"Here we go!"

"Loukas is Greek, as you might guess, with a smile to break your heart. He runs a youth hostel in Rethymnon. Now, at 34, I am obviously not a youth –"

"You are in spirit, Orly."

"Thank you, Nikki! He must have sensed that within me, because before long he offered me lodgings free of charge."

"In his bed?"

Orla blushed prettily, and even though she had put on a few pounds in recent years, Nikki and Diane suddenly saw sweet little Chava telling Tevye about her new love, a Russian soldier. "Of course not! I stayed on one of the bunks in the youth hostel for two nights and paid for both nights. But Loukas had the most breathtaking cottage he wanted to show me, on the top of a hill overlooking the Adriatic. He rode me up there on his motorbike -

what a thrill! The wind in your hair, the dangerous turns! At one point we came across two men slaughtering a goat. The entrails were falling out onto the ground as we rode past.

"Ugh!"

"Yes, but how primal, don't you think? Life at its most fundamental. In ancient days they would take the entrails and offered them to the gods on an altar."

"Okay, so Loukas," urged Diane.

"So, we rode a bit further, and then Loukas stopped and asked me to wait while he tidied his house for a moment. Girls, I have to tell you something. In that window of time waiting for Louka's return, I experienced a Perfect Moment. You know how every once in a blue moon something will happen, some random thing, that causes you to realize that the moment is perfect in every way and will never happen again?"

The girls' expressions were unreadable.

"Well, I had one of those moments, right there! I walked to the edge of the hill and stood there, looking out at the Adriatic. It was pale teal blue, with little cloud feathers threaded through here and there, as if an artist had painted them with a tiny bristled brush. It was a hot day, but a breeze played over my skin and it felt like a thousand cool, loving hands caressing me. In the air was the smell of the carob trees, do you know that scent? It's like chocolate. Breathe it in, and you are instantly intoxicated." Diane made a mental note to get a carob tree. "In the distance, I could hear the lambs baa-ing. There I was, every one of my senses absolutely vibrating with the knowledge that a lovely young man was coming back for me, and I knew that I was experiencing a moment of absolute perfection." Diane and Nikki's eyes were wide. "Then I heard the distant hum of Loukas's motorbike and here he was in his cut offs, ripped tee shirt and green flip-flops, impossibly handsome with this dark skin and luminous eyes. He took me up to his rustic cottage, and we made the most profoundly beautiful love together. I stayed there for three weeks, and each day was better than the last."

There was only one thing to say to these stories of Orla's, and Diane and Nikki generally said it in unison.

"Wow."

"It's the greatest love I have ever known," pronounced Orla solemnly, her multicolored eyes filling.

"Even better than Antonio?" asked Diane. Antonio was Orla's Italian race car driver.

"Oh, Antonio!" Orla closed her eyes. "What a beautiful, soulful man. But I have to say yes, even greater than my love with him. Of course, passion is hard to measure, isn't it, after the fact? It seems delirious, unending, impossibly intense at the moment, but afterwards? Well, you guys know."

Diane glanced quickly at Nikki, then down at her drink.

"But oh no, what am I saying? Diane, how are you? I know you've been sick and I'm so sorry. Did you get the flowers?"

"Yes, they were beautiful, thank you."

"Nikki told me you and Tony broke up. What happened? I mean, can I ask?"

What had happened was that sometime after celebrating her wonderful Shakespearean casting at the Spanish restaurant with Tony (where they were the only customers, Diane remembered later) she had started to feel very ill. Assuming it was the flu and with deep regret, she begged off of the first day of rehearsal for "Much Ado." Tony had kissed her on the cheek, said he would make do with the understudy and see her the next day. Twenty-four hours later, she was no better and had to bail on the second day's rehearsal as well, and then the third and the fourth. At first, she and Tony spent time on the phone so he could fill her in on the day's events, but by the fourth day he was completely immersed in rehearsals and too tired to talk. Finally, on his day off, he came back to Manhattan. She waited for him eagerly all day, but he didn't appear until late in the afternoon. The moment he kissed Diane, she smelled another woman's vaginal juices on his mustache.

Diane didn't really feel like describing to Orla the horrible shock of realization at what she was smelling, nor Tony's insistence that she was delusional, nor the hours of mutual accusations and, finally, his shamefaced confession. She didn't want to describe the lunacy of, days later, being told to bring his valuables, (a leather jacket and a book of Shakespeare sonnets) to his fucking therapist's office, who spoke to her on the phone in a reproving tone that suggested that *she*, Diane, was the malefactor. Nor the physical misery that finally led her to hail a taxi for the hospital, noticing for the first time in the cabbie's rear view mirror the sickly yellow of her face. (Her walls were mustard color, who knew?) The test result showed she had contracted Hepatitis A, most likely from that fucking paella in that empty restaurant. It is a disease which lasts weeks, if not months, which meant she had to withdraw from the best casting of her life. It took another month to get back on her feet, relying on unemployment insurance and the sympathy of her mother to keep herself afloat.

"We just went our separate ways. It was a growing thing," was Diane's mild response. Nikki, who knew better, fingered her earring and said nothing. She had been shocked when Diane had told her the story over the phone, and fully meant to rush into the city to bring her some of her chicken noodle soup, but she had so much to do with Mimi's schedule and her own busy affairs that she didn't know how she'd find the time. Horrified at the duplicity of which men are capable, she sent a floral bouquet then rushed into Gordon's study and threw her arms around him, a display of affection which surprised him, as Nikki had become rather cool to the idea of physical contact lately.

As if Orla knew what Nikki was thinking, she turned to her. "Gordon is going to be sorry he missed Dreamgirls, don't you think?"

"He is, and he sends his apologies. He wants to make it up to us by treating us to lunch tomorrow."

Diane looked at Nikki in surprise. "He does?"

"In fact, he's chosen the location, if that's okay with you guys. He has a business meeting downtown tomorrow morning and since we talked about poking around in the village... I mean, only if you want to."

"Of course we do!" exclaimed Orla, who was still trying to make up for the bridal shower and would be for a few more years.

"Sure," Diane responded weakly.

"Orla, how do you always manage to have these fabulously romantic adventures?" asked Nikki.

"I don't know, "replied Orla, looking a bit quizzical herself. "I guess I'm just open to them."

"Anybody had any good auditions lately?" Diane felt the urge to change the subject. "I've kind of given up on the whole thing myself, at least for now."

"I had a Maxwell House audition," responded Orla. "But it was such a hassle getting over to Madison Avenue from my job."

"You have a job? A job-job?" Diane and Nikki exchanged surprised looks.

"Yeah, in Chelsea. You know that travel agency temp job I've been doing? I thought for sure they were going to fire me because I spend a lot of time going to auditions and Greece and stuff like that, but I out-book everybody, and today Isaac – that's my boss - asked me to stay on full time. Why not, right? I can always quit. I really like making stressed out people happy, and he promised he'd be flexible about my auditions."

"You like it, huh?"

"I do! I send people off on their dream vacations, help them change their lives. It's called Triple A travel, but bleh. If it were my place, I'd call it the Great Escape."

"Perfect!" crowed Diane, and lifted her glass. "To the Great Escape!"

The next afternoon the three young women stood between two immense buildings clinging to one another as a fierce breeze whipped their clothing around their bodies, making them laugh. Out in the harbor, the Statue of Liberty raised her torch in approval.

"Isn't it fabulous?" yelled Orla loudly. "The way these buildings were built, it creates a crazy wind vortex. I feel like I'm flying!"

"I feel like my clothes are being ripped off!" yelled Diane.

"This is better than sex!" shrieked Nikki, which caused Orla to laugh and Diane to wonder. They endured it for a bit longer, then ran into the North Tower. Orla led them to the elevator.

"Oh God, the things I do for love," muttered Nikki, holding her hand to her throat. Diane looked at her quizzically. "Gordon took me here on our first date. I didn't have the heart to say no, he was so excited to show me the city and I was thrilled to be with him. But you know how I am about heights. Now he wants to come here, September 11th, every year. It's romantic, I guess. Sweet that he wants to share it with my friends. But ugh."

Diane suddenly felt a little dizzy herself. They approached the elevator that would take them to the 107th floor, and stepped in. During the stomach-droppingly fast ride Diane took Nikki's hand, which caused Nikki to look at her in surprised appreciation. Finally, the doors opened, and they were in another world.

The long and cavernous elevator lobby was entirely lined with mirrors etched in various nautical designs — sailing ships, harbors. Their reflections were everywhere, even on the ceiling, which made it feel like being inside a fun house. Next to each elevator door was an enormous quartz geode, the kind one only sees in Natural History museums, set upon a mirrored pillar.

"Is this kitschy, or cool?" said Diane.

"I think it's amazing!" responded Orla.

By now, Diane's heart was beating with anticipation. The three women made their way down the hall and round the corner to a stunning sight – the entire island of Manhattan, laid out before them in all its concrete and glass glory through the enormous floor-to-ceiling windows. The restaurant itself was impressive, with its dark wood paneling, gleaming brass bannisters, leather banquettes and immaculately uniformed wait staff, but Diane barely saw them.

From across the room, Gordon half stood and raised his hand. The three women made their way past handsomely dressed patrons and a white-uniformed waiter with a heavily loaded dessert cart to a table placed right before the windows.

And that's the last thing Diane remembers about Windows on the World. Not the food they ate, or what they talked about. Not what they did later, or how they parted. Just Gordon Barone, rising to meet them, and the entire city – high rises, bridges, the Hudson River leading to the vast sparkling ocean, laid out behind him, as if at his command.

Three weeks earlier, on a warm and humid August day on 45th street, a pale and sweaty Diane lay in her apartment on her velvet chaise, feeling very unlike Greta Garbo. Every time she got up, even just to go to the bathroom, there was an enormous water balloon suspended from between her breasts that bounced painfully as she walked. Was she going to die? She had lived so little of her life; it seemed enormously unfair to die now. God dammit, she had the worst luck! Why did things come so much more easily to others? Nikki was married already, well-to-do, with a beautiful child. Orla was somehow free to reject all the parameters of society and do as she pleased. Why was Diane the only one who had to grapple with reality-based issues like disease, heartbreak, and no money? Diane basked in a brew of self-pity for a good long while, indulging her penchant for compare-and-despair. Finally, she gazed down at her yellow writing pad. Was this any good? Didn't matter, there was nothing to do but write, unless she wanted to watch TV, and the reception was hopeless. The scene she was writing had just two characters, but Diane was thinking she might get bold and have a third person knock at the door.

Just then, someone knocked at her door.

Startled, Diane rose and hobbled painfully to the deadbolted, double-locked door. "Who is it?" she called out tremulously.

"Gordon," was the reply. Gordon? Nikki's Gordon? What was he doing here? She was too exhausted to run a comb through her hair, but she threw her robe on, removed the security pole, unlocked the deadbolt and opened the door.

Gordon loomed large in the doorway, making Diane wonder if she had recently shrunk. His black hair was in its perpetually mussed state — was it cowlicks? He was in his business suit, as always, and in his arms was a large paper bag.

"Sorry, Nikki couldn't make it, we've got a pile of little girls at our house and — God, Diane, you look terrible."

"Thanks."

"Get back in bed. I'll dole some of this out for you."

"No, no, you've done enough."

"Get in bed. Please."

Too tired to protest, Diane meekly got into bed even though she'd been spending the day on the chaise. She accepted a bowl of matzoh ball soup from Gordon and spooned it into her mouth, listening to him wash dishes in the kitchen, bag up her garbage and put it by the door.

"You really don't have to do that."

"Of course I do, you're an invalid. Nikki really should have described this better."

Wondering how Nikki had described it, Diane looked around her apartment and realized for the first time that all of her plants were dead. When did that happen?

"The walk upstairs was interesting. Black walls. A hypodermic needle. I came into the building behind a drag queen."

"Tall, black? Probably Rochelle."

"This apartment is huge, though, by New York standards."

"It's the reward for making it past Armageddon."

Gordon came out of her kitchen, wiping his hands on her "I HEART NY" dishtowel. "You're like that tragic character in La Boheme. What's her name?"

"Mimi."

"Really? No. Mimi?" He seemed perplexed. Mimi was the name of his daughter. "So, tell me, Diane, what do you need?"

"Peace in our times."

"No, seriously. Prescription refilled or something?"

"It's Hepatitis A. You just stay hydrated and, after the worst is over, try not to be bored to death."

He glanced down at her yellow pad. "You're writing."

"Trying to."

"A book?"

"A play."

"I see. Makes sense. You can't audition for anything right now, so…"

"That's my thinking."

"Want to read me something?"

"God, no!"

"Come on. I just did your dishes. You owe me."

Diane felt trapped. Did she owe him? Maybe she did. Against her will, and because she was a bit curious herself how it sounded, she started to read. It was bizarre to be saying the words she'd so carefully chosen out loud. Diane wondered if it would rob her of the ability to keep writing, as if letting the genie out of the bottle. Gordon stood listening, still holding the dish towel. After a moment, he lowered himself onto her wingback wicker chair, draping the towel on its arm. Then he started laughing. Diane had never heard anyone laugh at something she had written. It was shockingly gratifying. She came to her last words and looked up.

"That's great! Painfully funny! How does it end?"

"I don't know."

"You'll figure it out." He grinned at her, and Diane wondered why she had ever found him evasive and dull. "You've lost a lot of weight, you know. You should be eating more."

"Okay." Diane pulled up the covers self-consciously. "The soup was good."

"You need more than soup. Can you hold anything else down?"

"I'm not really motivated to try."

Gordon looked at her meditatively. "Okay!" he said suddenly, and rose. "I can see you are gainfully occupied, which is a great way to heal." He went back into the kitchen, rummaged around some more and came back with a flower vase filled with water and a glass, which he set next to her. "This is a pitcher."

"It's a vase. Your wife sent me flowers."

"For our purposes, it is a pitcher. I want you to drink all of this water today, then call Nikki tonight and tell her how you are feeling. Deal?"

"Deal. Thank you, Gordon."

"My pleasure."

After he left, Diane continued to write for a bit. Then she reached over to the wicker chair, grabbed the "I HEART NY" towel and placed it over her eyes, inviting sleep.

A day later, Diane's phone rang. "Gordon says you look terrible," said Nikki. "Are you worse?"

"I don't think so."

"I'm worried about you. Should you go back to a doctor?"

"No. I'll be fine, Nikki. I just need rest."

"We're coming to the city in September, ostensibly for a romantic weekend, but really I'm coming to see you and Orly. Do you think you'll be better by then?"

"Of course."

"We're going to stay at the Plaza!"

"Cool!" Diane started to get a headache.

"Orly wants us all to do something girlfriendy like see a show. I would love that, but I'm worried you won't be up to it."

"I will, I promise. How's Mimi?"

"Oh, my little lovebug! She's so extraordinary, Di. She says the most precocious things." Nikki then went on to list all the extraordinary things Mimi had said that week, and Diane stared down at her script. Maybe one of these characters should be an overly doting mother. By the time she got off the phone she was so exhausted she fell into a dead sleep.

The next day, Gordon called.

"I'm in a phone booth on the corner. There are no drag queens to let me in."

Diane put her key in a sock, opened the street side window (the only one that opened,) and saw him standing below in a navy pea jacket, blue jeans and Timberline boots, holding a bag of groceries. It was the first time she'd seen him out of uniform. She tossed the sock and he caught it in one hand. There would be only about two minutes until he made it up the black stairway of death. She brushed her hair and put on her flannel Lanz nightgown with the tulips on it. The bell sounded just as she was pulling it on over her head.

He came in as if he had lived there for months, walking straight to the kitchen with his bag of groceries. Diane tagged along behind as he produced an uncooked chicken, potatoes, broccoli, salad fixings, ice cream and a bottle of wine.

"I can't drink the wine."

"It's for me. I'm making you a meal," he announced. "At least one of these items will appeal to you. Lie down, I'll tell you when it's ready."

Diane lay on the chaise, and this time she did feel a bit like Garbo. He took off his pea coat, rolled up his sweater sleeves, and went to work. It was amazing how his vitality changed the atmosphere of the apartment. He hummed standards as he cooked, sometimes singing snatches of the lyrics – "It Had to Be You," "Our Love is Here to Stay," "I Did It My Way."

"You have a nice singing voice."

"Do I? That's odd."

"I don't even know if the oven works."

"It works. The chicken's on at 350 and roasting nicely. Your color is better. You're drinking the water?"

"Religiously."

"Good girl."

Diane attempted to concentrate on her play. The characters were having an argument about free will versus destiny. She had no idea where to go with it.

"I was in town for a meeting," said Gordon from the kitchen.

"Ah," responded Diane. "What do you do again?"

"Commercial real estate developer."

"Right. I hope you weren't involved in that horrible Broadway mall they're trying to put up. They knocked down five gorgeous theatres for that piece of shit, can you believe it?"

But Gordon was singing again. After a few minutes he came out of the kitchen with his glass of wine and sat in the adjacent chair. Diane very much wanted to start the conversation off on the right note.

"How's Nikki?"

"Good. She's all excited about this fair coming up at the elementary school. You know Nikki, so organized, so capable. They've put her in charge of everything."

"Please thank her for sending you over here. Really. Above and beyond."

Gordon rose, went over to the window and looked down to the sidewalk where he had caught the sock. "This is a terrible neighborhood."

"I know. I have a gift for picking out terrible neighborhoods. Sometimes it feels like they pick me."

"I could help you find a better place."

"Thanks, but I lose a lot of money if I break the lease."

"C'mon." Gordon sat down on the edge of her chaise and looked at her meaningfully. "Seriously, Diane, you're too good for this. You deserve better."

Diane was in a sea of speculation. What was going on here? Gordon had never taken the remotest interest in her. On the rare occasions when he was included in the threesome's gatherings, he had repeatedly gazed at his watch and left the room for various obscure reasons. Now, he seemed — what? Attracted to her? Why? She had seldom felt so uncomfortable. What was it about Diane now that made her different from who she was before? She rose to put her soup bowl in the kitchen. Immediately he reached out.

"No, let me take that. You look so frail."

That was it. She was frail. Delicate. Weak. Waifish. Afflicted, like Agnes of God. The opposite of the current Nikki who, as the years passed, seemed more and more capable, robust, energetic. Could that be it? Could her own weakened state be causing him to feel — what? More of a man? A devilishly wicked idea came to her, rendered more plausible by the intense boredom of confinement and coupled with the green-eyed monster of jealousy. Diane, in a move she was eternally to play over in her mind in later years, decided to play with fire a little. When he came back into the room she rose, then staggered a little as if losing her balance. Gordon rushed to her side, catching her up in his arms.

"Sorry, just… the bathroom."

"Sure." Gordon puts his arm around her waist, supporting her as she made her way across the room. She leaned into him a little. "I'm kind of weak."

"Yes. I've got you."

Oh, man. It was a turn on. It was such a turn on Diane didn't know what to do with herself, and was grateful for the privacy of the bathroom. She sat on the toilet trying to regain her composure. His arms were so hard and strong; did he work out? Had he felt that seismic jolt when they touched, or was this all in her head? Where was he now? Would he be waiting outside the door, or was he in the kitchen? Or maybe he had gone home, leaving her dinner in the oven. After a decent interval, she flushed the toilet and came out again.

He was waiting.

Diane took a few steps toward the bedroom, but instead of taking her arm he scooped her up Sleeping Beauty style and carried her to the bed, placing her down gently. "Let me see your body," he instructed in a tone that brooked no argument. Diane hesitated, then slowly raised her nightgown, exposing her lower torso with its clean (thank God) white panties. He placed his large, manicured hand on her ribs, and her breath caught. "You're like a child," he commented. "We have to get some meat on you." He pulled her nightgown back down and went to finish making dinner, which he served in bed. He sat watching her as she ate.

"That's not enough. Have another bite," he commanded, and she did, even though it was starting to make her nauseous. When he deemed her done, he washed her dishes and left.

Diane lay on the bed, her heart beating in wonder and alarm. What had he activated within her? And how did she turn it off?

Three weeks later, Nikki announced that Gordon would be joining them for lunch at Windows on the World and Diane panicked. Those two afternoons had been very stimulating, and a great distraction from illness, but she was well now, and back in her right mind. It seemed to her expedient to beg off on lunch. After all, she had the perfect excuse: too much excitement from "Dream Girls" and Joe Allen, wanted to make sure she didn't relapse, etc. She picked up the phone and dialed.

"Orly!"

"Dianasaur! I'm still singing those songs, aren't you?" Diane drew a blank. The only song she could think of was "I'm Just a Girl Who Can't Say No."

"Yeah! Listen, about lunch tomorrow —"

"I'm so excited! I've only been to the World Trade Center once but it's so cool. And later tonight, I thought we could go to the Village Vanguard and hear some jazz, Wynton Marsalis is going to be playing."

Diane loved Wynton Marsalis.

"Nikki really needs this. She adores Mimi, but she's been stuck on Mommy duty for four years, and you know Gordon's not good for much." Diane suspected Gordon was good for something, but didn't respond. "Though I guess I should stop saying things like that. I feel badly about what I said that day at Nikki's bachelorette party. Obviously, they've stood the test of time."

In your mid-thirties, a three-year marriage equated to standing the test of time.

The only thing Diane remembered about that lunch at Windows of the World, aside from the astonishing view, was that she desperately tried to avoid eye contact with Gordon. Yet it seemed that every time she glanced his way, he was glancing hers. Then they would both look away.

Three days after that lunch, as she both hoped and dreaded that he would, Gordon called. A client had given him tickets to the opera, and Nikki was too busy to join him. Would Diane like to go? Diane had no interest in opera, but like a robot programmed by some evil scientist, she said yes.

She dressed carefully, and was pretty sure she looked fantastic in the black sheath that had always been a little tight on her until hepatitis made her svelte. She met him at Lincoln Center, and of course he was standing before the fountain, ejaculations of illuminated water shooting up dramatically behind him, framed by the Met with its amazing Chagall wall hangings. It was hilarious, the man's knack for standing in front of dynamic settings.

They had great seats, orchestra center. The opera was impressive but long, and might have been really good, but Diane's body was vibing too much next to Gordon's to concentrate. He never touched her, their knees didn't even graze, but it was as if there were invisible molecules dancing between them. When it was over, they went across the street to the Saloon and had a drink. What did they talk about? Diane doesn't remember. What she remembers is the timbre of his voice, so deep and vibrant, and the intent way he looked at her, as if he were contemplating what to do with her next.

They took a taxi back to her apartment and still didn't touch in the cab, in fact they sat quite far from one another. When they arrived, she didn't say, "Would you like to come in?" He simply got out of the cab and walked into the building beside her, accompanying her up that long hellish stairway. And that's when it all began.

He was gentle, at first. At the days progressed and Diane's energy grew, he was less gentle. They grappled with one another like animals in the wild. She found she could wrap her legs around him as he pinned her to the wall like a butterfly and it made her feel like a gymnast. He hit places within her that she didn't know existed, filled her in a way that was excruciatingly good. He toyed with her, tantalized her, made her beg for it (she cringed about this later) and God bless her faithless feminist heart, she loved it, all of it. One day, he took a large cucumber out of his grocery bag, bigger even than his erection, and said, "You're going to take this." Diane nodded and obeyed. Afterwards, they cut it up and ate it in a salad. She was shocked at herself that she was willing, even eager, to follow his lead in all this. What was happening to her? Sex with Tony had been tame and (she supposed) very British, and previous lovers had, she realized now, also been quite conventional. This was new and exciting and, in Diane's mind, the very last time it was going to happen. Until it wasn't.

After a while they started having conversations to fill time between rounds, and found one another not uninteresting. Diane's dry wit made Gordon laugh, and Gordon possessed an ironic sensibility she found intriguing. He was smarter than she had at first given him credit for, conversant on politics, (though they disagreed on almost everything,) and they shared a love of rock and roll. They liked to turn the stereo up and sing loudly to the Rolling Stones, or Led Zeppelin, or even (his idea) Bruce Springsteen. If there was a neighbor across the hall, Diane never saw them and never heard a complaint.

"How did this happen?" she asked one warm spring day three weeks later, as they were lying in bed. The sun was streaming in through Diane's purple curtains, staining the flank of Gordon's body a gorgeous mauve. She suspected she would never forget that color, that long muscular leg.

"I don't know," responded Gordon. "I was just bringing soup."

"You're not my type at all."

"You're not mine, either, except for your body."

"The only novel you've read is by Ayn Rand."

"Actresses are very shallow people."

"You don't have an artistic bone in your body."

"You make arrogant, blanket statements that only reveal your ignorance."

"In some ways, you're not even a very good person."

"That is true," said Gordon, and they fell back into one another's arms.

And the guilt. Oh, the guilt was crushing. Diane felt as if she were carrying around heavily sloshing buckets of hot tar in a yoke over her shoulders. Every time she talked to Nikki on the phone, she wanted to cry or even throw up afterwards. Occasionally, she did both. Most of Nikki's conversation was about the wonders of Mimi, Nikki's role as head of the PTA, her pottery class, and the Spanish she was taking because one day she wanted to go to Costa Rica. She rarely talked about Gordon, or if she said his name, it was something like, "Gordon disagrees with me about that," or "Oh, here's Gordon, late as usual, I have to run." Maybe she didn't care about him anymore? Maybe she didn't mind if someone else was using his body? Because that was all she was doing, Diane told herself, using his body until it became less interesting to her and she found someone else. Nikki was so busy, and she sounded happy and very preoccupied with Mimi and the joys of motherhood. Still, Diane lugged those buckets of tar, and couldn't escape the noxious smell of shame. This would end soon. She'd find a way to make it end.

1989

Two years and a few months after his diagnosis, Paul Barnes died. He had outlasted expectations, but no one survived AIDS for more than a few years back then and everyone knew it. Will, who called to give Diane the news, said with some bewilderment that he himself was still testing negative but that Young Michael was not doing well. "We weren't lovers, you know, Michael and me. I know everyone thought we were, but we were just friends." His voice was filled with fear.

The minute she heard, she called Nikki. If she had known how hard Nikki was going to take it, she would have gone to her personally. Nikki started sobbing as if a stuck valve had just been opened, as if she were hearing about her own death in an alternate universe. "Keening" was the word that came to Diane.

"It could have been me, it could have been me," she kept saying, and "Thank you, Lord, for giving me this life with Gordon which I do not deserve. Thank you! Thank you!"

It was weird and rubbed Diane the wrong way. Shouldn't they be thinking about Paul in this moment? She couldn't get off the phone fast enough, but it also solidified her thinking about her own part in this distasteful melodrama.

The next call she made was to Gordon at his place of business.

"Gordon Barone."

"We can't do this anymore."

"Diane? What's going on?"

"Nothing. Everything."

"Let's talk. Meet somewhere and we'll talk about it."

"It needs to stop, Gordon. You know it, too, there's nothing to talk about."

"I think there is. Look, I'm cancelling my appointments, meet me at —"

But Diane hung up. The ugliness of it all was just too much for her. She was tired of hating herself, of feeling unclean and sinful. It had to end.

Paul had been mistaken in his prediction that Diane would never see him again. When she heard from Will that the end was near, she had gone to visit him at Roosevelt Hospital.

He had his own large room, Diane guessed for fear of contamination, with a window onto 59th Street. The nurses came and went briskly, heavily covered in gloves and masks and offered Diane same, but Diane had read up on it; she knew you couldn't get the disease from breathing the same air, so she refused. She didn't want Paul to think she was afraid.

She thought she was prepared for what she was to see, but there was no preparing for Paul's appearance; he looked like the living dead. His once-beautiful eyes stared out from sockets deeply embedded into his head. Most of his hair was gone, and he had the Kaposi's Sarcoma that she'd heard about; purple skin lesions all over his body. His naked leg poked out of the sheet; it looked like an unearthed bone.

Diane approached Paul's bed with a broad smile on her face, carrying an armful of long- stemmed flowers.

"Well, if it isn't my Irish Tzeitel. Come here, darling, let me look at you." Diane approached as far as she dared, trying not to let her smile slip. "Still with the fabulous hair. You should put it up, you'll look like a Gibson Girl. Is life treating you well?"

"I'm fine. You know, auditions, rejections, the usual. Paul, I'm so — I just wanted you to know that I'm so —"

"I know. It's a horror show, isn't it? I believe my ingenue days may be finally over." Diane's laugh was more like a gasp. "Good, thank you for laughing. I'm so tired of the gloom and doom. Are you still acting?"

"Yes, but it's losing its charm. I find I enjoy writing more these days."

"Plays? How delightful! Write a role for me, why don't you? A sad, glamorous clown of a man with a convincing butch side. What kind of flowers are those, darling? I'm not seeing very well."

"Calla lilies," Diane said, with a twinkle of a smile.

"Oh my God, she remembers!" Paul cried, taking the flowers from Diane, cradling them tenderly and slipping into his famous dead-on impression of Katherine Hepburn in "Stage Door."

"The Calla lilies are in bloom again, such a strange flower! Suitable to any occasion. I carried them on my wedding day and now I place them here in memory of something that has died."

It was uncanny; gazing down demurely at the flowers held so wistfully in his left arm, Paul *was* Katherine Hepburn. The nurse came in to find Diane doubled over with laughter, and Paul looking quite delighted with himself.

His funeral was at the West End Synagogue. The place was packed with many actors but also with friends from the Jewish community. Doris Schmidt, who had played Tevye's wife Golde, was there and she looked bereft.

"He was my best friend. Whenever he played Tevye, he always asked for me as Golde. He called me almost every day, it's like we were married in another life. I just don't know what I'm going to do without him."

Diane wondered how she had missed the deep friendship between the two of them. She had been so involved in her own personal drama back then, she hadn't even noticed. She vowed to herself to be more observant in future, and was glad to see people smiling at the large bouquet of calla lilies up front, sent from "Your Stage Door Janey."

It seemed a lot of people felt that Paul had been their best friend. The actors playing Lazar Wolf and the Rabbi hugged each other tearfully. Will sat in a pew by himself, looking stricken and bewildered that he was still healthy, when so many of his friends were not. Diane found Orla and they sat together. Diane scanned the room for Nikki, and found her sitting on the other side of the temple clutching Gordon's hand and staring straight ahead, as if mentally willing herself to be somewhere else.

Orla turned in her seat and saw Young Michael standing in the back, accompanied by a young male friend who held onto him protectively. Michael was impossibly thin, with a lesion on his face and sunken cheeks that made her baby-faced suitor Fyedke suddenly look like an old man.

When the service was over, Orla went over to give Michael a hug. He held his hand up. "Thanks, Orla, you don't have to."

"Hugs aren't contagious."

"Still." Michael gave his friend a nod, and he moved away to allow them to talk.

"I'm so sorry, Michael. Is there anything I can do? Just name it."

"Maybe… would you mind calling my mom when this is over?"

"Calling your mom? Isn't she…" Orla stopped herself, and swallowed. "Sure. I'll call your mom."

"Thanks. It will make her happier to hear it from you." Michael borrowed a pen and wrote his mother's phone number on the back of the funeral program, while Orla's heart broke. They stood there in silence for a moment, and she was about to turn away when he spoke again.

"I just wonder – I just wonder what it's going to be like. To go from alive to dead. That one moment is what I'm curious about. The rest of this is just… bullshit."

I think it will be beautiful, Michael," Orla said. "I think you will find the most exquisite peace."

Michael looked momentarily hopefully. "Think so?" Orla nodded with absolute certainty, her eyes never leaving his, then reached out to hug him. This time, he let her. Then, she put his mother's number in her bag, and they parted.

On the other side of the room, Nikki had just spotted Michael, and her eyes were wide with shock. Urgently, she grabbed Gordon's arm and pulled him out the side door of the temple.

Diane made her way outside and sat on the steps. She saw Nikki speaking to Doris and thought she should run to catch Will, who was walking away from the temple, his hands jammed into his pockets. But she just couldn't seem to get up. She crouched over her feet and stared at the sidewalk for a moment.

"You okay?" Hearing Gordon's voice, Diane sat up stiffly.

"Yeah. Just… examining the mica."

"You look like you're going to throw up or something."

"I'm fine, thanks. Healthy, strong, in need of nothing."

Gordon hesitated, then sat down beside her. "I've never seen Nikki so upset. I know she liked Paul, but she's been just devastated by this. I can't get her to talk to me about it."

"There's nothing to talk about. She's sad."

"You'd tell me if there was something more to this?"

"More? I don't know what you mean."

There was no need for Gordon to know the whole story; she knew how he'd react. Fine for him to have a sexual history, but for Nikki? She mentally willed Gordon to stand up and move away, but he continued to sit there.

"I like your hair up like that. Kind of old fashioned. You don't usually do that."

"Gordon. It's over."

"I know it's over." Gordon said with some exasperation. "I can still worry about you, can't I?"

"No," responded Diane resolutely. "I am not the one who needs you, Nikki is. Go be with her." Gordon didn't move. She felt it necessary to turn and look him directly in the eyes.

"Please."

Gordon stayed a moment longer. Then he rose and rejoined his wife.

1977

Living in the world of make-believe agreed with Orla. The story of a young girl who finally finds her true family after being stuck with the mad caprices of a crazy woman for years resonated with Orla, and she loved being at the theatre watching the others create that story. Even though she had found a piece of family in meeting her grandmother, it wasn't quite the fairy tale ending she had dreamed about. Mona was a tough cookie, and though clearly fond of Orla, wasn't there supposed to be a male counterpart in this story? The father who had been searching for her all his life and suddenly appeared? Or maybe someone who had been there all along, who knew everything about her and cared deeply but for some reason couldn't reveal himself? Orla was ever waiting for that miraculous day.

As for Janita, she was beginning to regret that she had invited Mona back into their lives. It wasn't that her mother had gone back to her disapproving ways, in fact quite the opposite. Having Janita, and particularly Orla, back in her life had given Mona a new sense of purpose. She had, without too much trouble, found them a duplex in Hoboken, an accomplishment which filled her with an unusual sense of pride. She started to participate in their daily lives in a way that Janita never expected. She took Orla to voice class, and to rehearsals when Janita wasn't feeling up to it, which was rather often. By then, Janita had started to realize what a fifth wheel the parent of a child actor was. She had to be there because of labor laws, but there was nothing to do but sit in a folding chair in the rehearsal room for eight hours and talk to the other mothers - dreadful, ambitious back-biters, each of whom thought their daughter should be playing the role of Annie. They were deeply suspicious that Orla had been cast so quickly after getting into town, and looked at Janita as if she must have slept her way to the top or something. They made their own children nervous, gossiped endlessly, and were competitive to a scary degree. Mona got along with them better, so Janita gratefully agreed when her mother offered to relieve Janita every now and then.

When the show opened and was the hit of the season (which was very exciting,) and when, early in the run, the little actress playing Pepper had to have her tonsils out and Orla got to play the role for a week, Janita was there every night and that was a lot of fun — Orla was so good! There was a little incident with one of the other actors who was a bit of a perv, but Janita straightened it out and it was like it never happened. But then the original girl returned, the excitement died down, and Janita became bored again. She gave herself the assignment of making sure there was a hot meal on the table when Orla got home, but this meant she had to have her mother for dinner, too. Janita would sit there smoking a cigarette as Orla and Mona related the day's activities; who was nice (Andrea, who played Annie;) who to steer clear of (Dorothy, who played Miss Hannigan) and all the other minutiae of a life in the theatre, which Mona seemed to be enjoying as much as Orla.

"And Mr. Charnin says Andrea is maybe gonna sing a number at the Tony Awards!" enthused Orla.

"Can you imagine? On nationwide TV. Millions of people watching."

"I'd be scared to death!"

"Better keep up with those singing lessons. You may end up playing Annie yourself some day!"

Janita was starting to wonder if coming to New York had been such a good idea after all. She missed the California weather and the laid-back west coast vibe. New York was so nervous! Everybody was always doing something, all the time, and if you weren't *doing* something they seemed to think there was something wrong with you. Even Simon, who had been so much fun in San Francisco and actually did get into the chorus of "Annie" playing a citizen of Hooverville, could talk about nothing but "the business." It was so *boring!* Janita started toying with the idea of taking Orla out of the show and going home. Broadway wasn't all it was cracked up to be, in Janita's opinion.

Janita had gone out, ostensibly shopping for groceries but actually to meet the guy who sold her weed, and Orla and Mona had just come back to Hoboken when the phone rang.

"Hello?" said Mona brightly. There was a pause, then a male voice said, "Janita?"

"No, this is her mother, Mona. Who's calling?"

"This is Jack. Janita's husband." Mona's brain did a double take. Her husband? Janita had never said anything about a husband. She had heard Orla mention someone named Jack once or twice, but thought it was a friend of hers in San Francisco. How to react? Mona decided the best course of action was to be friendly.

"Oh, hello Jack! How nice to meet you. Janita's not here right now, she's just out getting groceries."

There was another pause. "I see. So, Mona, is it? How are you feeling today?"

"Oh, we're having a wunnerful time! We just got back from the matinee, and there's no show tonight, so Orla can rest. Are you gonna come out and see the show?"

Whereupon, Jack replied, "The show?" And Mona realized she had strayed into uncharted territory. Just then, Orla came into the kitchen and said, "Who ya talkin' to?" Between Mona and being a stage orphan, she was starting to sound like a New Yorker herself.

"Oh, here! I'll let you talk to Orla, she's right here!" said Mona, and thrust the phone at her granddaughter. "It's Jack!" she whispered, and she saw Orla go pale and run out of the room. "Oh, sorry, I was mistaken. Maybe you should call back later?"

When Janita came home with groceries, Mona helped her unpack them and put them away. Then, with a tone that she hoped sounded neutral, she said, "Your husband Jack called."

Janita, who was just putting away the tuna fish, froze, her hand still extended toward the shelf. She turned slowly and stared accusingly at Mona. "I told you never to answer the phone!"

"Janita, why didn't you tell me you were married?"

"Because it's none of your business!"

"None of my business? I'm your mother!"

Orla, who was hiding in her bedroom, heard the ensuing argument that took place between her mother and Mona. It was the most sustained fighting she had ever heard from Janita, who by now would normally have gone into one of her narcoleptic trances.

"He'll never take me back now! You've ruined everything!" Janita wept. Then Orla heard her grandmother slam out the kitchen door. Orla waited a bit, then crept into the kitchen and found her mother sitting at the kitchen table, a lit cigarette dangling out of her slack mouth, her expression bleak and comatose. Orla gently removed the cigarette and helped her mother into bed.

2023

After a few false starts, Sunjay and Orla finally spoke on the phone.

"Swamy Deshpande?"

"Yes. Hello. Miss Nevins?"

"Oh, please call me Orla. Am I pronouncing your name correctly? Deshpande?"

"Yes, but perhaps it will be easier if you just call me Sunjay."

"Oh, thank you! Like the first bird of the morning! Isn't this wonderful that we can speak to one another from so far away, Sunjay? Mumbai sounds like such a strange and exotic place!"

"I'm in Houston, remember? I wrote in my email--"

"Oh yes, yes, that's right. Sorry, I'm a little forgetful these days. So much going on, I'm just crazy busy! Isaac is flat out mean to me these days, and Homer ate some chocolate which scared me to death."

Sunjay now supposed Homer to be a pet of some sort. "Of course. I had a friend whose monkey died of chocolate poisoning."

"Oh, are monkeys allergic, too? And there must be so many of them in Mumbai!"

This appeared not to be the moment to reiterate that he was in Texas; Orla seemed a bit flustered and he felt he must put her at ease. "Many monkeys, yes." He responded. "I do hope that your Homer survived the experience well."

"Oh yes, I took him to a clinic and they washed out his stomach."

"That is a relief. It is my wish that my services be of some use to you even though, due to the circumstances of your childhood, you are not able to provide me with your exact time of birth or its location."

"I'm so sorry. Like I said, my mother burned down the house where we were staying in Hoboken while I was doing Annie. Jack called her, and they got into a fight, and Mommy got so upset she fell asleep with her cigarette."

"Ah."

"I knew it, too. I turned to Mona that night -- the orphans were just about to do "It's a Hard Knock Life," -- and I turned to Mona and said, 'Mommy's gone.' And Mona thought that I meant she went back to California, but I knew it was more than that. I could feel the empty. And Mona felt so bad about it that a year later she died, too, just bang like that. So, after that I got emancipated! But anyway, sorry about the birth stuff."

Sunjay could not follow most of this, but perhaps it didn't matter. "Please do not apologize, Miss Orla! All is well. I have prepared a horoscope based on your date of birth alone. May I deliver it to you?"

"Oh yes, please! I can't wait!"

Sunjay cleared his throat and read from the speech he had prepared based on the information gleaned in his Astrology reference book, which he refused to think of as Astrology for Dummies. Such an insulting name for such a very good book.

"Being born on May 23, you are a Gemini. Faith in the goodness of humankind make a person born on this date stand out as a special individual."

"Oh!"

"You are generous, ready to talk down any enemy and help those you find who are in need. This is, of course, a wonderful quality in a person, but it can also be their weakness. Sometimes a Gemini doesn't know when to stop, and the love they share with the world may not be reciprocated. This can leave you feeling hurt, and drained of emotion, even hurt by those you care for."

"Oh, that is so true! And what a beautiful voice you have, Sunjay. So resonant!"

Sunjay swelled with pride. "Thank you."

"But I'm kind of confused."

"By your horoscope."

"No; by your voice. I am looking at your picture right now, and your voice is different from what I imagined. I imagined a much thinner voice, higher in pitch than yours. Perhaps even a little nasal."

Sunjay was stunned. Orla's description exactly fit Mr. Bhandari's voice, which was indeed somewhat nasal and more of a tenor. How did she know this? Doubts about Orla's legitimacy re-entered his mind, and a dark suspicion occurred to him. Was she perhaps in the employ of Mr. Bhandari? Did he see his own picture online, become angry, and decide to punish Sunjay by hiring someone to expose him? Was he planning to sue Sunjay? That would be horrible!

"I — I'm so sorry, Miss Orla, but I'm afraid I must terminate our conversation for the moment. A situation has arisen. A circumstance beyond my control."

"Oh, what a shame, I'm so enjoying this! Another time, then. But I'm sorry, I still haven't figured out how to use this Venmo you talked about. Can I send you a check?"

"NO!" said Sunjay, louder than he intended. "It's quite fine, we will call this session complimentary."

"Sunjay, this is getting silly, I can't keep consulting you for free. Just let me send you a little something, please!"

Sunjay reflected. If this woman sent him a small amount of money, what would the harm be? He had just given her a horoscope reading; it was a legitimate transaction. But he obviously couldn't masquerade as having Mr. Bhandari's face anymore. If "they" were watching, he needed to come clean. "Miss Orla, I feel I must confess something. You have guessed the truth; the face I have posted on my website is not my own."

"Oh!"

"It is the picture of a man I admire greatly, a Mr. Bhandari. Unfortunately, my face is one of great ugliness and I felt I could not use it."

Orla sighed deeply. "Sunjay, it makes me so sad that you don't like your own face! I am sure that it is much more attractive than you yourself feel. We do that to ourselves sometimes, don't we? Run ourselves down, when the truth is frequently something much more pleasant."

Sunjay found himself trying to guess what Orla looked like, and how old she was. Her voice was quite high pitched and chirpy, almost like a child's voice, but the content of her conversation seemed to indicate someone older. All he knew was, there was something very comforting about talking to her.

"Miss Orla, I will email you my address in Houston, if you desire."

"Oh, that would be grand!"

2025

As Diane approached Orla's building, she had a heavy presentiment. Perhaps it was the fact that it looked shabbier than she remembered it, although the restaurant below still seemed to be thriving. It was rent controlled, so the window decor varied widely, ranging from elegant curtain installations to what looked like bedsheets. She pushed through the revolving doors and approached the desk where stood the latest doorman, a middle-aged Latino man with a nametag on his jacket that read "Apollo. '

"Hi, I'm here to see Orla Nevins. 14B?"

"She not here."

"Do you know when she'll be back?"

"They take her away." He said this so casually that Diane gasped.

"Take her away? Where?"

"Hospital."

"Oh, my God. Do you know which hospital?"

"No se. Maybe Roosevelt?"

"Who took her away?"

"Ambulance. Her people say she no come back."

"What people?"

"Relatives." Diane tried to think if Orla had ever mentioned having relatives other than her mother and grandmother, but could come up with nothing.

"And what about Harvey?"

"Who?"

"Her partner. The man who lives with her."

"Mr. Gluck?"

"Yes, that's right. Mr. Gluck."

A janitor had come into the foyer while they were speaking and was mopping the floor. The doorman spoke to the man in Spanish, then turned to Diane.

"He die."

Diane stared at the doorman dumbly. "Die? He's dead? When?"

Again, an exchange in Spanish. "Four month ago."

Diane's head was reeling. How did she not know this? Why did Orla not tell her? "Can I leave a message for the relatives? Do they come back here?"

"Si. They come. They get her things. They say she no come back."

Diane stumbled out of the building trying to make sense of this flood of information. Harvey was dead, and Orla was in the hospital. Why? What had happened? Had she been sick? Diane dialed Nikki's number, but it went straight to voicemail. Maybe she was talking to this Sunjay guy. Feeling in dire need of coffee to sharpen her wits, Diane ordered a latte at Starbucks, sat on a park bench by the 72nd street subway, and thought back to the last time she had seen Orla in person.

It had been two years ago. Orla had flown out, impulsively and at the last minute, to see Diane's play in Los Angeles. Surprised and thrilled, Diane went to pick her up at the airport. She waited the longest time for Orla to come out, circling Arrivals again and again trying to get Orla on the phone. On the fifth try, she rounded the American terminal and saw Orla standing outside, animatedly chatting to a young woman. Diane rolled down the window.

"Orly!" she called. Orla turned away from the girl and her eyes widened in surprise.

"Diane!" What are you doing here?"

"I'm picking you up!"

"Really? Wow! You didn't have to do that!" Orla said a few more words to the young woman, they both hugged with great affection, and Orla rolled her suitcase to Diane's car.

"How did you think you were going to get to the theatre?" Diane asked once Orla was settled in the car.

"Oh, I would have found my way."

"Do you even know where the theatre is?"

Orla laughed. "That was the sweetest woman I was just talking to. She's coming here to go to UCLA! She lives in Ohio but she's really not comfortable with the political climate there, so even though her parents didn't want her to, she applied to UCLA. Imagine her delight when she got in!"

The entire drive to North Hollywood, Orla talked about the young woman on the plane. Diane tried to interject a little something about the play Orla was about to see – she really couldn't believe Orla had flown all the way out there just to see it, and was very moved by the gesture – but she couldn't get a word in edgewise. That young woman had really preoccupied Orla's attention.

"I told her we should meet up for a drink afterwards."

"Tonight? Does she live in North Hollywood?"

Orla laughed. "I don't know!"

Diane looked at her quizzically. "I want you to be prepared, honey, this is just a small theatre, and it's LA. It's not important."

"What do you mean, it's not important? It's theatre!"

"Yeah, but Los Angeles theatre is different. For actors, they're hoping someone will see them and put them in a TV show. For playwrights… well, I don't know what it is. You certainly don't invite your agents to it, they just treat it as your cute hobby."

"Oh, that's ridiculous! This is your play! It's important!"

It was lovely to feel that kind of support from her friend. They arrived at the theatre, and Orla was bubbling with excitement. She loved the space, she loved the neighborhood, she loved the people behind the ticket counter. Diane was pleased at all the approbation, and couldn't wait for Orla to see the play. Her actors were top notch, and she felt she had directed them well. Sometimes a cast gels, sometimes it does not; it's a mysterious alchemy that you can't force. This cast had gelled.

Diane had seated them in the second row, center. Perhaps a bit close, but she wanted Orla to be able to appreciate the nuances of expression. The lights began to dim. Orla squeezed Diane's hand and winked. The show began.

Ten minutes into it, Diane heard a snort. She turned to see Orla, sound asleep, her chin on her sternum. Horrified, Diane gave her a little nudge. Orla startled, nodded to Diane and resumed watching the show. But it happened again. And again. Finally, Diane felt she couldn't keep nudging her anymore. She cursed herself for putting them so close to the stage. The spill from the stage lights revealed Orla's face to the world (and to the cast;) an older woman, probably deeply bored, sleeping through the show.

When the ninety-minute show was over, Orla woke up and started to applaud enthusiastically. "Wonderful!" she enthused. "Just wonderful!"

The rest of her visit was similarly bizarre. Orla spoke a great deal about her dog, about the girl on the plane (who they never had drinks with,) about the exotic trips she had planned for the future. But she never said another word about the play.

In retrospect, Diane wondered why she hadn't called Nikki to report on the visit. It had been disquieting, to say the least, but then Diane got busy with other things and kind of forgot about it. After all, Orla had always been unpredictable.

The doorman had mentioned Roosevelt Hospital, which was as good a guess as any; it was nearby. Diane decided to walk the eleven blocks to the hospital and inquire. It was funny; if it were LA, eleven blocks would be unthinkable. Not only would she drive it but, once there, she would circle the parking lot to find the slot closest to the door. It was good to be back in the city. It felt healthier somehow. The crisp air, the people rushing around, the taxis whizzing by. The air of expectation.

Yes, the city had changed but, in some ways, it had the same intoxicating buzz it always had. You always had the sense that, at any moment, something thrilling could happen to you.

1990

"Wake up, Diane Daly! You're the toast of the town!" Diane hadn't answered the phone when it first rang, she was too hungover from the opening night party the night before. But she recognized the voice on her machine as being the Artistic Director of the theatre, and he sounded urgent. It caused her to jump out of bed and take the call before the guy could hang up.

"Hello? What? Could you repeat that?"

"The reviews are a rave! The show is a hit! Congratulations!"

Diane could scarcely believe it. She'd been having terrible fights with this man, who wanted her to change the ending of the play, and told her she was making "the biggest mistake of her career" by insisting on keeping that ending. He had been reluctantly friendly when introduced to her friends last night, spending most of his time with the actors (and probably saying, "Don't blame me, I wanted her to change the ending.") But now the reviews were out, and to Diane's delight every critic singled out the beauty of the ending as one of its high points.

On the phone, the Artistic Director had apparently forgotten that there was ever any disagreement between them. Suddenly, she was his new favorite playwright who he'd like to commission for the next season. (At a later audience talkback, he himself referred to the "enormously moving, almost magical ending." Diane marveled. How do people do this? Instantly revise their thinking and pretend they never felt any other way? She almost wished she were that malleable, except that she also loathed that quality in people.)

Diane hung up in a kind of daze, reflecting on the previous night. Orla and Nikki had been there, of course. Orla brought her new beau, an older man with a comb-over, just a little taller than Orla (which means very short) who tended to peer at people, or perhaps his glasses just needed adjustment. His name was Harvey, and he had a deep, drawling voice, like an American Alan Rickman. Everything he said (which wasn't much that night) tended to catch Diane off guard and cause her to puzzle over what he meant. At intermission he came up to her and said, "So. Voltaire was right, eh?" And walked away.

Gordon came with Nikki. Diane noticed he was starting to go a bit grey, but it suited him. He was sporting a beard and had let his hair grow longer, which tamed his cowlicks and made him look a bit like Eric Clapton. He wore a black turtleneck under a brown suit, and brown suede Hush Puppies. Diane felt that she was perhaps noticing a bit too much about him, and looked away.

The show went very well, and the applause afterwards was fulsome but not enough to lead Diane to believe there would be raves in the morning. After the show, Harvey came up to her and said, "A triumph of form over substance!" To which she would have taken offense, except that he was beaming at her approvingly through his cloudy spectacles. Gordon said nothing, just smiled and gave her a thumbs up from afar. They all went out after the show for drinks and to discuss the play. Diane thought Gordon might weigh in at this point, but he was in an extended conversation with Harvey. Audience members kept coming over to her and saying how much they enjoyed it. Diane felt a bit stunned by all this praise. She had been laboring in the fields of constant rejection as a writer for so long, it all felt like a bit of a joke.

"But enough about the play. Tell me about what's going on in your lives!" she begged Nikki and Orla, when it all got a bit too heady.

"Well, I'm a partner now at the agency," announced Orla demurely.

"No!"

"I am! Isaac asked me if I'd like to buy in, and I said I'd think about it, but only on the condition that I could change the name of the agency."

"To Great Escape?" guessed Nikki.

"To Great Escape!" Orla nodded happily.

"Amazing!" Diane raised her glass. "To Orla, and Great Escape Travel! Long may they prosper!"

"How much was the buy in?'" asked Gordon, who hadn't raised his glass.

"Gordon," said Nikki reprovingly.

"Oh, I'd rather not say," Orla demurred.

"Did you have a lawyer look at the contract?"

"I didn't need to. Harvey looked it over for me." Gordon, who had just experienced a conversation with Harvey, looked skeptical.

"I'm a CPA," Harvey explained to the others. "It's all totally *sui generis.*"

Diane and Gordon exchanged a look. It was the first eye contact they'd had in a long time.

"I can have my lawyer give it the once-over, just to make sure," Gordon offered.

"Oh, thanks, Gordon, but I'm fine! Let's talk about Diane — what a show!"

Later, as they were getting ready to leave, Gordon made his way over to Diane. "*Sui generis* means unique."

"Oh God. Should we be worried?"

"I think we just have to hope this guy Isaac is a straight shooter."

"How many straight shooters run businesses in this city, in your opinion?"

Gordon declined to answer. "The play was really good, Diane. Smart, funny, perceptive, just like you. I know I don't get the right to be proud, but I'm proud of you." He took her hand for a moment, and Diane's pulse inadvertently raced. He released it and moved away. Watching him, Diane reflected on the men she'd dated in the past three years. Some of them looked really good on paper — a journalist with a commitment to social issues, a doctor who volunteered with Médecins Sans Frontieres, a novelist whose stuff was actually worth reading. She had almost moved in with the novelist, but then decided there would be too much competition. And anyway, none of them did that "thing" to her that Gordon did. Every time their eyes met, Gordon's and hers, it was as if he were reaching inside of her. How could she marry a man who didn't do that to her? Wouldn't such a marriage be doomed?

On the other hand, (in addition to the small issue of his being Nikki's husband) Gordon was a real estate developer, for God's sake. He worked in a reprehensible field; the feverish overbuilding of commercial real estate in Manhattan these past years was changing everything about the city she loved. The Marriott Marquis alone, which is what became of the Broadway mall idea, depressed the hell out of her; a soulless monstrosity, as predicted. Still, as she watched Gordon amble back to the table to sign the credit card (even just the way he walked, holy hell) she found herself thinking, would it be such a terrible thing to be in contact again? What if they just had coffee?

Nikki, looking radiant in a way Diane hadn't noticed until that moment, came up and took her arm affectionately. "Diane, I didn't want to announce it at the table, but guess what? I'm pregnant again!"

Diane's mind was suddenly drained of all thought, her body of strength. "Oh. Wow."

"Can you believe it?" Nikki beamed. "After five years, I thought maybe I couldn't have children any more, but I'm four months along now and I feel great!"

"Wow, Nikki," Diane repeated dumbly. "That's great!"

"Thanks, honey, I knew you'd be happy for me. Orla was worried--" Nikki stopped herself. Diane looked at her curiously.

"Orla was worried what?"

"Well, you know. She's so sensitive to people's feelings."

"She thought I'd be jealous? Honey, I'm thirty-two, I have plenty of time to have a baby if I want to, which I'm not even sure I do."

"That's what I said! And now you're a big successful playwright – I'm the jealous one!" But Nikki did not look jealous. She looked the picture of complacent self-satisfaction, at least in Diane's opinion. No. Don't do that, she warned herself. This is your friend. Maybe your best friend.

To atone for the sin of covetousness, Diane grabbed Nikki's hands and started to sing a Kool & The Gang song. "Celebrate Good Times, Come On!" she warbled, and did a happy dance. Nikki laughed and danced with her. Orla, seeing them, broke away from Harvey and joined in, even though she didn't know yet what they were celebrating. When Nikki leaned in and whispered, "I told her!" Orla shrieked with delight and sang all the louder. It looked, from the outside, like an incredibly happy moment for all three of them, and the other customers smiled indulgently at the disruption. Across the room, Gordon turned and watched with a wry smile.

Later that night, on the street, Diane waved to her friends as they went their separate ways. Then she turned and went back into the bar. An hour later she was still there. "You sure now?" the bartender asked, when she ordered yet one more Long Island Iced Tea. "I'm sure, she responded. "I need my Great Escape."

Six weeks after the show opened, Diane was offered a job writing on a television series on the west coast. It was an easy decision to make. She gave up the Heavenly Hellhole, packed her things, and moved to Los Angeles.

2025

Roosevelt Hospital was abuzz with activity. At the crowded hospital intake desk, an overtaxed Black woman searched Orla's name on her computer as Diane tried to ignore the heavily breathing man in back of her. The temptation to turn around and tell him to back off was almost irresistible. "Orla Nevins…Yes, she was here. She was with us for five days, and then discharged to another facility."

"What was her diagnosis?"

"I'm not at liberty to discuss that. I can tell you that she was suffering from dehydration."

"What facility did they take her to, can you tell me?" The woman sighed, tapped a bunch of other keys, then looked up at Diane. "Meadowbrook mental care. In Yonkers."

Diane's heart sunk. She had been afraid it was something like this. Ever since Orla's visit to California she had felt uneasy. Why had she not been more attentive to what was going on with her?

Extricating herself from the mass of humanity, she made her way outside to call Nikki, who this time picked up right away.

"Hey! I just remembered, Orla joined a church. Do you remember the name? She was all about how open and progressive it was. Maybe if we search all the Unitarian churches in the area —"

"Nikki. Orla's in a mental care facility."

Nikki was dumbfounded. "Mental care? That can't be right. She was fine the last time I talked to her."

"Six months ago."

"Yeah, but — can a person slide that far that fast?"

"I think she was sliding before we realized it. There's something else, Nikki. Harvey is dead. He died four months ago."

"Oh my God. And she didn't tell us? Oh Diane, something really is wrong. We have to go to this mental care place."

"We?"

"Of course. I'm coming out on the next flight I can find. Don't do anything til I get there."

Diane breathed a sigh of relief. Doing this alone was very stressful; she needed moral support. Plus, she was just now realizing how much she missed Nikki.

1990

At five months, Nikki felt the baby move. It wasn't like Mimi's first kick, which she barely recognized as such. She had thought there was a thread or a hair on her stomach, and was plucking it away when she realized it wasn't a thread; it was Mimi. But this movement, this kick, perhaps, had force and intention. The baby was declaring itself. "I am here!"

"So you are, "she said to her belly fondly. "So you are."

The psychic connection between her and this burgeoning life felt tangible. Sometimes the baby was very active at nighttime, when she was desperate for sleep, but she knew how to calm him. (She was sure it was a boy.)

"Okay, settle down now, Mommy needs to sleep," she would think. And quite soon, the baby would comply and go to sleep, if one is not already asleep when suspended in amniotic fluid. Certainly, it would calm down and just be.

If there was tension between Nikki and Gordon, and there was from time to time, the baby would become quite active and thrash around. Nikki always felt consoled by this, as if baby was expressing physically what she felt.

"Yeah! He's being a jerk, right?"

But Gordon, in spite of the serious financial setbacks he had been experiencing with the recent savings and loan crisis, was actually delighted by the pregnancy, and doing all he could to make Nikki's life easier. He did the laundry for the first time in their marriage, for instance, and insisted on being the one to make breakfast so that Nikki could sleep in.

"How's Toughy?" He would ask when she came down in the morning.

"Doing a little morning dance," she might reply, or "Toughy's playing football with my tummy!" Gordon would laugh, and insist on feeling his son for himself by placing his cheek against Nikki's stomach. Nikki loved this; it was as intimate an act as had occurred between herself and Gordon in a long time. When the baby kicked, they both laughed in delight.

One morning, Nikki came downstairs looking a bit bewildered. "How's Toughy?" asked Gordon.

"I think he must be reading," she responded.

"He knew his mom needed a good night's sleep." Gordon kissed her and they had breakfast. But the next morning Nikki came down, and the look on her face was something Gordon had never seen.

"I think something's wrong," she said, and they went to the hospital.

The baby's heart had stopped, for no reason that anyone could provide. They induced labor; Toughy was indeed a boy. A beautiful, perfect boy, except for the fact that he was dead.

A deep chasm erupted between Nikki and Gordon. They both felt equal grief, but they absolutely could not share it. Nikki felt that Gordon had played a part in creating the stressful environment that "killed" her child. Gordon resented Nikki's seeming conviction that she was the only one suffering.

"For fuck's sake, I lost a child, too!" he shouted at her one evening when Nikki refused to budge from the sofa for eight hours straight and Mimi came in to him crying about being hungry. It was at this point that they hired the nanny.

Nikki didn't want to blame the loss of the child on Gordon, on his reckless speculating and constant blanket assurances, in spite of her worries, that everything was going to be just fine. Everything clearly wasn't fine; no one was renting those buildings he borrowed so much to build. Gordon spent his nights pacing back and forth, back and forth; she could hear him from their bedroom (which he seemed to never be in) and it drove her wild with anxiety. So yes, maybe it was his fault, in a way.

She sank into a deep depression. Even the sight of Mimi playing the Sugarplum Fairy in the school's production of The Nutcracker couldn't pull her out of the deep well of pain in which she resided. She tried medication, this new drug Prozac everyone was talking about. It put a bit of a dent into her misery, or rather distanced her from it somewhat. She found she could function enough to fake it, and that was the important thing since she didn't want Mimi to think there was anything wrong with her mother. But the void was still there.

In Los Angeles, Diane had landed on a show that was both challenging and satisfying to work on. It was a family show, fairly intelligent, kind of heartwarming, lots of drama. People who watched the show prided themselves on how many boxes of tissue they went through crying. Her showrunner was a cheerful, very capable older woman named Clara, who had been around the block many times and knew how to handle "the guys upstairs." At Diane's first network notes session, the comments that were given were so clueless that Diane had to work hard not to convey her disdain. Masking her feelings wasn't one of Diane's skills, but she knew the importance of neutral note taking. Her agent had told her about a writer who was fired because she sat with her arms folded during a notes session, which led the network to tell her agent she was "difficult." But Clara faced the executives with body language that did not suggest she thought they were idiots, and before Diane could even register the implications of the mess that the network was making, Clara would say, "Yes! Good note! I've got the perfect way to address that," even when she didn't. Later, the writers would gather and figure out a way to do damage control and, with Clara's guidance, it usually worked out well. Diane was learning a lot.

The day that Orla called her at work, Diane's attention was pulled in about five directions. As the writer/producer of the episode that was currently filming, she was going to be needed on the set as often as possible. She was also part of the team that was location scouting the episode, her input was required in casting, and she had been assigned another episode, the outline for which was expected by the end of the week. So, when Orla called her in the middle of the day seemingly to chat, Diane was not really there for it.

"I'm worried about Nikki," Orla said. "She's just not herself."

Diane was studying a "day out of days" as she walked down the hall to her office. "Well, who is these days? I'm personally in the middle of going crazy. One of our locations just fell through, and the guy we cast as the sweet twinkly grandpa turns out to be kind of a perv."

"Yikes."

"What's this about Nikki?"

"Something's wrong, I think. Ever since the miscarriage - "

At the word 'miscarriage," Diane stopped what she was doing. She knew about it, of course. She and Nikki had spoken at length numerous times after the fact, but somehow even though Nikki referred to it as "the death of the baby," Diane had a hard time envisioning it as anything more than a very late period. This was no doubt due to the fact that she herself had never been pregnant, and knew nothing about the seismic changes that took place within a woman even in the first months. This was revealed to her in force when at one point, fully six months after the tragedy, Diane had said to Nikki, "Oh well, I'm sure there will be another one." This statement, which was meant to sound encouraging, released a completely unexpected torrent of anger from Nikki about her, Diane's, ignorance and insensitivity. She knew enough now, when the word 'miscarriage' was spoken, to be careful.

"Okay, wait, Orly. Just a sec." She closed the door to her office and sat down. "Sorry. Start again."

"Ever since the miscarriage, it feels like Nikki is just going through the motions. She says all the right things, but the emotion behind them feels missing, you know? And her voice is so dead. She sounds almost robotic sometimes."

"Well, you two are on the phone, right? She's in Westchester, you're in Manhattan."

"Yeah. She doesn't come into the city anymore, that's the other thing, but you can tell a lot about a voice on the phone. For instance, I can tell that you're super stressed, but feel guilty about something and want me to think you're not being insensitive."

Wow. Bingo.

"Okay Sherlock, so what do you think we should do?"

"I think she needs a Great Escape. I think we all do. What would you say to us all taking a house in Italy for a week after your shooting stops? I'm a partner now at the travel agency, people keep offering me a week here, a week there, hoping I'll recommend their place to my clients. Right now, there is this really cool place in Florence I'd love to get a look at."

"When you say 'all of us' —"

"The three of us with our guys. Harvey, Gordon… You're still with Ben, right?"

She was still with Ben. She had met him at a film festival in Sundance, Utah. He was a film editor, probably younger than she, though they hadn't specifically compared birthdates yet and wasn't looking forward to the moment when they did. He was tall with sandy hair and an infectious slightly gap-toothed grin. They both loved skiing, they both loved dining out, and after a while, it seemed they were starting to have feelings for each other. Why not invite him? She didn't particularly like the idea of Orla's new boyfriend, Harvey, being in the party; he was so weird. But Gordon — well, as far as he went, it had been almost two years. Her current feelings toward Gordon were sympathy for the loss of his child and pity for his current business losses. That wasn't a terribly sexy combination.

Now that she had money for the first time in her life, she and Ben flew first-class to Florence, which was lovely with its endless wine, soft pajamas and open-out beds. Diane joked that she never wanted to get off the plane. Ben was sweet and funny and easy to be with. They spent the first day and night in the Brunelleschi hotel with its view of the Duomo to get over their jet lag. Heaven.

The next day, the rest of the gang came. The property owners had provided a limo to take them all to their destination, which turned out to be large palazzo-like farmhouse Orla had found just a few miles outside of Florence. It was beautifully restored from its sixteenth century origins, with stone archways, Greek columns (added on, Diane guessed, to create the palazzo vibe) and all modern conveniences. A splendid centuries old mulberry tree grew on one side of the house. On the other side down a gentle slope was a lap swimming pool flanked by cypress trees on one side and acres of vineyards cascading down the hillside of the other. A grove of olive trees was beyond that, and in the distance was what looked like hundreds of acres of forest.

"It's okay, I guess, if you like perfection," commented Diane as the six of them marveled at the view. In the distance, they could see people working in the vineyard.

"The place is part of what they call 'Agrituristo,'" said Orla. "A working farm that caters to tourists. They passed a law in 1985 allowing farmers to make money and preserve the land by offering accommodations to tourists, and they get big tax benefits. Of course, not everybody has a gorgeous house like this to offer. A hundred years ago, this was the property of some old famous guy, a count or something. I have to look that up again."

"Who knows?" speculated Harvey. "Perhaps Marcilio Ficino lived here!" They all looked at him blankly. "Marcilio Ficino," he repeated, as if he had just said George Clooney. "The Florentine philosopher of the fifteenth century? He asserted a defense for the immortality of the soul."

"Oh, <u>that</u> Marcilio Ficino!" said Gordon, and Diane couldn't help but laugh.

Harvey winced, as if Gordon had just farted loudly. "Ficino is considered the most important advocate of Platonism in the Renaissance. Your loss, I'm afraid, if you haven't heard of him."

Gordon turned toward Nikki, hoping to exchange a look, but she was gazing in another direction; the pool, it seemed.

Orla took Harvey's arm and beamed at the others. "And the best part is, all the food they serve us this week has to be locally sourced, which means fresh, fresh, fresh!"

It was clear Orla was already working up her sales pitch for when she got back to the travel agency. The place truly was a find; she should have no trouble convincing her clients to stay there. Ben squeezed Diane's hand and grinned at her. She nudged him back playfully, then noticed Gordon looking at them. Gordon, caught in the act, quickly busied himself with bringing in his and Nikki's luggage.

To the others' surprise, Nikki had not insisted on bringing Mimi. Sensing her mother's distant mental state, the child had bonded with her nanny, an extremely efficient German woman who seemed to dote on Mimi, and the child was happy to stay home with her. For Nikki, this was a relief; she found it exhausting to play the happy game all day long. It was May, and the weather was still a bit cool, but Nikki fully intended to get her laps in in that pool. Lately, she had found that prolonged swimming helped her to think more clearly and lighten her mood.

Orla and Diane approached Nikki, who was staring down at the pool in an almost alarming way. "You okay, Nick?"

Nikki looked up and smiled convincingly. "Yeah, great, this is so great. It was wonderful of you to arrange this, Orly. Did Gordon give you our check?"

"Check? This is a completely free week!"

"Free? All six of us?"

"Hey, I'm a honcho at "Great Escape" now. You wouldn't believe the perks I get."

Relief washed over Nikki's features. "Oh, wow, so it's true. I wasn't sure… sometimes Gordon can play a little fast and loose with… We really wanted to come, but it's been tough lately."

"I know. Isn't it lucky this came up?"

Nikki hugged them both, then went into the farmhouse. Orla and Diane exchanged a smile. With Diane's TV money and Orla's new standing at the travel agency, it was no problem for them to split the cost.

"This is gonna be good."

"Yeah. It's gonna be very good."

Every day the couples would go off on their separate expeditions, then reconvene on the patio under its luscious grape arbor for supper. Diane and Ben rented bikes and rode about the spectacular countryside sampling local wines and practicing their nascent Italian. Harvey and Orla went to the Convent of San Marco so Harvey could experience the ancient building where all the great philosophers of the Renaissance went to meditate. Gordon found himself a golf course, Nikki spent an inordinate amount of time in the pool, and one day all six of them took in the Uffizi.

As they wandered the galleries of the Uffizi, they came upon a Botticelli painting, "Primavera." Harvey was in raptures. "Ah, yes! All of these figures are borrowed from Lucretius — Cupid, Venus, Flora, Spring, Zephyr, they all represent the renewal of life. And look at the three muses! How remarkable -- these nudes look exactly like you girls! Do you see it?"

Diane, Nikki and Orla leaned in for a closer look. The ladies in question, all blondes with curly hair and soft, corpulent bodies bore no resemblance to any one of them.

"Well, that's certainly my ass!" quipped Orla. They laughed and moved on.

In the evening their host, Francesca, a busty, gregarious Neapolitan lady with a booming laugh, served the most amazing meals -- Florentine steak, Pizza Napoletana, Piedmontese agnolotti, all accompanied by fruits, cheeses, and the wines of the regions. Diane observed Nikki starting to relax, and even laughing a bit. But it was strange, the more Nikki relaxed, the tenser Gordon seemed to become. Through an upper window of the house Diane could see him pacing back and forth on the phone in front of the pool — he had acquired one of those amazing remote telephones that allowed you to speak anywhere. What he didn't realize was how well sound traveled over water.

"Then we should sell it.......I don't care about the loss, I need capital and I need it now!" Diane closed the window.

On the last day, five of them went to the Palazzo Vecchio. Gordon stayed back at the farmhouse to take care of some business, which the others feared meant more shouting around the pool. The group approached the W-shaped Piazza della Signoria, with its copy of Michelangelo's David. Their guide was Harvey, who in only a few days had fashioned himself into an expert on All Things Florence.

"Savonarola was hanged and burnt here in in this square," he informed them. "In his sermons he preached against the immorality of the age, and death was his reward."

"Well, there was a bit more to it than that, right, honey?" commented Orla. "That guide said he tried to take over Florence. He forced the citizens to burn all their nice things – mirrors, jewels, cosmetics, fine clothing."

"Sounds more like a campaign against women," commented Nikki.

"And the clergy," quipped Diane, and Ben laughed.

Harvey continued undaunted. "They burned books, manuscripts of secular songs, paintings, sculptures, musical instruments. They did it every month. Bonfires of the vanities, they called them."

"Ah!" said Nikki. "Like the movie."

Harvey appeared to be making a monumental effort not to roll his eyes. "There were excesses, to be sure, but Savonarola helped bring down the House of Medici. That could only be a good thing."

"Soldiers raiding your homes?" responded Nikki. "Taking all your worldly possessions, and punishing you if you resisted?"

"It was a debauched time. It needed purifying." Nikki shrugged, and looked away.

"Oh, Harvey," responded Orla, swatting him playfully.

"Oh, Vomit," he responded with a wry smile, and moved away.

"*What* did he just call you?" Nikki was incredulous.

"Inside joke," Orla responded, and followed.

The five of them wandered the gallery en masse for a while, then found themselves splintering off into different exhibits. Finally, Diane and Ben slipped away and went to a café.

"That Harvey's a fun guy," said Ben dryly.

Diane laughed "Orla sees something in him we don't, I'm afraid."

"Where did she find him?"

"At a place called Esalen in Northern California. Orla said she wanted to experience her Dynamic Aliveness."

"I'd say she's pretty dynamically alive right now."

"Yeah, Orla's great."

"And yet she comes back with this guy?"

"Yeah, I don't know. They live together in her tiny apartment. No idea how they make that work. He makes her happy, that's the important thing."

"That's true, who are we to judge? You never really know what attracts people to each other. For instance, I'm fascinated right now with your lips." He kissed her, and she cuddled up against him. "But please, don't let me get stuck in the same car with Harvey."

"Promise." Ben stretched his long legs out under the café table for a moment. His reddish gold hair caught the sun. Diane noticed two women walking past and eyeing him appreciatively, but Ben didn't notice them; he was focused on Diane.

Diane was starting to realize that Ben made her happy, too

In the museum, Orla, who had noticed the others drifting away from them, turned to Harvey and smiled sweetly. "Harvey, you are a fascinating man and it's really cool to listen to your thoughts on guys like Savonarola. But Nikki has barely spoken on this trip, and you just shut her down in front of everyone. If you do that again, I will kill you."

Harvey looked at her in surprise. "Oh. Okay."

"Thanks, hon." Orla kissed him affectionately, and they moved on.

When they returned to the villa, Francesca had made them a delicious Ragu al Napolitano, with thick cuts of pork in the sauce the way they make it in Naples. The sun was setting, lending a golden glow to everyone's skin; the evening felt blessed. Orla and Harvey were in conversation about some philosopher, Ben had encouraged Nikki to describe her marvelous finds at the market in town, and Diane was making it her business to polish off the bottle of Chianti.

"Who would like more Ragu?" Francesca came bursting in with a large replenished bowl.

Gordon lifted his plate compliantly. "How can I say no to you, Francesca?" Francesca laughed, moved in back of Gordon and started to heap Ragu onto his plate. As she leaned over to serve him, Diane distinctly saw Gordon lean his cheek against her plentiful bosom and give it a nudge. She laughed quietly, nudged him back with said breast, and retreated with the bowl.

Suddenly Diane's wine went sour. She watched Gordon, watched Francesca, observed three moments of further visual contact between them, and put down her glass.

"So, Gordon. Take good care of your "business" this afternoon? Get a lot done?"

Gordon wiped his mouth before responding. "I did, yeah. Thanks for asking."

"That's good. What did you accomplish while we were at the Palazzo? I'm just asking, because it was so great and I'm sorry you had to miss it."

"Thanks for your concern, Diane. I was on the phone a lot, telling my business associates about the tempting opportunities here in Italy." He winked at Francesca. Diane flushed with anger and poured herself a fourth glass of wine. Nikki, facing away from Gordon, overheard this last and turned toward him.

"Gordon. You're not thinking of buying property here?"

"Why not? Place could use a little developing, wouldn't you say? Not enough luxury hotels, for one thing."

"I see," responded Diane coolly. "So basically, you want to fuck Florence the way you fucked New York City."

Gordon put down his glass. "Excuse me?"

Orla, who had been talking to Harvey, instantly caught the sudden change in atmosphere and turned toward them.

"Jesus, Gordon," persisted Diane. "Look what you and your ilk are doing to Times Square already."

"My ilk?"

"You're trying to rob it of all personality, all character."

"I see. So, you prefer to have peep shows, sex clubs, drug addicts hanging out on every corner. You prefer that to luxury hotels and relative safety."

"I don't think it's a binary --" started Ben, but Diane cut him off.

"Luxury hotels like the Marriott? Is that what you want, to put a fucking Marriott in Florence? They tore down five exquisite theatres in midtown to build that monstrosity. What would you like to tear down here, Gordon? The Palazzo Vecchio?"

"Don't be an idiot."

"Those Broadway theatres were priceless landmarks!"

"They were falling apart, rat infested! I don't know why you got so incensed about them. Picketing in the middle of a snow storm!"

"It meant something to me!"

"So, you decide to freeze to death for no reason along with all those other morons, stopping progress, costing good people hundreds of thousands of dollars!"

"Good people? Like you? HAH! Don't kid yourself, baby."

There was a silence. Suddenly Diane realized the others had stopped talking, and that she had just done something very stupid.

Nikki dabbed her mouth with her napkin. "I didn't know you were at the protests for those theatres, Diane. The Helen Hayes and the Morosco, right?"

Diane put down her wine glass. "Uh, right."

"Gordon, how did you know about it?"

Instead of responding, Gordon reached for the bottle of wine and poured himself a glass. A Milky Way of shooting stars began to form in Diane's peripheral field of vision. The ensuing silence felt like an eternity.

"We were just talking about it the other night," said Orla. "While you were swimming laps." Diane looked at Orla in surprise; she was a study in neutrality.

"Yes. I was defending 'my ilk,'" Gordon added smoothly. A gentle but unconvinced bubble of laughter circulated around the table.

"I wrote an article once on the postmodern philosopher Michel Foucault," offered Harvey, oblivious to all. "He opines that architecture sets the life of society, and should be implemented as a way of understanding one's values and culture. I'm not sure where the Marriott Marquis fits into that paradigm, but —"

"S'cuse me," said Diane, who rose and dashed to her room. She washed her face, drank as much water as she could, and brushed her hair hard. After a time, Ben came in. He went to sit in the chair in the corner and watched her in the bathroom, brushing her hair. Diane found it impossible to turn and acknowledge his presence.

"So. You and Gordon, huh?"

"Me and Gordon? What do you mean?"

"Come on. That wasn't the way casual friends talk to each other. And it certainly wasn't the way one talks to the husband of your best friend, unless you're fucking him."

"I'm not fucking him! Jesus, Ben."

"But you were, at one point. Right?" Diane felt the room spinning again. She grabbed the rim of the sink and sat down on the toilet. "Yeah. That's what I thought."

And that's how it ended with Ben.

FOUR MONTHS PRIOR to the trip to Italy, Orla was just finishing a sale with a lovely couple who were taking a trip to Israel for their fiftieth anniversary, when Harvey came into the travel agency. His gaze alighted on Orla and he took a seat, never taking his eyes from her. Debbie, one of the other travel agents, came up and asked if she could help him, but he shook his head no; he would wait for Orla.

Orla saw all this as she ran the couple's credit card, thanked them graciously for choosing Triple A, and wished them a happy holiday. The whole time she was thinking, where have I seen this guy? He was pretty memorable, even if she couldn't place him. A short man with arms that faced forward like Fred Flintstone, a few strands of hair tortured across his nearly bald pate, and tremendously bushy eyebrows. Yet for all that, there was something endearing about him, at least to Orla. She had some kind of positive association about him that she couldn't place. When her clients had gone, Harvey made a beeline for her desk.

"Hello! Do you remember me? Harvey Gluck."

"Uh, remind me?"

"Esalen, three weeks ago."

"Oh, okay!" Orla did have a dim memory of him now. He was always standing in corners with his arms crossed, frowning. But he wasn't frowning now, in fact he seemed positively giddy, in his fierce looking way.

"It took me awhile to find you, Esalen is not in the habit of giving out addresses, but I remembered that you said you worked at a travel agency in New York, so I did a little research."

"You checked all the travel agencies in New York?"

"Just Manhattan. It wasn't that hard. Your first name is unusual. If they said they didn't have an Orla working there, I hung up. But this one did, and here I am!"

Orla tried to remember; did they have a conversation about travel? Did she promise to book something for him? Parts of Esalen were a blur for her, because in spite of the many experiences with her mother as a child, Esalen was the first time she had ever done Ecstasy.

"Well, isn't that nice! What can I do for you?"

"You can let me take you out to lunch."

"Oh!"

"After all, we both just went through something transformative. I personally feel the need to process some of it after the fact, and you are the exact person I would like to do that with."

"Gosh, Harvey, I…I have some appointments coming up, so I won't be taking lunch 'til late."

"That's fine. I'll wait. I'm so very glad to see you again!"

Harvey smiled at her brightly, causing his intense eyebrows to look even more intense, then turned and resumed his seat at the door. Flustered, Orla went into the coffee room and poured herself a cup. How to get rid of this guy? She didn't want to go out to lunch. In fact, she never took lunch, she just brought a sandwich and today it was a nice tuna salad. But she had lied about having appointments lined up, and if he sat there long enough, he'd realize that. What to do?

Isaac came in, refilled his still-full coffee cup and started stroking his Fu Manchu mustache in a way that set Orla's nerves on edge. Everything Isaac ever did seemed like a cover for what he was actually doing, which was usually spying on everyone else.

"Who's that guy?"

"What guy?"

"The weird guy sitting by the door."

Orla deeply resented Isaac's knee-jerk assessment; he did this all the time. Suddenly she felt protective toward Harvey.

"He's my brother, in from Michigan. He's going to take me to lunch."

"Oh. He looks nothing like you."

"We have different mothers," replied Orla.

"He got the shitty genes," replied Isaac, and went back out.

So, now she was committed to lunch with Harvey. She went over and told him her next appointment had cancelled, and she had a little time.

They walked to the Empire Café, an art deco style dining car on 10th Avenue. Harvey, who it turned out was new to the city, praised her choice of lunch venues and compared it to an Edward Hopper painting, not exactly an original comparison. He was an interesting conversationalist, however; he saw things in a different light from most people. Often it was an inaccurate light, but to Orla that wasn't so important; it provided perspective. For instance, there was a very tall and surly Native American man working in the kitchen; when they entered; he was yelling at a waiter.

"Sorry," said Orla as they took a seat in a booth. "He's kind of known for being temperamental."

"It's a recognized trait of the Lakota nation," responded Harvey. "I don't believe he thinks he's yelling; he probably thinks he's having a pleasant conversation."

"FUCKING IDIOT!" yelled the cook from the kitchen.

"How do you know he's Lakota?" asked Orla.

"The cleft in his chin," said Harvey. Orla turned to look at the man; she could see no cleft. They ordered, and Harvey sat back and beamed at her in his frightening way again.

"Orla, Orla, Orla. You have an unusual name. What does it mean?"

Orla smiled. "It means Vomit."

Harvey's eyes widened. "Vomit? In what language?"

"Irish. If you put an accent over the O, it means Golden Princess. But my mother didn't do that. So, my name means Vomit. She didn't know that, I learned it on a trip to Ireland."

Harvey started to laugh, and his seal bark of a laugh was even more unsettling than his smile but Orla just had to join in.

"Such a fine line between guts and glory! And what an amazing person you are! I can't believe I found you, Orla without the accent. Wasn't Esalen a revelation?"

Indeed, it had been. Orla had been invited to Esalen by the Institute after she called to inquire about the retreat for a client, who had read something about it in Playboy magazine. One of the few perks of the AAA Travel was that the "senior agents" got to visit a hotel or spa occasionally, all expenses paid by the establishment. Orla was only a senior agent by virtue of the fact that so many of her co-workers had quit, generally because they couldn't stand working for Isaac.

The woman who answered the phone at Esalen was warm and forthcoming; in a relaxed and appealing voice, she told Orla that Esalen was an alternative philosophy and technique intended to raise self-awareness and human potential involving philosophical and psychological means. She said an experience at Esalen would include Holotropic breathwork, ecstatic dance, somatic therapy and rejuvenation in their hot tubs overlooking the ocean. The only one of those things Orla had ever heard of was a hot tub, but "ecstatic dance" sounded fun; she thought it might be worth a visit.

Since Orla didn't drive, she arrived by bus from San Francisco. She was completely stunned by the rugged natural beauty of the Big Sur coastline, delighted by the workshops (even the one where a girl sat in the middle of a room banging a cushion and screaming out her pain) and the illuminated mineral water hot tubs overlooking the Pacific Ocean were a spectacular experience, particularly late at night. Everyone was naked. No one indulged themselves in small talk, they went straight to discussing their inner child or tantric sex or the nature of God. On the second night a lovely young woman offered Orla a spoonful of something she called "Adam," and for the next eight hours Orla roamed the property in a state of ecstatic awareness, much of which she didn't remember afterward.

"I must tell you, Orla, the pinnacle of my time there was the intensely pleasurable experience I had with you," said Harvey. Uh-oh, thought Orla, calculating the date of her last period. "I had just come out of a workshop, and I was feeling a certain amount of self-loathing. I had somehow been coerced into confessing unsettling things about my father, and it produced a distinct sense of discomfort within me, as if I had somehow betrayed him. He was a harsh man, but a hard worker and always provided for our family. His feelings about me — I was not his favorite child, to say the least — did not merit my taking him to task in front of an audience of strangers and though they were kind, I regretted speaking out. As I walked out of the workshop, I toyed with the idea of going home, and was on the verge of doing so when you appeared, seemingly out of nowhere, in a flowing white dress, your lovely feet bare, a luminous smile on your face, as if you had known me a long time and were delighted to see me again. You gently placed your hand on my breast and said, 'I can see into your soul, and it is so, so beautiful.' Do you remember that?"

"Um…"

"You gazed at me with those eyes of yours, so different, so haunting, took my hands and started to dance with me. There was no music, but you were humming something so happily that it was easy to join in with you. We danced together for a good ten minutes to the music that you were humming."

"Wow. Okay."

"And it meant so very much to me, to be able to do this freestyle dance with you, without self-consciousness, which for me is extraordinary as I am normally not the most spontaneous of men. Then you stopped humming, dropped my hands, kissed my cheek, and ran off. It altered the trajectory of my actions that day, and perhaps for the rest of my life."

"Oh, my!" exclaimed Orla.

"Do you remember me now?"

"So, that was you!" She had no memory of this, but why burst his bubble?

"Yes! This is why I had to see you again, to thank you for that moment. Even if I never see you again, Orla, I traveled all this way just to thank you."

Indeed, it had been a quite a challenge for Harvey, finding Orla. All he had had to go on, when he woke up and discovered that she was no longer at Esalen, was that her name was Orla, she was a travel agent, and she lived in New York. He had heard this in the group circle on the first day when they said a few things about themselves. Of course, this could have meant she worked anywhere in the state of New York, but there was something about Orla — was it a worldliness, or an other-worldliness? - that convinced him she dwelled in the Big City. The internet was in its infancy, but Harvey was an academic (of sorts) and as such had connections with a number of universities. Accessing a colleague's computer, he got a list of all the travel agencies in Manhattan and cold-called each one of them, until he found the Orla he was looking for.

"You did all that, just to find me?" marveled Orla.

"It was worth every moment," replied Harvey. "I feel like I've been looking for you my whole life."

This comment deeply resonated with Orla who, all her life, had been waiting to be found. In spite of her initial reluctance, she started to see Harvey in a different light. She was impressed by his breadth of knowledge, or anyway what seemed to her like a breadth of knowledge. He could quote quite a few philosophers, and could point to any building in the city and give you an authoritative account of its architectural origins. "Beaux Arts," he declared the Chrysler building, although Orla had heard somewhere that it was Art Deco. "Brutalist, but by a Japanese guy" he designated the World Trade Center. Orla accepted these pronouncements as fact.

A few weeks later, Orla's noxious boss, Isaac, proposed that Orla buy into the travel agency business, and it seemed natural to consult Harvey about the advisability of doing so. She did not like Isaac, but she loved the agency, and she had the money to do it because she had inherited some money from grandma Mona and, thanks to her stepfather Jack's early advice about computers, had invested it in a company called Apple; it seemed to be doing fairly well. Harvey asked her a few questions about the agency, perused the month's bookings (but nothing else) and opined that it was better to have money in a productive business than let it sit in the stock market. Accepting this wisdom, Orla wrote Isaac a check for two thirds of her inheritance and became co-owner of what she now insisted be called the Great Escape Travel Agency.

Harvey made it a habit to pick Orla up at the end of the day's work to walk her home. Spying on them through the venetian blinds, Isaac was scandalized by the intimate way Orla behaved with her brother in public, but since she had pretty much saved the agency by buying in, he decided not to mention his thoughts on the subject. This was difficult for him, as Isaac was not accustomed to self-restraint. He eased the strain by redoubling his vitriol toward the lesser employees.

Harvey was so dazzled by Orla that everything made him happy. For him, finding her had been like finding the holy grail. The delight he experienced at the success of his treasure hunt put a rose color to everything else that happened to him in Manhattan, including being mugged at knifepoint in broad daylight two weeks later on his way to meet her.

Orla could see him through the windows of the agency, staggering across the street with blood streaming down his face. She ran outside.

"Harvey! What happened??

"I guess I was mugged. Two young Hispanic guys ran up to me with knives in their hands and demanded my wallet. I told them I didn't want to give it to them, and one of them punched me. Isn't that strange? They were holding knives, but they punched me."

"Oh Harvey! Are you okay?"

"I hit the pavement. My face hurts. They have my money and all my identification, but you know what? I feel strangely liberated. I am stripped down to my basics now, like Diogenes!"

Concerned he might have a concussion, Orla convinced him to stay with her until he got back on his feet. Since Harvey had not said where he had been living up to that time, Orla was surprised to see him arrive carrying only a backpack and a few books. She was worried about his opinion of her modest digs, which were small even by New York standards, but Harvey was delighted by the accommodations.

"This is perfect! Diogenes lived in a wine barrel in an Athenian marketplace and was the happiest of men!" He crowed.

Harvey stayed in Orla's apartment for three months, and it was very pleasant at first. Orla would go off to work, Harvey would write all day and when Orla came home, there was always a delicious, if spartan, meal on the table prepared by Harvey's hands, which they would eat sitting at her miniscule café table in the corner by the only window, affording an extremely partial view of the Hudson. Orla would talk about her work, Harvey would tell her how his article was coming, and it was all very convivial. Harvey had some strange habits, though. He saved string, for one thing, rolling it into a larger and larger ball. He also flattened out aluminum foil and reused it until it was in tatters, put the day's undrunk coffee in the refrigerator for the next day, and never threw away leftovers. This ran rather counter to Orla's habits, which were more careless and occasionally extravagant. She liked to dine at the rather pricey restaurant downstairs, for instance. It was fun being welcomed by name and brought the wine they knew Orla liked before she ordered. When she brought Harvey down there for a meal, however, he became deeply uncomfortable.

"Why a tablecloth? They'll just have to wash it. Wouldn't a plain wooden surface suffice? Why are these people eating so much? Look at these portions, it's disgusting! Americans are a country of swine!" It was one of Orla's first clues that not all was perfect about the match.

Harvey Gluck was born and raised in Kentucky, but through diligence and the watching of television had acquired the speaking patterns of William F. Buckley. He had matriculated at the University of California at Berkeley, but found the school "prosaic" and dropped out. This did not prevent him from claiming he had a bachelor's degree on his resume, and for a while he taught at the University of Arizona until an unfortunate incident caused him to leave the school precipitously. Orla got the impression the incident had something to do with the intolerance and vacuity of the dean, but beyond that Harvey would not say. He claimed his main source of income stemmed from his writings for philosophy publications, but in the three months he lived with Orla, no checks ever arrived.

Once the first flush of joy at having found Orla receded, Harvey's mood slowly began to shift. Orla would come home bubbling over with tales of the lovely people she had met at work and the marvelous trips she was sending them on, and Harvey's responses turned quite judgmental, deriding the wealth of certain individuals who had nothing better to do than to burn precious carbon traversing the planet. His attitude softened temporarily when Orla broached the idea of a trip to Italy. Though initially reluctant, he began to see the possibilities of witnessing for himself the sites where the great philosophers had lived and worked. Once Orla offered to pay for his trip, it seemed expedient to accede to her wishes.

Although the others on the trip never would have guessed it, their time together got off to a rocky start. Orla had been thrilled, and Harvey appalled, at the luxurious room they had been given, with its enormous white bed and private terrace overlooking the pool and vineyards. It felt like ridiculous overkill to Harvey, and Orla's explanation that the company wanted to impress her so that she would book more clients into the property only irritated him further. Commercialism, he felt, was going to be the downfall of America and he wanted no part of it. Orla steadfastly refused to ask for a smaller room, and finally accused Harvey of trying to ruin the vacation. Aggrieved that she saw him in this light, Harvey partially relented and a compromise was achieved; Harvey moved his suitcase out onto the terrace and slept on a cot, which they requested from housekeeping.

"Ridiculous. Ridiculous!" Orla muttered to herself when, after having made fitful love, Harvey would then go out onto the terrace to sleep. It was nice, however, to have that comfortable big bed to herself.

Harvey enjoyed himself in Florence, in his way. He took pleasure in relieving the others of their ignorance on historical, philosophical and architectural matters, and found many of his own previous convictions reinforced regarding the greatness of Italy. Dante's concept of the Divine Order seemed to him reflected in the symmetry and mathematical order of Renaissance architecture. He was less fond of the Baroque period with all its frou-frou, and frowned disapprovingly when Orla said she liked it. (When Harvey frowned, it was as if his entire brow collapsed, so you couldn't miss it.) He held forth on Lucretius and his unfortunate treatise on the pursuit of pleasure as the guests were lolling happily in the pool, and forgave them their indolence with the news that this hedonistic Roman Lucretius had also been the first to hypothesize the existence of atoms. Diane and Ben found that it was time to go in for a nap.

Harvey proved that he could be both interesting and an intense bore within the space of ten minutes. Orla, who had been looking forward to spending time with Diane and especially the grieving Nikki, found herself instead being dragged to various architectural wonders in Florence to hear Harvey expound upon their impact upon philosophy, or vice versa. Conversation that Orla had found sparkling and amusing three months ago began to seem repetitive, as did Harvey's love-making, which now seemed to have two gears – first, and fifth.

The epic altercation between Diane and Gordon at the table the final night of the holiday went unnoticed by Harvey, who had been at the moment paging through a book trying to find a quote from Giordano Bruno to read aloud to Orla.

"Bruno posited the existence of alternate universes in the 16th Century, Orla. Can you imagine? Let me read you what he said...."

But Orla had had quite enough of Italian philosophers. She turned her focus to the accelerating tension between Diane and Gordon, was confirmed in her hunch that there was something going on between them, and jumped in to save the holiday from ruination.

"We were just talking about those protests the other night," she said, coming to the rescue at an extremely awkward moment and sparing herself another conversation about Giordano Bruno. Harvey was slightly miffed to have his discourse interrupted, but it was hard to tell what was going on with Nikki. It's possible her grief over the loss of her child was so intense that she might not have even registered the tension between her husband and Diane. After the others had left the table, Nikki had ripped off her shift and gotten back into the pool.

Harvey was not someone who was sensitive to conversational nuance. He had been told by Orla, however, that Nikki had lost a child. That, added to the fact that Orla actually threatened his life should he cross Nikki in any way caused him to take extra care in her presence. Walking in the garden the next day in thoughtful contemplation of what he would have for lunch, Harvey came upon Nikki sitting on a bench under a tree, crying. He would have retreated instantly, but Nikki saw him before he could do so, and smiled apologetically.

"I'm sorry. I thought I was the only one here."

"It appears I am here, too," responded Harvey. "How awkward for both of us."

There was a pause. "I'm very sad."

"Yes. I see that. Schopenhauer wrote that we shouldn't reject sadness, as it is an inherent characteristic of the human condition."

"I'm afraid I don't get the option to reject it."

"Actually, you do, but then you might go mad. For those who cannot process the shock of grief, I believe madness is the only option."

"I'd rather not go mad. I have another child at home."

"Then it seems to me you are behaving exactly as you must. The paradox of grief is that it is both a horrific experience and a profound opportunity to gain self-knowledge."

"Who said that?"

"I don't know. I hope it was me."

Harvey nodded to her respectfully and retreated. Nikki felt her spirits lift for the first time in many weeks. Later, she found Orla, and reiterated to her what a lovely experience this holiday was. She also mentioned that she quite liked Harvey.

"That's nice." responded Orla. "He's driving me out of my mind."

The fact was, though Orla was very good at having brief, intense romantic relationships that transported her body and soul, she was not as good at having them stand the test of time. Harvey had already lasted longer than seemed advisable to Orla. Even back in New York, their domesticity had been making her feel antsy, and the saving of string and tin foil and all that nonsense made her feel as though she were becoming her grandmother Mona, who had lived through a depression. Harvey hadn't lived through a depression — what was wrong with him? Orla was ruing having asked Harvey on the trip at all, particularly with so many handsome young Italian men everywhere. She had half a mind to call Antonio, her race car driving lover (except for the fact that he was now married with a baby.)

When they got back to New York, the inevitable Talk took place. Orla told Harvey his hermit-like behavior and endless diatribes were wearing on her. Harvey accused Orla of having a "convenience mentality," whatever that meant. It was decided that Harvey must find another place to live, whether in the city or not was up to him. Harvey took his rebuff philosophically. In fact, he cleverly turned it around and presented the situation as if it were he who was ending the relationship because he couldn't abide Orla's moral hypocrisy in having a friend like Diane. (Orla regretted ever having told him about Diane and Gordon.) Harvey left behind the suitcase that Orla had bought him for the trip to Italy, snatched up his backpack and his books, and walked out the door. Orla breathed a sigh of relief.

Later that night, though, lying in bed, Orla found that she missed him.

FOUR MONTHS AFTER the trip to Italy, Nikki and Gordon were no further along in coming to grips with the turn their lives had taken. For Gordon, the trip had been a welcome diversion. It temporarily relieved the tension between himself and Nikki, and it also relieved him of the domestic responsibilities he had taken on, since Nikki was essentially not functioning. It had not, however, relieved him of the spiraling costs of his business, or the woes of the banking crisis. Or the fact that Diane had been there with her new lover. Gordon did not expect to be as agitated by that as he was. Diane looked happy. She looked carefree, successful, and beautiful; Gordon deeply resented it.

Gordon's feelings about Diane were so complicated that he seldom allowed himself to think about them. From the first moment Nikki brought him to that lunch at Marvin's Gardens, Gordon could feel Diane sizing him up. It made him deeply uncomfortable. Women did not generally size Gordon up; they deferred to him. A lot of men deferred to him, too, but to have a woman like Diane scrutinizing him the way she did — this was unusual, and a bit offensive. He knew he was there to make a good impression on Nikki's friends, that she placed a lot of value on their opinion, and at that point Gordon was quite entranced with Nikki so he put a lot of energy into that lunch. He felt (incorrectly) that he had won Orla over; she was small and cute and seemed to like everyone. But this Diane. At one point he glanced at his watch to calculate how much longer he could decently stay, and when he looked up, it was into the eyes of Diane. He felt a jolt; it was as if she could see right through him, had discovered what a fraud he was and found it mildly amusing. Not knowing how to react to the moment, he winked. It instantly felt like the wrong response.

When he saw her, months later, at the rally to save the theatres, he felt that same jolt. What the hell is this woman doing? He watched her for a while, marching in the snow with her picket sign (and, as mentioned before, considered and rejected the idea of giving her his gloves.) She seemed absolutely sure of herself, filled with passion and indignant fury: A strong, angry woman. He found it a bit repulsive and moved on.

Then she became ill. Gordon was extremely reluctant when Nikki asked him to look in on Diane, and he put the visit off for a number of days until Nikki insisted. When he saw where she lived in midtown, with its drag queens, drug addicts and hookers, he almost laughed. Perfect. He pushed the buzzer once but didn't hear anything. He was about to turn away when one of the drag queens came out and let him in, so he had to trudge up those bleak, black stairs.

When Diane opened her door, he was shocked by her appearance. All evidence of her seemingly cock-sure nature was gone. She was skinny, her hair was dirty, she looked on the point of fainting. For a moment, Gordon wondered if she had become a drug addict herself, especially as Nikki had said it was hepatitis. Yet her intense vulnerability was moving to Gordon. The loss of her power caused him to look more closely at her, and what he saw drew him. She could die here, he thought, and no one would know. When he arrived a few days later laden with groceries and she seemed so glad to see him, he felt like her savior. He cooked her a meal, and he sang as he cooked it. Sang! He never sang at home. What was happening to him?

Gordon was not, by nature, a philanthropic man. He gave to no charities, and was exasperated by liberal ideology. His desire to help Diane had nothing to do with Christian charity, and everything to do with the fact that he was becoming hopelessly ensnared in a complicated web of feelings for her. He both loved and hated that she could see into him. He both loved and hated (himself) that he was having sex with her. He saw himself as a man of principle, a family man like his father, and his relationship with Diane shattered that self-image. He didn't need her. He was sure he didn't need her. So why was it impossible to stop seeing her?

Gordon knew that, at this point in their marriage, his presence felt like an annoyance to Nikki, a distraction from the enormity of her pain. Would he say she was wallowing in that pain? It's impossible, cruel, heartless to accuse a woman of wallowing when she has lost a living being that had been sharing her body, but to Gordon, the answer seemed to be yes.

As for Nikki, the chasm that had opened up within her was so enormous that she could not see to the other side of it. Why, she wondered, had she been saved from having AIDS only to live a life that was this bleak and without color? Why couldn't she love her remaining child the way she had before? Was it because she was afraid Mimi, too, would expire without warning in a completely senseless and random way? She went to bereavement support groups for women who had lost children, and though she listened carefully, it seemed that no one truly captured what she was experiencing. This child she had carried had been talking to her, from within the womb! It had been sharing her thoughts; she could tell by the way it moved within her. Nikki felt that she understood for the first time what it must feel like to have a twin. It was the warmest, most companionable feeling, and suffused Nikki was a happiness that she hadn't felt… well, ever. Her early days with Gordon had been exhilarating, but it was always very clear that they were two separate people who shared the goal of settling down and raising a family, and that they had met at a good time to do that. There's nothing wrong with that, in fact Nikki supposed that was how most people in the world experienced love. But the love she had felt for the child within her superseded all that. With the loss of this baby, Nikki felt that she had also lost half of herself. She only half-existed now.

Sometime after Diane moved to California, Gordon suggested to Nikki that they move, too. Nikki didn't really care where she lived, so she went along with his plan to move to Colorado, where apparently new business opportunities existed. She did all the things you were supposed to do to relocate to a new state, and did it all by rote. Who the fuck cared.

1998

It was a balmy Sunday afternoon in June. Orla had just spent a wonderful few hours at the Village Vanguard listening to a friend of hers, a jazz pianist named Kenny Kirkland. Kenny had started out as a client of Orla's. She had put together a number of wonderful trips for him, which he never took because another tour would always suddenly come up for him and he'd have to cancel. He almost never asked for a refund. Orla loved listening to him play, because he could make magic out of anything. Kenny told her once that in jazz there are no wrong notes, that what seems like a wrong note can be made into a right note easily. This concept appealed to Orla, who was lately feeling as though some of her missteps were becoming more difficult to quickly fix. Her business relationship with Isaac, for instance, was still deteriorating, her "grand passions" seemed to be a bit less magical these days, and she found that she thought of Harvey rather more often than she expected. When she listened to jazz, however, and particularly Kenny, unintentional moves were quickly made intentional and incorporated into the fabric of the music. She loved that. She doubted, however, that it was as easy for other pianists as it was for Kenny. Sitting at a table with Kenny's jazz buddies, she somehow blended right in with them, as was her way. A trumpet player at the table, hoping to be called upon to sit in, was particularly cute, and they exchanged numbers. You never knew when you might need a jazz trumpet player in your life.

She came out onto Seventh Avenue and walked over to Washington Square Park to watch the parade of activity that always goes on there. A man in a red sweater was blowing bubbles with an enormous bubble wand, and children and adults alike were dancing around popping the bubbles with glee. An enormous bubble wafted slowly toward Orla; she watched in fascination as it got larger and larger, and when it was very close, hovering over her like a space ship, she felt as if she could see complex civilizations lying within its tensile surface. Orla imagined millions of little creatures on the surface of that bubble, living lives that – who knows? – to them may have seemed very long. The bubble quivered in front of Orla a moment longer, and then poof! It disappeared, as if it never was. Orla stared at the place where it used to be, lost in thought. Then her gaze drifted downward, and she saw someone walking toward her that looked familiar. He had lost a lot of hair, and the youthful jaunty gait was gone, but she recognized what was left of that handsome face.

"Will?" Will, who had been apparently deep in thought, looked up, recognized Orla instantly and smiled in delight.

"Oh my God, it's little Chava! How are you, Orla?" They embraced, and Orla could feel how skinny he had become.

"I'm good, thanks. I'm great, actually. I'm a travel agent now. Just got back from a cool trip to Tokyo."

"No kidding! Send me somewhere wonderful."

"I will! But first tell me how you are."

"Well, it's been a wild ride. I'm not an actor anymore."

"So, that makes two of us. What are you doing now?"

"I'm a psychiatrist."

"The big one! That takes a lot of school."

"A lot of school, a lot of studying, many hours, but it was worth it."

"What set you on that path?"

Will's demeanor turned somber . "I just never understood why so many of my friends were taken, but I wasn't. It felt like — like I must have been saved for a reason. I know that sounds like woo-woo bullshit."

"Not to me, it doesn't."

"Don't get me wrong, I did it as much for me as for the people who became my patients. It's incredibly rewarding. It can also be exhausting, depressing, frustrating. But it was the right move. Not to say I won't get back to theatre someday. Life is long, at least longer than I at one time thought it was going to be. And right now, mine is a lot happier."

"I'm so glad."

"How about you? You a married lady now?"

"Oh gosh, no. I don't know if that's going to be in the stars for me. I enjoy the rotation too much, you know?"

Will laughed. "I know exactly! And what about Diane and Nikki? You ever see them?"

"All the time. Paul was right, something about that show makes people bond for life."

"Paul….God, what a loss. And Young Michael. I feel so guilty for urging him to come to New York."

"Don't feel guilty, Will. Our paths are preordained. It was going to happen, nothing to do with you."

"I don't actually subscribe to that, honey. If I did, I wouldn't be in my current field."

"Oh. Sorry."

Will laughed. "Don't apologize! Vive la différence! I finally got it, you know. I'm HIV positive, but there are so many ways to address that now. There was nothing for Paul and Michael, that really haunts me sometimes." They gazed down at the sidewalk, a silent prayer. Then Orla looked up brightly.

"But you're okay?"

"I'm thriving. Thank God for modern science. Every day I'm alive is a miracle."

"I have that thought, too." Orla smiled. "Every day."

2000

When the TV show on which Diane wrote was cancelled after three respectable seasons, Diane took a few meetings around town and considered herself enormously lucky to land on a cable network show that was a critical darling of the industry. She wrote an episode that won a Writer's Guild award and was told by a co-executive producer that she was one of the best contributors "in the room," which is where the writers break the stories for each episode. Things were breezing along nicely for Diane, except for one problem; she had failed to respond to the advances of the showrunner, Mike Winstead. Therefore, she was fired.

She had heard about Mike from other writers; his flirtatious nature, his actions with women that could easily be termed harassment. She knew, too, that he had a volatile temper and she had managed to steer clear of any contact with him outside the studio, until one day he asked her to accompany him on a trip to Lake Arrowhead, where the Writer's Guild planned to celebrate him for his many accomplishments. He was expected to give a sort of writing seminar to the other writers in attendance, a fifty-minute presentation of How He Worked, and he confessed to Diane that the notion terrified him. He had no idea how he worked, or how to communicate how he worked to others. He impressed upon her how important it was that she accompany him to Arrowhead to help him put together the presentation. Diane felt cornered, and knew that to decline was to be ostracized, so she agreed.

On the limo drive out they brainstormed ideas, or rather Mike rambled on in his usual disconnected fashion and Diane, notebook in hand, tried to make sense of it. Mike was a smallish, middle-aged man with an obvious combover, and somehow Diane was counting on his obvious lack of appeal and her comparative height – she had at least three inches on him – to protect her. When his arm strayed onto her side of the backrest once or twice, she made a point of chatting to the limo driver, to remind Mike that there was a third person in the vehicle. By the time they got to Arrowhead she had some idea of what Mike could say, and spent the first night typing out bullet points for him. The next morning was a meet-and-greet breakfast with the many other writers who had gathered for the event. There must have been a hundred of them, and all of them wanted to be able to say that had their picture taken with Mike Winstead. Diane sat off to the side eating her bacon and eggs and forcing herself to smile at people she didn't know as they passed. She felt fortunate to be on a hit TV show, especially when there were so many people who couldn't even get their foot on a rung of the ladder. She had the feeling she was no better than a lot of these writers, just luckier.

That afternoon was Mike's presentation, and to Diane's relief it went pretty well, in spite of the fact that he raced through

Diane's bullet points and after twenty minutes said, "Why don't I take some questions now?" The audience was more than happy to ask questions; it was a way for them to get onto his radar. When the presentation was over there was a sunset cocktail activity, and then dinner, and then after-dinner drinks, and in retrospect Diane realized that was when she should have gone to her room with stomach flu or something. Instead, she hung around talking to other writers, who had by now realized that she worked on Mike's show and found her interesting. It was flattering. Diane found she enjoyed talking to these young writers, even if their burning ambitions were very much on the surface of every conversation.

But she had been told about Mike. She should have left the party. Perhaps the fact that she saw him across the room in intimate conversation with a pretty young redhead who laughed delightedly at everything he said gave her the courage to stay. Idiot.

As the two of them walked across the expansive central lawn of the conference center to their rooms, (which were side by side, unfortunately,) Mike was in high spirits. Adulation suited him, and he started to wonder if he should make a habit of giving presentations.

"With your help, of course, Diane. You are my right-hand gal, you know. My gal Friday. I couldn't do a thing without you."

Diane hated the world "gal," but she laughed self-deprecatingly and thanked him for the approbation. He put his arm around her, best chum style. Diane knew this playbook well, and her red alert signal sounded. She saw other writers heading to their rooms and desperately hoped one of them would run up to Mike and ask for an autograph or something. No such luck. She manufactured a large yawn.

"Wow, I'm exhausted, what time is it?" It was only 9:45.

"Why don't you come in for a nightcap?" said Mike.

She was sunk.

It played out like a movie she'd seen before. She declined the nightcap with some half-baked excuse. He went to kiss her goodnight, then tried to turn it into something else, forcing Diane to extricate awkwardly. Laughing apologetically as if it were all her fault and she had led him on in some vixenish way, she dashed into her room and closed the door behind her. Leaning her head against the door, she thought, I'm so fucked.

When it came time to renew her contract, she was informed by a co-executive producer that her work had been substandard and she was being let go. In spite of her suspicions that this might happen, it came as a shock. She was indignant; she said that she didn't believe the reasons for firing her and listed the many reasons she was an asset to the show. Finally, (and she will always regret this) she alluded to Mike's behavior with her at Arrowhead. The co-exec rose and left her office, and that was that.

Diane kept trying to tell herself that it was a good thing, because it released her to do other things like writing that novel she always wanted to attempt, but each morning she woke up feeling like an abject failure. That feeling was exacerbated when she learned that the redhead in Arrowhead had been hired onto the show.

Following this, her agents started to act strange. Apparently, "things were said" when they brought her name up as a possible hire, things that caused her agents to lose their enthusiasm for her. "That network won't see you," she was told, and "We can't get 100% behind this project you want to pitch." When she said she'd be happy to rethink the pitch, she was told that wouldn't be necessary. Diane's anxiety spiked; this town was incredibly tough, and once a person was seen as "trouble" or "difficult" -- Correction: Once *a woman* was seen as "trouble" or "difficult," she was toast.

Making things worse still was the fact that Diane's mother was devastated. Marilyn had never been prouder of her daughter than when she got that job, because the series was about publishing in New York in the 1950's, which had been Marilyn's world. As a former editor in Manhattan, she gave Diane all sorts of tidbits about life back then, and was absolutely delighted when something she said made it into an episode. It created a wonderful dynamic between Diane and her mother, one they had never enjoyed before. The day she had to tell her mother that she'd been let go was one of the worst of her life.

"But why?" Marilyn kept saying. "I thought they loved you!" Diane just couldn't bring herself to say, "Because I wouldn't fuck Mike Winstead." Her mother and she had gotten close, but not that close, and her mother was an old-fashioned woman. Diane couldn't bear it if her mother said something like, "What were you wearing that night?" or "You weren't leading him on, now, were you?"

Diane wondered if her mother might not be even more depressed about it all than she was. She certainly didn't seem herself lately on the phone.

Then one night Marilyn called Diane, and her tone seemed brighter. "Diane, I have decided to go to Mexico, and I want you and Bruce to come with me!" she announced. Bruce was Diane's younger brother, thirty-six to Diane's thirty-eight. His wife had left him recently for her physical therapist (she had broken her leg skiing) and Bruce was absolutely blindsided by it all. He had moved out of his house and into a studio apartment on the south side of Chicago to prepare for the ugly divorce proceedings to come, and from the way he sounded on the phone in conversations with his mother, Marilyn was worried he was drinking again.

"Why Mexico?" asked Diane.

"Because Mexico is fun! And I think we could all use a little fun. I've booked us on a cruise to Puerto Vallarta."

"What? Without even asking me? How do you know I'll be free?"

"Honey, you're out of a job; you're free. And if you're not, I'd like you to make yourself free, Diane, please."

"You'll never get Bruce to go."

"He already said he will, and now I need you to say yes, too. Come on, darling. I know you've been blue lately, and frankly I could use a boost, too. I don't want to go into it now, but there are issues I'd like to discuss with you and your brother."

Feeling trapped, but knowing it was useless to struggle, Diane agreed to the trip. She was pretty much in awe of her mother. When Diane's father died suddenly in a car crash, the whole family had gone into extended grief mode. Marilyn had been completely blindsided. She had been living the suburban life for over twenty years, and had left all thoughts of being a "career gal" behind. Diane and Bruce were surly, angst-ridden teenagers, incapable of processing their grief and, to add insult to injury, Diane's father had let his life insurance policy lapse. There was nothing for it but for Marilyn to re-enter the work force, so she sent out a battalion of resumes and got one response back from a city magazine in San Diego. She moved her two miserable children there from Chicago and, within five years, they had promoted her to editor-in-chief. It was astounding that a woman in her fifties, given all the pressures of an industry that was as misogynistic as any other, was able to pull something like that off. It helped that they had been so impressed with her New York credentials, but Marilyn was a juggernaut. Once she took that job, she was an unstoppable force. Diane wished she had half her mother's drive.

When they convened in San Pedro to board the cruise ship, Diane realized that her mother's worries about Bruce had been well justified; he looked absolutely vagrant in his baggy-assed jeans, stained jacket and unkempt beard.

"Oh, dear. Oh, dear," said Marilyn as he approached them. When Diane hugged him, she knew that her mother's suspicions about alcohol were correct.

"How was your flight?"

"Don't ever fly United," he responded, and they boarded the ship.

Diane had never been tempted to go on a cruise, and now she knew why. There were people everywhere, hundreds of them at all times unless you were in your stateroom, where Diane would have stayed for the entire trip (it had a nice balcony) if she weren't compelled to come out for meals. The casino, with its headache-inducing blinking lights and non-stop sound effects, was open twenty-four hours a day. The pools were filled with screeching children. Lunch was presented in the large dining hall by grinning waiters and waitresses who were required to dance out conga line style with huge platters of food to the accompaniment of blaring pop music; then you were meant to help yourself cafeteria style. Diane felt so sorry for those waiters, who she knew were out-of-work actors.

Bruce spent a good deal of time in the casino, which worried Marilyn. "You know he has an addictive personality!" she complained, which caused Diane to wonder why her mother thought it would be a good idea to put him on a ship with bottomless alcohol and a casino. When, at her mother's prompting, Diane joined Bruce in the casino, she noticed that he confined himself mostly to the quarter slots of the one-armed bandits, which brought Marilyn some relief. Still, that can add up.

When they made port at Cabo San Lucas, they disembarked to find a marketplace had been set up alongside the ship. Marilyn was delighted; a fast and easy way to buy gifts. It seemed clear the cruise ship people were hoping the bulk of their passengers would visit the marketplace and come right back to the ship, but Diane had cabin fever. She walked into town and found a place renting motor scooters. "Bike path!" said the young rental guy, pointing back toward the beach. But Diane headed inland.

After a few miles, it became clear why they wanted tourists on the bike path. Soon enough the palm trees, greenery and festive shops gave way to rocky terrain, dusty unpaved roads, shanties and lean-tos on the sides of the road. Listless people sat on the stoops of their dwellings, looking up in dull curiosity as she rode by. Piles of trash flanked the road; children ran around barefoot and often naked in the trash looking for hidden treasure. When she came upon a man squatting by the side of the road taking a dump, she decided it was time to turn around. Only ten minutes away. Less. It was as if the country had erected a stage set at the harbor, behind which lay the real country. Diane wondered if most countries did this.

Back on the cruise ship, the festivities had resumed. Many of the passengers were returning from their shopping spree carrying hand woven baskets they would never use, wearing puka shells they would throw away. The music started, and the waiters danced the food in for the umpteenth zany time. Whee! Happy Times were Here Again!

Diane skipped lunch and took a nap.

When they hit Puerto Vallarta, Marilyn decided they should all have dinner at one of the luxury hotels along the coast. Diane and Bruce obediently put on their best clothing (which meant Bruce put on a jacket) and followed their mother off the ship.

They entered the lobby of the Fiesta Americana, a huge parabola of a building facing a cove. Their gaze was instantly drawn by the enormous palapa thatched roof soaring overhead. How many natives did they hire to create that intimidating structure? Diane hoped quite a few, and made mental notes for Orla. Marilyn led them to the ultra-elegant Thai restaurant she had chosen. Diane was surprised at how well her mother seemed to know her way around. After they had ordered and received their drinks, Marilyn leaned back and sighed, looking around the room wistfully.

"Your father brought me here. It was our 'empty nest' vacation. Bruce had just gone off to Rutgers, and we felt we needed a little fun. You kids were so busy with your lives, you probably didn't even know we came here. We thought it was going to be the beginning of many such trips." Diane and Bruce's father had died the following year. Diane put her hand over her mother's and Marilyn smiled at her sadly. Then she turned to Bruce.

"I want you to tell me how you're doing, Bruce."

Bruce sipped his rum and coke and gazed at his mother blandly. "Great, Ma. I'm doing great."

"You don't look like you're doing great. Diane, does he look like he's doing great?"

"I'm Switzerland, Mom. I have no opinion."

"You look bloated and unhappy. Now, I know what Connie did was a shock - "

"Nope. Not talking about that."

"—but you're too strong to let something like this upset the entire apple cart of your life. You're smart, and creative, and have so much potential. I'm not going to say anything more about this, after all, we're on vacation – "

"Good."

" -- but your sister has experienced a serious setback lately, too, and she's not letting it ruin her life." Diane wondered how her mother thought she knew this. "I want you two kids to stay more in touch. I want you to become closer, and lean on each other more, okay? I think Diane would like you to do that, wouldn't you, Diane?"

"Sure."

"So, will you do that for me, children? Will you make an effort to be closer? For me?" Diane and Bruce looked at one another. This was starting to be a weirder conversation than usual.

"What's up, Mom? Is there something you want to tell us?"

"Well, yes, actually. I was going to wait until after we'd had our lovely dinners, but since you ask, I have recently been diagnosed with cancer." Diane gasped, and Bruce put down his drink. "I know, isn't that a bore? They may have caught it early, or they may not have. It's all a little cloudy at the moment, but it does make one think. Of course, the first thing I think about is you children and how you will fare if, you know –"

"Mom, when did this happen?"

"About a month ago. If I've seemed a bit gloomy, that's why."

Bruce went around the back of his mother's chair and leaned over, embracing her from behind. Touched, she rested her cheek on his arm.

"It'll be okay, honey."

"I love you, Ma."

"I know." They stayed like that for a long moment, with Bruce hugging her and Diane holding her hand. Finally, Bruce stepped away.

"I'll be back. I just need to use the —" Bruce left the room. Diane imagined him crying in the stall of the bathroom, because that's what she would like to be doing at the moment.

"Oh dear, I've ruined dinner," said Marilyn.

"No, no."

"Their Caribbean paella is delicious, you have to order it."

"I will."

When Bruce came back, Diane guessed he had splashed water on his face because his shirt was wet. He had also acquired an entirely new attitude.

"Okay." He sat down forcefully. "So, what do you need from us, Ma? What can we do? Shall I move back home, or —"

"No, honey, I don't think that's necessary, at least not at this juncture, but thank you for offering. I'm not really a sentimentalist, as you know, I don't believe there's going to be some angel on a white unicorn waiting for me at the pearly gates of heaven." Diane wondered what religion that imagery came from. "And I'm not into the idea of pain. It seems to me when it's time to go, you should just go, not bore everyone else with your aches and pains. So, with that in mind, I wanted to inform you two of something. There is a little envelope scotch-taped to the back of the Renoir print in my bedroom. You know that painting of the luncheon at the boating party, the ladies with their lovely hats?" Diane and Bruce stared at her, bewildered. "I know you remember it. Anyway, in that envelope is a little red pill. Just a little capsule, wrapped in a bit of tissue inside an envelope with a Ritz Carlton emblem on it. When it gets to a certain point, and you will know when that point is because I will tell you or it will be clear in some other way, I want one of you to promise to give me that pill."

"A — a suicide pill?"

"Well, if you want to call it that."

"They make suicide pills?" Bruce was appalled.

"Well, you have to know who 'they' are, but yes."

"How do you know who 'they' are?"

"I've done my research. You have to bite down on them. If you swallow them the whole thing takes a lot longer, but if you bite down --"

Diane's eyes filled with tears. "Mom, this is horrifying!"

"All right now, let's not make too much of this. I'm only saying 'if', not 'when.' And right now, I feel absolutely fine, so this is only hypothetical."

"I can't kill my own mother!" Diane wailed, and the diners at the other table turned to look at her.

"Oh, good lord, Diane, count on you to turn this into something dramatic. I'd like us to have a nice holiday, if you don't mind. Can you both just promise me?" Diane was weeping now, but, somehow, she nodded. Marilyn turned to Bruce. "Can you promise me, Bruce?"

"Let me think about it, Ma, okay? This is kind of…. big."

"Of course. And look! Our entrees have arrived. Yum!"

Diane's mother died eighteen months later. It was a stroke, Diane was told, which took her out in "one swell foop," as Marilyn would have jokingly put it. Diane was grief stricken, of course, but also, upon reflection, relieved that she didn't have to make that horrible decision with the suicide pill. Could she have done it? Could she have lived with herself if she had done it?

Bruce had risen to the occasion. He had given up the apartment in Chicago, quit drinking, and moved to San Diego to be closer to his mother. Diane drove down when she could, but it was Bruce who became Marilyn's prime caregiver, and it was her illness that provided him with a new lease on life because, while there, he fell in love with the visiting nurse. On the phone with Diane, Marilyn reported the progress of the relationship with delight.

"I think he's going to propose to her, I really do! Why didn't I think of getting sick sooner?" she crowed, and Diane marveled at the enduring power of the maternal instinct.

While Diane and Bruce were cleaning out the house for an estate sale, Diane went to her mother's bedroom, took down the Renoir print and turned it over. There was the Ritz-Carlton envelope, taped by its flap with its opening facing forward. She reached inside the envelope and took out a ball of tissue, inside of which was a little red capsule. It looked more like a decongestant than an agent of annihilation. She put the pill back in the envelope, removed the envelope from the back of the framed print, and pocketed it.

2023

Sunjay's phone calls with Orla were going very well. After much consideration, Sunjay had determined that she was not, in fact, with the FBI, and relaxed more into his role as an authority on All Things Astrological.

It was Sunjay's high school friend Scott who had introduced Sunjay to the idea of forming his own horoscope website. Scott himself, a failed salesman for a window and door company, had gotten the bright idea of forming a fake profile on a dating site, presenting himself as a handsome forty-eight year old military man looking for love with an older woman. Once he "hooked a fish," as he put it, he told them he was posted in some far-off country but was being reassigned to the states soon. He would then move the conversation to WhatsApp, claiming it was a demand of the military that he conduct personal relationships in that manner. On the third phone call (if things were going well) he would tell the fish that he was falling in love with her. Older women were very lonely, and self-conscious about no longer being young and beautiful, Scott said. Keeping the conversation on the phone worked for them because they often presented themselves in their photos as being younger and more attractive than they were, so they were none too anxious to expose that fiction.

The next thing to do was to have a big emergency – a medical emergency was often good, because older women understood medical issues. Scott liked to use the story that they had finally found a liver for his sister for her transplant, but there was not enough money to cover the cost and if they didn't get the money extremely soon, the liver would go to someone else and the sister would die.

"You would be amazed at how fast they fall for this. The urgency is the thing, Sunjay, you've got to create an emergency so they don't have time to think about it."

"And this works?"

"Buddy, I cleared 250 K this year."

"Wow!"

"You're Indian, right?"

"Uh, yeah."

"Yeah, I can tell by the accent. And you're not – I mean, sorry, but you're not that great looking. Here's what you should do. Horoscopes are a big Indian thing, right? Like, nobody wants to go to some white dude to get their horoscope done, they want to go to somebody who looks exotic. You should do a horoscope version of what I'm doing and make a killing."

"Astrology? I don't know anything about it."

"Doesn't matter. I'm not in the military. Google it."

Bearing in mind Scott's instructions, the next time he talked with Orla, Sunjay tried to figure out a way to introduce the idea of falling in love. The only problem was, he was kind of enjoying the dynamic between them that had developed already, and was nervous about spoiling that. Orla was very intuitive; if Sunjay had had a bad day, she could always read it in his voice and would get him talking about it.

"What's the matter, Sunjay? You seem a little down."

"Oh, no, I am fine! I am thinking about you."

"No, you're not, something has happened. What is it?"

This conversation happened just last Thursday, after Sunjay had been pulled over by the police and given a ticket for driving with a broken tail light. It wasn't just the ticket; the cop had pulled him out of the car and slammed him up against the hood, patting him down looking for weapons. Weapons! Sunjay was a man of peace; he had no weapons.

"Oh no! That must have been so terrifying! How could he do that to you?"

"It's Texas. They can do a lot of things. Now I have a moving violation, and I assure you I am a very good driver."

"I'm so sorry, Sunjay. You're such a good person. This shouldn't have happened to you."

In a strange way, Sunjay *was* kind of falling in love with Orla. Not in a romantic way, but in the sense that she made him feel good about himself in a way that was unusual to him, and he would like to perpetuate that feeling. If he took all her money, the next step was to ghost her. Sunjay didn't want to stop talking to Orla.

"Let me pay for that broken tail light, will you?"

"I already paid for it."

"How much did it cost?"

Sunjay looked down at the receipt from the repair shop. "Two hundred and thirty-eight dollars and eighty-five cents."

"Boom! Done. Check is in the mail. Now, tell me what's in the stars today."

2001

By the time of the World Trade Center disaster, Nikki's marriage to Gordon was collapsing, too. Terrifying to think that the two of them might have been in that building, as the tradition of celebrating their first date on or around September 11 had persisted for some years. Traditionally, Gordon would have gone there for a business meeting with his fellow masters of the universe, then joined Nikki at Windows on the World for lunch. Which means that in an alternate reality, he would have been stuck in that building when the plane hit, and she would have arrived in time to see the building crumble.

Nikki imagined the person she might have been had that happened. It would have been terrible, terrible, too tragic to even speak of for some time. Then, slowly, she would find that she was able to speak about it to her closest friends. Gordon would be forever enshrined in her mind as a kind, caring husband and excellent father who made the world a better place. She would eventually start to see other men, and always she would be comparing them to Gordon's abundant virtues, but finally she might find a man who, though not Gordon's equal, would help her find a few sunbeams of joy in this life. It would be this man who would see her through to the end of her days. Maybe he'd be younger than her; yes, that would be nice. Someone younger and deeply supportive, to help her forget Gordon.

Instead, the motherfucker was alive and having an affair.

It took her awhile to understand what was going on. She was not suspicious by nature, so when she found tickets to the new Broadway play, "One Flew Over the Cuckoo's Nest" in his jacket pocket and he told her he had taken a client to see it, she thought no more of it. When Gordon frequently had to go out of town for long weekends to look at property for possible building sites, she was too busy to spend time thinking about it and rather enjoyed having their king-sized bed to herself. But when he was stuck in the bathroom with painful constipation one day and asked her to bring his phone up to him, and she looked down and saw the words, "I love what you do to my body" in a text, well, there was no way she could mentally accommodate that into her daily life. She tried; she glanced away quickly, slipped the phone through the door to Gordon and said nothing, partially because she could scarcely believe or process what she had just seen, partially because he was in a vulnerable position on the toilet and it seemed unfair to confront him at that moment, but mostly because she knew that by saying out loud what she had just seen, she would forever alter the chemical composition of their marriage, and she didn't think she could handle a shakeup like that.

She needed time to process this. She needed to get away from everything for a while. Mimi would be fine; she was fourteen now, and hated everything about her mother. The phenomenon of being reviled by one's child was, Nikki knew, a natural part of growing up, but every derisive look, every dismissive comment from Mimi was like a dagger into Nikki's heart. She adored Mimi, she still thought there was something magical about her, so to have this magical creature find her repugnant was almost more than she could bear.

And now, Gordon. Yes, she needed to take a break not only from her family, but from the horrors of living so close to the greatest catastrophe that had ever happened on American soil. It had happened a month ago, but people were still walking the streets in shock, still being atypically kind to one another, a disturbing trait in a New Yorker. She decided to visit Diane in Los Angeles.

She hadn't seen Diane in four years, but they spoke fairly regularly on the phone and Diane always sent a card on her birthday as well as Mimi's. From their conversations, it always sounded as if Diane was on the brink of having something wonderful happen with one of her scripts, she was always "taking meetings" and "taking lunch" and "pitching the studio." But it didn't sound as if much of it had led to anything. Her firing off the popular TV series was the real shame; Diane had told Nikki all about that and Nikki had urged her to sue the network or report the showrunner to his union, but Diane told her that was a sure way to end your career forever. To Nikki, it sounded as if that might have already happened.

Nikki was met at the airport by Diane in the PT Cruiser she had bought during the flush years (which looked cool, but turned out later to be a piece of crap.) She looked great; athletic and slightly tan with sun-streaked hair that put Nikki in mind of a lioness.

She and Diane picked up where they left off, as if no time had passed, the way close friends tend to do. Diane took her to all of her favorite places; hiking in the canyons, breakfast on the beach, Wolfgang Puck's, they even went on the Universal Studios tour. But Nikki could sense an undercurrent of unease within Diane; she wondered if it was something personal, or the fear they were all feeling following this brutal attack on American soil. It was all too ugly; they had talked about the tragedy on the phone and wondered why the rest of the world hated the U.S.so much (without doing the research to get the answer.) For the moment, they both just wanted to try to have fun and forget their worries, but finally, one night at dinner, Nikki was tipsy enough to spill her suspicions about Gordon.

"I think Gordon is having an affair."

Nikki expected compassion, but was surprised to see the blood drain from Diane's face, as if she had reported Gordon's death.

"Oh Nikki, I'm so sorry."

"Did you know?"

"No, of course not. What makes you think he's having an affair?"

"It's been a growing awareness. Do you remember that evening in Italy, when that woman Francesca made a big meal for us and you and Gordon quarreled?" Diane nodded. "I think he was having sex with her."

"Oh."

"I mean, I can't be sure, but that was the first time I started to suspect things."

"That was some time ago."

"I know, and I had kind of convinced myself I was imagining it. Until last Thursday."

Nikki related the incident with Gordon's cell phone. "Obviously, I don't think it's the woman in Italy. That was just the first moment it occurred to me he might be capable of such a thing. I don't know what to do, Diane. Do I confront him? I hate ugly scenes, but the thought of knowing about it and not telling him also seems impossible. What if he leaves me? I couldn't take it if he left me, Diane.

"He won't leave you."

"I could understand if he did. I'm not the most pleasant person to live with these past few years. Sex just seems pointless to me now, and I get so impatient with his tired old stories. Why do men think they have the right to bore people with the same long anecdotes over and over again? They can't possibly think they're being entertaining."

"They just need to talk sometimes."

"What if he leaves me?" Seeing tears form in her friend's eyes, Diane put her hand over Nikki's comfortingly. (Hugs were not really Nikki's thing, unless they were "hello" or "goodbye" hugs, so Diane didn't attempt that.)

"You know, Nick, this could be just a midlife crisis thing. These things burn out sometimes and the marriage manages to survive. But let's say there is someone else. Do you feel that you could possibly forgive him? If, for instance, he admitted it and vowed it would never happen again?"

Nikki struggled with this. "I don't know. You didn't forgive that terrible director you were with. Tony."

"No. But Tony was a schmuck. And I didn't have his child."

Nikki's stomach lurched. "Oh God. It would kill Mimi if we broke up. She would blame me, of course. But to forgive him….How can I trust that it would never happen again? I've had suspicions about him in the past. Little things like coming home late and ticket stubs, you know? But I never had this kind of proof. Ugh! What a skank! How can he be attracted to a woman who would write something like that?"

It was excruciating. Diane had been imagining a conversation like this with Nikki for years but, in her imagination, it had been the opportunity for her to find the courage to come clean about her own "dalliance" with Gordon years ago, fall to her knees and begged her friend's forgiveness. She knew Nikki would be shocked at first, but gradually she would come to see that her friendship with Diane was more important than a momentary indiscretion that had taken place in the past. She would recollect that they had all been very immature back then, that they had all made a lot of foolish mistakes (and this would cause Nikki to think of her own regrettable incident with Paul and Michael) and, seeing Diane's penitent face, Nikki would offer her absolution for her sins and all would be well.

There was only one problem: It wasn't in the past. It was still going on with Gordon. And it had never really stopped.

Diane had tried so often to end it over the years. After the AIDS scare, after Nikki's miscarriage, during her own mother's illness; these death-related events always reminded Diane that she, who had no particular religious convictions, was destined for hell. But Gordon had his hooks in her like a drug, and seemingly hers were in him. Those "business trips" Nikki spoke of were often to Diane in Los Angeles. She had seen Gordon struggle over the years with his addiction to her, possibly with less soul-searching but definitely with a sense of guilt.

"Why do you make me come to you? Why can't you let me go?" he yelled once in frustration during one of their fights, which amazed her because she felt the exact same way. If she were to have seen herself as a character in a film, or read about herself in a book, she would have hated that character and rooted for her to come to a bad end. How could she do this to her best friend, and for all these years? What kind of she-devil would do this? She struggled with self-hatred. She went to a therapist, hoping the woman would help her find a way to extricate from Gordon, but instead she claimed to find nothing to blame in Diane and provided her with some kind of "love will find a way" bromide that disgusted her; absolution was the last thing Diane wanted. She wanted flagellation, finger-pointing, denunciation, and instead she got a lot of head nodding and "How do you feel about that?" Diane started to suspect that this was a technique therapists used to maintain a healthy client base, so she quit going.

Orla was the only person Diane confessed it to, immediately after the debacle in Italy, but of course Orla already knew. They had been lying on Orla's Murphy bed playing with her latest pup, Schatzi, when Diane suddenly blurted out the whole story. Orla nodded, as if she herself were telling the story.

"Mm-hmm."

"Orla. You knew?"

"To tell you the truth, that's why I tried to get Nikki to change her mind about marrying Gordon. I could tell from that first lunch at Marvin's Gardens that he was more suited to you than her."

"That's not true! He's not suited to me. He's not well-read, his interests outside of making money are nil, and he's a Republican for God's sake. I honestly don't know how it's lasted this long. He's like an addiction I can't quit."

"Maybe you should stop trying."

Diane looked at Orla in surprise. "What?"

"Your relationship with him has gone on for almost as long as his with Nikki. There seems to be a kind of stability there, wouldn't you say?"

Diane shook her head firmly. "No, Orla. I can't go through my life being in love with a close friend's husband. That's just weird. I need to get on with my life. I mean, what if I want to have children some day?"

"Do you?"

"No. But I might, some day."

"I'm just saying stop beating yourself up, Diane. You're a little too good at it."

So, Diane tried to stop beating herself up, but guilt is something that Catholics do extremely well, and though Diane was not Catholic, she and her brother had spent a summer at her very Catholic grandmother's farm in Maine. (In retrospect, Diane suspected her parents were going through a rough spot.) This grandmother taught her and Bruce the Our Father and the Hail Mary and spoke often of the evil of mortal sins. Funny how early indoctrination can come back to haunt you.

Diane's attempts at quitting Gordon followed the pattern of many people trying to quit smoking, or shooting drugs. She would be having some success with it, start to acquire a little self-respect, do some dating, maybe even meet someone with real potential. And then something would happen in her life; a career setback, or her mother dying, or something that made her feel weak and vulnerable, and suddenly Gordon would appear, as if he had sniffed out a wounded animal. Because from the very first day that's what he loved, Diane was convinced, her vulnerable side. Her weakness. That's why Diane guessed he kept his distance during her successful years; he felt diminished when she was flying high.

"That's bullshit!" Gordon said when she proposed this theory to him. "You're the one who rejects me when you're flying high. You don't need me anymore, so you take a powder."

Well. Maybe that was partly true. During the TV years she had sworn off of Gordon quite successfully. Who knew anymore what was true? Diane often wondered; if she had met Gordon first and married him, would he now be playing out these same scenes with some *other* Other Woman? It made Diane's head hurt to speculate.

Gordon had asked her to marry him once. He flew into town one day and announced that he had made the decision to leave Nikki so that they could be together.

"Are you high?" shouted Diane. "You can't marry me! I would *never* do anything like that to Nikki!" At which point Gordon started laughing derisively, she started to hit him, he grabbed her wrists and pinned her to a wall and it ended up in sex again. Oh, God. What a tangled web we weave.

So now, here she was with Nikki, listening like a good friend while Nikki told her about the skanky woman who was having an affair with her husband and all Diane could think was, she's right; I am skanky. I am, without doubt, the lowest form of female life there is.

"He's changed in other ways, too, Diane. He used to have this kind of "Fountainhead" attitude toward his work. You've read that, right? Ayn Rand. She was a fascist, of course, but her ideas about the nobility of architecture and city building and the struggle for individualism — Gordon was really inspired by her. Now he's building affordable housing, for God's sake!"

Diane smiled. For this, she did not feel guilty at all. Gordon had reappeared over a year ago, after she was fired off the show and in a weakened emotional state. Nikki must have told him the whole sad story, because suddenly he "just happened" to be in town and wondered if she wanted to take a walk on the beach. It had been a long time, probably four years, since she had kicked the Gordon habit, but she was hurting and desperately needed the boost of seeing him again.

He met her in Malibu, and the minute he got out of his rented BMW and started walking toward her, all tall and handsome in his faded jeans and Ralph Lauren polo, Diane could feel the pull. She knew he was prepared to play the role of the strong male savior again, but this time, she wanted it to be different. He held her in his arms (God, it felt good) and then immediately started talking about her "plight."

"We can't let that asshole get away with this, you've got to sue. Let me take care of this, Diane. I know a lawyer --"

"I don't want to sue. I just want to leave that whole thing behind me."

"You're making a mistake, Di."

"Let's just have a nice walk on the beach, okay?"

So, they walked. It was an exquisite day, not a cloud in the sky and the ocean sparkled appreciatively at the sun. The tide was going down, so they took their shoes off and walked barefoot in the nice squishy sand. The pelicans flying overhead always made Diane feel their connection to prehistoric times; they looked so much like the flying dinosaurs they were. She shivered with enjoyment, and Gordon took her hand.

"Cold?"

"No. It's a beautiful day."

"I expected to find you sad."

"Disappointed?"

"Don't be an idiot." They were back on their familiar terrain. They went to a beach restaurant for drinks, and Gordon made his pitch for being back in her life.

"It's no good, Di. We're both miserable when we're apart."

"Speak for yourself."

"Okay, I am speaking for myself. I'm miserable when we're apart. I know you won't let me leave Nikki, but if I did it anyway —"

"If you leave Nikki, I will never see you again, I swear to God."

Gordon leaned back and looked at her appraisingly. "Why? Because your love for Nikki is so deep that you don't want to hurt her? Or because your self-esteem is so fragile that you can't bear to be perceived as a home wrecker?"

It was a question that went deep. "Can't both be true?"

Gordon considered this. "Yes. Both can be true."

"I can't let you leave Nikki, Gordon. My reasons for that may be good, or you may be right and I am just an insecure coward. But I miss you. I knew I was going to lose this battle the minute you called."

"It's not a battle."

"It's always been a battle. You knew I'd lose it, too, that's why you're here."

Gordon smiled ruefully. "It's not a battle, Diane. It's two people who love each other."

Diane had no answer for that. The waiter came, and they ordered food. Then they stared out the window watching the waves pound up onto the shore; the show that never closes. Finally Diane spoke.

"It's got to be different this time."

"Okay. In what way?"

"There has to be something good that comes out of it."

"Besides happiness?"

"I don't mean for you and me. I mean for the world. Or anyway, our little part of it."

"What do you want?"

"I want you to change the way you do business."

Diane then laid out her proposition. She would let Gordon back into her life if he proved to her that he was capable of building something other than luxury hotels and golf courses, and she wanted him to do it right there in California.

"What do you want me to build?"

"Something for the common good. Affordable housing. Senior living. A rehab center. I don't care, as long as it doesn't cater to the one percent. If you can do that, I'll welcome you back."

He looked at her incredulously. "Diane Daly, are you bargaining with me?"

"I am," said Diane. "Let's do a deal."

And so, they did. Gordon threw in with a non-profit affordable housing developer in California. With his clout and expertise, building increased exponentially. He was still building the high-end stuff; he had a hotel going up in Laguna Beach that was breaking ground as well. But Diane took comfort in knowing that her life of mortal sin was also spawning something good.

It continued that way for a number of years. There were months when Diane didn't see Gordon at all, and a long patch during her mother's illness when she couldn't see him. But they were always in touch, and met when they could. He was with her at her mother's funeral, and if Bruce wondered why he had never heard about this man his sister was clearly in love with, he never said anything. "My friend Gordon," was how she introduced him, and then Bruce never heard about him again.

This episode with Nikki was too close a call, and it demonstrated to Diane just how delusional she had been, trying to convince herself that Nikki didn't care for Gordon. Nikki cared. She was terrified he was going to leave.

Diane drove Nikki back to the airport. On the drive, Nikki said, "I'm not going to confront Gordon, not yet at least. I couldn't bear for Mimi to suffer over any of this."

"That sounds right," said Diane. "Give it some time. See if he changes."

Before Nikki got out of the car she turned to Diane. "I'm so glad we did this, Di. I don't know what I'd do if I didn't have you to talk to." She hugged Diane briefly but fiercely and Diane watched her go into the terminal, knowing she had been given a reprieve she didn't deserve. You don't get that many lucky breaks in life.

She got out her phone and called Gordon.

"So, another excommunication."

"The repercussions are getting worse and worse. I feel like shit, and you should, too."

"I'll never feel like shit about us, Diane. But you're calling the shots here, as usual."

This enraged Diane. "Why do you say that? You're the one who won't let us go. Let me go, Gordon, please! For once in your life, think about someone other than yourself!"

Gordon picked Nikki up at the airport, which was a surprise because usually they both just took Ubers or a car service. He seemed a bit somber, but he was attentive, inquisitive, and interested in hearing about Nikki's trip to California. Nikki thought of how cold and distant she had been toward him before she left, and wondered if Gordon had been worried that she was thinking of leaving him. This new Gordon was a welcome relief; she was glad she hadn't immediately thrown accusations at him. Divorce was a terrifying prospect to her. She would do anything to avoid it.

A few weeks later, Nikki sneaked a look at Gordon's phone while he was in the shower. There were no racy texts, just a whole lot of work-related messages. What happened to the skanky woman, she wondered? Nikki guessed it was one of those one-night stands a man lives to regret, like Michael Douglas in "Fatal Attraction." In her mind, the skanky woman looked like Glenn Close.

In the months that followed, Nikki and Diane chatted frequently. Diane told her about the new guy she was seeing, a cinematographer. "That's pretty much all you meet out here is people in the industry. The chances of me meeting a doctor or an architect or a mathematician are pretty slim."

"Were you hoping to meet a mathematician?"

"Only if he can carry a tune."

Nikki laughed and repeated Diane's quip that night at the dinner table, but only Mimi thought it was funny. As the days passed, Gordon became quieter and more irritable. Every conversation he and Nikki had seemed to end in some kind of trivial spat. When he wasn't at work, he spent all of his time in the guest house out back, only coming in for the occasional meal. Even Mimi, who had reached the age where she was generally oblivious of her parents, noticed it. "What's the matter with Dad?" she asked one evening during another dinner without him, and Nikki had no answer other than, "He's been working very hard. He needs his rest."

But Gordon was more than tired; he seemed empty. He went about the motions of the day, but didn't seem invested in anything. One night, when he was asleep and Nikki was still awake reading, Gordon started to cry. It was the strangest sound, so plaintive and vulnerable, as if he were a child who was lost and scared. Nikki was deeply unsettled by the sounds he was making and jostled him out of the dream. "Gordon!"

"Oh, sorry," he said, in his worldly empire-builder voice, the one she was used to, and went back to sleep. Nikki tried to go back to reading, but that little boy lost voice stuck in her head for a long time afterward.

One night when Mimi was at a friend's house for a sleepover, Nikki and Gordon went out to dinner. It was a restaurant Nikki had been looking forward to, and the kind of place you had to book at least a week ahead. Sitting opposite one another, Nikki did a running narration on what she thought of the décor, the menu, the service so far. Gordon just sat there staring at the dessert menu, not seeming to take in his surroundings or listen to what Nikki was saying. It was so goddamn exasperating that finally Nikki said, "Gordon, are you planning on leaving me?"

Gordon looked up from his menu, surprised. "What?"

"I just need to know. I can't take the suspense any longer."

"I'm not going to leave you, Nikki."

"Why not? You're obviously not happy. Sometimes I think you hate me."

"How can you say that? I don't hate you. I'm just… I don't know…" Nikki waited for him to finish the sentence, but apparently he wasn't going to.

"You're just what? Bored? Unhappy? Miserable? That's the message I'm getting. That's the message Mimi is getting, too. If your life is so awful, why don't you change it?"

"I can't. I'm here for you, Nikki. I'm sticking it out."

"Wow. That's really romantic, Gordon. You're sticking it out. That just makes me all tingly inside."

"That's not what I--"

"Look, I know you haven't been faithful to me. No, don't even try to protest. I suspected it, and then I had proof. And I was very upset by it for a while, but I decided not to say anything because I could see you were trying to change. What I don't understand is, if you're so unhappy, why do you stay with me?"

"Because I – I love you."

"I wish you could hear how unconvincing that just sounded."

"Nikki. I don't claim to be the best husband in the world."

"Well good, because that would just be silly."

"I'm trying my best, I really am."

"But why, Gordon? I just don't understand why."

Gordon looked down at the table. "I'm doing it for love, Nikki. I don't expect you to understand. I don't know any other way to explain it."

2006

Diane decided to marry her cinematographer. It felt like the right thing to do. They had been together now for a few years. He was smart and knew a lot of cool people and as a result her social life had blossomed exponentially. Suddenly, she was going to red carpet events, hobnobbing with famous people and getting to wear the kind of clothes she only saw in magazines. He introduced her to a producer who hired her to do a rewrite of an indie film which actually got made and, although her name was not in the credits, it made her feel like she was still connected to the industry, and that felt good.

So, she was marrying her cinematographer. It felt silly to go through one's whole life without being married, even though Orla had never been married and she seemed perfectly happy, but Diane wasn't Orla and she had certain expectations of herself. Being married and successful were part of those expectations. Also, although she never talked about it, she was over forty now, which was like sixty in LA years and if she was ever going to get married, this felt like the outside of the envelope. Even though a lot of the people she was meeting seemed pretty vacuous and she came home some nights with a deep sense of existential dread, still it was pretty exciting to think about giving up her place and moving to his cool digs in Mandeville Canyon, which had a pool and a housekeeper and a panoramic view of Los Angeles from downtown to the beach.

And so, she was marrying her cinematographer.

"Oh, Diane! I'm so happy for you!" exclaimed Nikki. "Does Orla know?"

"I'm calling her next."

"And he's Jewish! So perfect for you!"

"Why is that perfect?"

"Oh, you know, you with all your Yiddishisms."

"Everybody who has ever lived in New York comes away with Yiddishisms."

"I don't think I did. Wait, is klutz Yiddish?"

"Yes."

"Well then, I do! He's kind of famous, right? I think I've seen his name in credits."

"Maybe."

"We're coming out for sure! When's the date?"

"Well, that's the thing, it's not going to be like that. We're going to keep it very private."

"Private? You're not inviting us?"

"I know that sounds weird. We're just going to fly to Hawaii and do it there. We already got the license, so you can do it anywhere."

"Oh. Wow. Okay." Nikki's deflation was palpable.

"It's his preference. I would totally go for a big blowout, but he has, uh, you know, family issues that make him want to keep it private." This, of course, was not true.

"Well okay, but can I throw you a party or something?"

"Umm… What if you and me and Orly met at a spa or something?"

"Yes! Let's pamper the bride! This is so exciting, I'm kvelling! That's the word, right, kvelling?"

"Yeah, but it's not a three-syllable word."

"Hey! Gordon built a place years ago that had a great spa, what was it called? Gordon!"

"Oh hey, you know what, maybe not a —"

"Oops, I forgot, he's out jogging. I'll ask him when he gets home. It was in Ojai, I think."

"Uh-huh. Well, you know what, Ojai gets so hot. Maybe we should just — "

"Although now that I think about it, that was so long ago, I don't even know if it's still open. And Gordon is primarily focused on this affordable housing craze of his, so …"

There was a pause. "Still?"

"What?"

"He's still doing affordable housing?"

"Yeah. He stopped with the luxury stuff a while ago. It's funny how he's changed these past few years. It's not like he isn't a good breadwinner; he is. But he's shifted gears. Now he's all about housing being a fundamental human need, and social justice and the revitalization of communities. It's cool, I suppose. I just never thought it was his thing."

In the end, Diane did not marry her cinematographer.

2008

Isaac loomed over Orla's desk threateningly, waving a sheaf of papers.

"Idiot! You gave them back their fucking deposit?"

"Of course I did, Isaac." Orla tried to keep her voice calm. "His wife was diagnosed with cancer. He sent the doctor's diagnosis."

"Anyone can fake that shit, it was past the thirty-day cancellation period, way past. You are so fucking stupid!"

"Isaac, please don't talk to me like that."

"I'll talk any way I want. That was a twenty-five thousand dollar booking!"

"I see. So, you want me to say, 'Sorry, you're going to have to go to France anyway. Bicycling through France is really fun when you're getting chemo?"

"You are so fucking clueless, Orla. Do you know how much money you cost this agency with your bleeding-heart attitude toward every little excuse that comes down the pike? We are hemorrhaging money! Look at this balance sheet! Do you even understand how to read a balance sheet? Of course you don't, you're too busy giving money away!"

It was shortly after this conversation that Isaac decided to leave the Great Escape travel agency, cashing out on what he claimed was his and leaving Orla with seriously depleted operating funds. On the one hand, Orla was happy not to have to deal with his snark and hostility. On the other, she actually did not know how to read a balance sheet, or keep the books. The joy she took in Great Escape was the joy of changing people's lives for the better, not adding and subtracting numbers; she had counted on Isaac to do that stuff. For a short time, she hired an accountant, but his fees proved to be more than she could afford, so she tried to educate herself by going to a night school on accounting. For some reason, she just couldn't "get" what the teacher was saying, and she found herself getting frustrated and even angry. Maybe this was why Isaac was always so angry; maybe his soul had been destroyed by numbers.

The market crash of 2008 came shortly after Isaac ran off with more than half his share of the travel agency. Were Orla a vengeful type, she might take consolation in the fact that he placed all of that money in the stock market two weeks before the crash. But Orla didn't really care what happened to Isaac, she was merely grateful that she herself had taken most of her money out of the stock market and bought this business nine years ago. For this, she realized, she had Harvey to thank. Orla didn't consider that if she had left that money in Apple stock all those years ago, she would be a millionaire by now. All she knew was that suddenly, today, Harvey looked like a genius. She wanted to call and thank him, but she didn't know where he was. After they had broken up (was it really fifteen years ago?) he had simply disappeared with no forwarding address, and of course back then he hadn't had a cell phone. She thought of him often.

Orla had had a couple of other passionate flings after Harvey. She had met a painter in Barcelona and spent a glorious ten days with him. She still had the painting he made of her on the wall of her apartment, and they corresponded from time to time by old fashioned snail mail, as they both felt email would have cheapened the experience. She also met a scuba diving instructor in the Caymen Islands a few years ago who taught her the joys of coral reef exploration and had many land-based gifts as well, but the romance flickered out once she realized that going lower than twenty feet in a scuba tank was giving her terrible earaches and, on shore alone, her lover wasn't half as entertaining. As exciting as both men had been, neither of them had Harvey's intellectual gifts, nor his talent for cuddling and whispering silly things to her that made her laugh.

Orla went online from time to time to try to find a Harvey Gluck. It wasn't that common a name, but all she could ever find was one or two obituaries, a realtor in Key Biscayne, and a financial advisor; then it went to the composer Christoph Gluck.

One day, Orla was walking her latest pup, Trixie, a dachshund, in Riverside Park on a warm summer day in July, when coming toward her she noticed a figure that she was sure she recognized. A man about her height, with arms that swung forward like Fred Flintstone. His hair was thinner, in fact, he was almost bald, and he was dressed in a pullover shirt, waistcoat, jacket and tie. He looked like something out of the 19th Century. Orla slowed down so that he would notice her, and he looked up just in time.

"Orla!" he exclaimed. I was hoping I would one day run into you."

"Harvey!" she beamed. "You're looking very Victorian."

"Thank you. My father died, and left me rather a lot of money. It was unexpected, as he told me repeatedly that I was his least favorite child. But the fact is, Father was wealthy, and in an uncharacteristic fit of fairness, he divided his wealth amongst the four of us evenly. My older brothers were quite put out.

"I'm sorry about your father, but glad for you."

"Thank you! I'm not sorry about my father at all. Esalen revealed to me long ago that pain created by our parents is something we can overcome, if we work at it. I was a pompous ass the last time we were together, Orla. Convinced that money was the root of all evil. But I have money now and I can testify that it is not all bad."

"I'm glad to hear it."

"And you? You look wonderful. How have you been?"

"Good. Still at the travel agency. Isaac has left the business."

"Oh, but Isaac was a terrible man! I'll never understand why he thought you and I were brother and sister. He called me a pervert once."

"I'm so sorry."

They stood and talked for quite some time. It had been fifteen years, and they had much to catch up on. Orla confessed that she had missed him after their breakup, and Harvey told her he cursed himself daily for his stupidity. He saw in retrospect that he had behaved miserably on the trip to Italy, but that his pride had kept him from reaching out to her afterwards.

"I was being my father, Orla! I absolutely was, but I just couldn't see it. It wasn't until I spent some time in therapy that I realized how much my father affected the way I lived my own life. He was an impecunious man, stingy with both money and emotions, never saw the good in people. Imagine my shock when, in death, he suddenly became generous. I fully expected him to leave his money to West Point Academy."

They walked for a while and, though Harvey still waxed philosophical from time to time, it was not enough to annoy Orla. In fact, he seemed as charming to her as the first time they met, even more so. He told her he had bought an apartment on Riverside Drive and invited her up to see it. It was a building she had walked past many times but never considered much, shaped a bit like a medieval castle, with a rampart on top. From the spacious top floor apartment where Harvey lived, the unobscured view of the river delighted her, especially when she considered the very small slice of it she could see from her own apartment. Trixie wandered around sniffing everything, and finally settled down on a rug by the door as if it had always been her spot.

That was the beginning of Take Two with Harvey. It was ever so much better than Take One. They were older now, they had perspective and a sense of balance, and their expectations weren't as grandiose. Orla's never-ending quest for a Grand Passion had died down; now she was looking for stability, comfort and someone to say hello to in the morning. It was also wonderful that each of them had their own place so close to one another, it enabled them to feel both independent and interconnected. It was nice to miss each other, and then meet up on dates. The first time they had cohabited, Harvey had just been mugged (and Orla suspected he had been living on the streets before that, or in a shelter.) This time, she wasn't his protector; they were equal. There was definitely something attractive about being in a relationship with a man of independent means.

Diane and Nikki were delighted to hear the news about the return of Harvey. They had both noted the long stretch of single life for Orla, and her loneliness. She was forty-five now, perhaps not considered the optimum age for romance, and her worshipful adoration of Trixie had seemed a bit unhealthy considering that none of her dogs ever managed to live very long. It seemed her grieving period each time a pet "crossed the rainbow bridge" grew more intense with each one. Whatever reservations Diane had had about Harvey were dispelled the moment she heard the delight in Orla's voice. Loneliness was a bitch.

2014

To allay boredom, and to appease a certain survivor guilt that lingered within her, Nikki became very involved in the effort to end the AIDS crisis. She joined the Colorado AIDS Walk and Run, and every year she donated herself heart and soul into raising money to end the disease. The people she worked with were very grateful, as Nikki had deep pockets, and they chose to look the other way when she said things like, "I've never understood the gay lifestyle choice, but I hate what's happening to them." If they wondered what exactly motivated her to make this her personal cause célèbre, no one asked.

In addition to not understanding the gay "lifestyle choice," she now had a new concept with which to grapple. Nikki went to Instagram and looked up her daughter Mimi, who was now her son, Ray.

Why Ray? Nikki wondered what positive associations had inspired Mimi to take that rather prosaic name. It was bad enough that she was suddenly Nikki's son, but to have to call her Ray? Nikki mentally corrected herself; to have to call "them" Ray. This pronoun thing required a mnemonic device that was simply unavailable to Nikki, the same way so many of her passcodes were.

Today's picture of Ray on Instagram had them in a skull cap and nose ring, their head shaven as usual, giving the camera the finger with both tattooed hands. They were smiling, though; that was good. Nikki was glad they were past the phase where Mi…Ray posted videos castigating her mother for her ignorance and intolerance. *Their* mother. Shit. Impossible.

Gordon had handled all of it better than she. This surprised Nikki, as Gordon had been intolerant in so many other ways. Mimi had come home on a surprise visit from Oregon and told them both to sit down, which is never a good sign, but Nikki was too happy to see her daughter to worry. Then Mimi sprang the news.

"Mom. Dad. I want you to know that I am non-binary."

Non-binary. It sounded vaguely digestive, like being lactose intolerant, so Nikki said sympathetically, "Oh honey, is there anything we can do for you?" This set off a whole chain of events that labelled Nikki from then on as being prejudiced and intolerant, which seemed so unfair, especially since Gordon's response that day had been, "What the hell does that mean?" Mimi went on to explain (without any annoyance displayed toward her father at all, of course) that it meant she considered herself neither male nor female but rather both, which is why from now on she would prefer to be called Ray.

Nikki was too shocked to respond. She supposed Gordon was, too, because they both sat there for a long time, processing this. Then Gordon started to chuckle. It was a dark, ghastly chuckle; he did not seem truly amused.

"Great. Fine. You're Ray. That's perfect. Call me when dinner's ready." And he left the room.

"Is Dad mad?" Nikki's morphing child asked her.

"I think he just needs to think about it. I think we both do."

"Call Diane. She'll explain it to you."

"Why would Diane know more about it than we do?"

"She lives in California."

That seemed like a ridiculous reason, but Nikki didn't want to get into a fight. Mimi only spent one night with them, and Gordon left on a business trip the next day, so the two of them didn't really get to talk about it. Nikki brooded for a while, and then decided she would call Diane after all. To her surprise, Diane was completely prepared to have this conversation.

"Ray is not your son," Diane explained. "They simply want you to know that they are gender fluid, not exclusively identifying as either male or female, and have taken the name Ray as an expression of their identity."

"Did you know about this already? Did Mimi tell you?"

There was a bit of a silence on the other end. "No. I have worked with non-binary and trans people. It's more common than you think."

"How are you calling her "them" so easily? I'm completely confused."

"I know, Nick. It's a different world now from when we grew up. Maybe that's a good thing, I really don't know. But Ray is still your child, and they love you just as much as they always did."

"Oh God Diane, stop with the "they" stuff!"

"You're going to have to get used to it, Nikki. Ray needs your support right now. The danger here is that sometimes parents are so frightened and repulsed by who their children have turned out to be that they reject them entirely. Remember Young Michael?"

Even after all these years, Nikki flinched when Diane brought him up. "This is nothing like Young Michael! Mimi isn't dying, she's just claiming a new identity. It's not going to kill her!"

"Exactly," said Diane. "I'm glad you see it that way."

Nikki hung up, miffed at how in-the-know Diane's tone had been, but decided that there was really no option but to follow her advice. She loved Mimi deeply, whoever Mimi thought she was, and didn't want to lose her.

When Gordon came home from his business trip, he seemed much more relaxed about the whole Mimi thing.

"I've been giving this some thought, and I think it's really important we don't let this non-binary thing estrange us from Mimi. She's our kid, I mean "they're" our kid, our only kid, and I don't want to lose her. Them. Remember Young Michael? That kid at your friend Paul's funeral?

Nikki stared at Gordon for a long time with narrowed eyes. Finally, she said, "I'm glad you see it that way. I do, too."

In recent years, Nikki and Gordon's marriage had settled into something of a benign partnership. Nikki didn't question Gordon's business trips and, when he was home, Gordon made a habit of telling Nikki how attractive she was, how nice her hair was looking, how lovely that outfit, doing little things to make her feel good about herself so that they didn't have to think about how little passion was in the marriage. Nikki appreciated it. She enjoyed the occasional jewelry, she liked it when Gordon praised her before others at dinner parties or posted something nice about her on social media (she suspected they looked like the perfect couple,) and frankly she was relieved not to have to pretend to enjoy sex with him.

It had been difficult when Mimi had moved away; there seemed to be nothing to talk about with Gordon. Then Nikki joined an empty nest support group and discovered a whole community of new friends that occupied a great deal of her time. She took yoga, she joined a knitting group, she supported the local community theatre. Her friends were all very impressed that she used to act professionally, it made her something of a celebrity in those circles, which was nice. Now, when they had dinner together, Nikki could tell Gordon about all these activities and it filled the void nicely. In turn, Gordon would tell one of his stories about his early days in the real estate business, generally something about the great tycoon he first worked for who then fell on hard times, gloating a bit about his own relative success, and Nikki would nod her head and smile as if it were the first time he was telling it, not the twentieth. After all, as Diane had said, men just need to talk sometimes.

If there were other paths Nikki's life might have taken, she was determined not to think about them. There was really no point to it. She considered herself very lucky.

2020

Orla's life became considerably brighter once Harvey came back into it. He still looked at her as if he had just found living treasure, and she loved being loved. (Who doesn't?) Living apart made all the difference; when she had heard enough of Harvey's philosophizing, or became a bit irked on his authoritative dissertations, or could feel one of his mood swings coming on, she merely went home. The one thing they agreed upon was that freedom was everything.

Orla became involved with a Universalist church that embraced all faiths. She hadn't known such a thing existed until one of her clients recommended it, and she was delighted at the services, which mentioned no deity in particular and let your mind roam pleasantly during the sermons. She deeply believed in helping others, mainly because it caused her physical pain to see them suffer. She frequently handed out money to the homeless, but found that it was best not to do so around Harvey, who loved to engage her in a philosophical examination of her actions, for example: Who was it was she was actually helping by giving away money; them, or herself? Who cares? Did it matter?

Orla had various challenges with the business, which was subject to the vagaries of the economy, but in general people loved to travel and she had built up an extremely loyal client base, so her work life was happy. In addition, the small amount of Apple stock that she still had left when she bought the travel agency, which sat there for the longest time not doing much, had suddenly ballooned into a sizable nest egg. Any time her bankbook ran into the red and it looked like paying employees might be a problem that month, she merely replenished her coffers from her own account and breathed a sigh of relief. 2019 had been a very good year for Apple, and for Orla. (And for the homeless in her area.)

In January, there was a story about a health emergency in China, a virus of some sort. It wasn't clear if it started in a Chinese market (something about pangolins) or a lab, or what. Harvey was sure it started in a lab, that some virus had escaped, maybe intentionally, and was making its way toward them. But then, Harvey was always so alarmist.

Only a week later, everybody started hearing about the "Novel Coronavirus," and pretty soon anyone who was flying to the US from China was subject to screening. Then someone in Washington state died of the virus. Then a couple of people in Arizona, and California. Then Wuhan, China, a city of eleven million people, went into lockdown.

"Wow!" said Orla. "Can you imagine locking down an entire city? How does that even work?"

"It probably doesn't," commented Nikki. She, Diane and Orla were now communicating via their new discovery for three-way video calls, Zoom. For Orla, Zoom was a life saver, because it created the comfortable illusion that you were safe in the presence of friends, instead of what was starting to feel like a Stephen King novel. Every week she, Nikki and Diane would tell each other what was happening, share their fears, even have a few laughs. As she was in New York, Nikki in Colorado and Diane in California, it was the most regular communication the three friends had had in a long time, and it felt like a bit of sanity in an insane world.

"I'd hate to be in China right now," replied Diane. "Then again, I've never really been tempted to go, have you?"

"Oh, I've heard it's fabulous!" enthused Orla. "The Brownsteins went there last year and had a wonderful time!" Diane didn't ask who the Brownsteins were. Orla had gotten into the habit of talking about people as if everyone knew them; Diane assumed they were clients.

A few days later, an entire cruise ship was quarantined off the coast of Japan and they had given the disease a new name: "COVID 19."

"Catchy," quipped Diane.

"I don't know how you can joke," said Nikki. "People have died. Did you see what's happening in Italy? They're calling it a hotspot."

"And that's just the night clubs" said Diane in a Groucho voice, waving an imaginary cigar.

"Diane. Stop."

"Sorry. I joke when I worry."

"It's better than what Harvey's doing," said Orla. "He loves to catastrophize. This fits right in with his world view."

Days later, all the passengers on the Grand Princess cruise ship were stranded off the coast of California because half them had tested positive for COVID 19. A week after that, the US issued a "no sail" order to all the cruise ships.

In California, Diane and Gordon were watching TV. Some time back, somewhat against the will of both of them, they had resumed seeing one another. By now it was one of those old habits that felt so familiar it had ingrained its way into their DNA. It was no longer the crazy passionate affair of their first years, or the tortured guilt-ridden rendezvous of their middle years. It was more like having a favorite teddy bear that you had held so long it had been hugged into a different, possibly hideous but reassuringly familiar, shape; a shape you didn't notice had changed. Of course, they couldn't hug every night, but when they could, which was every few months or, if they were lucky, oftener, they clung to one another with the kind of relief a child feels that the teddy hadn't been permanently misplaced.

They had just finished dinner and were watching TV in her home when they heard the announcement that the health emergency was officially being called a pandemic. Diane, who had been feeling uneasy about it all day already, turned off the TV.

"You'd better get home."

"Honey, I've got a meeting tomorrow in Long Beach."

"After the meeting, then. This thing is serious, they're going to freeze travel soon."

"Surely not from California to Colorado."

"How do we know? You should really leave soon, Gordon. Nikki is going to need you."

"Don't you need me?"

"Of course. But she's your wife. Ray is your child."

"Ray definitely doesn't need me, they're quite happy in Oregon."

"Gordon, if we suddenly had to go into a lockdown of some sort, how on earth would we explain the fact that you are here with me?"

"Oh, so that's it. Still worried about your image as a home-wrecker."

"Yes! Fine! Have it your way. But seriously, go home."

Gordon took his meeting and stalled for a couple of days, but finally relented. She drove him to the airport and handed him a mask. "Wear this." He smiled and took it from her.

"I love it when you worry about me."

"I hate it."

"I know you do." He kissed her, a satisfyingly long kiss.

"How the hell have we lasted this long?"

"I wouldn't call it 'lasting'. You've excommunicated me more than once. We've gone years without seeing each other."

"Okay, what would you call it?"

"Mutual enslavement."

Diane laughed, they kissed again, and he went into the terminal. It felt suddenly to Diane as if she spent half of her life watching people she loved walk into that terminal.

He texted her from the plane. "*Half empty flight. A pangolin has the seat next to me, should I be concerned?*"

That night on Zoom, Nikki said, "Thank God Gordon's back from Las Vegas. He's such a freaking workaholic." That jerk, thought Diane. He told her he was going to Vegas? Probably thought too many trips to California would look suspicious.

Orla sipped her glass of Kombucha. "It's so cool that he's building homes for poor people now, though. How many has he built so far, Diane?"

Diane's heart skipped a beat. "Oh gosh, how would I know? A lot, right, Nikki?" What the hell was wrong with Orla? How could she ask her something like that in front of Nikki?

"Yeah," responded Nikki smoothly. "About a hundred and forty units so far, I think. He's also building senior centers, he says that's big business these days. I was surprised he wanted to do something so — well, charitable, as affordable housing, but it seems to give him a lot of joy, and an unhappy Gordon is not pleasant to be around. Plus, he tells me they're going to be giving him some kind of humanitarian award soon. That puffs up the ego nicely," she laughed.

The next couple of days were busy ones for Diane. The recent rains had initiated a leak from the roof into her upstairs bathroom. Gordon had climbed up there and tried to fix it, but he had only made it worse, so Diane had to get a roofer. You dope, thought Diane. You may be a builder, but you ain't no roofer.

At that moment, there was a ding on her phone. Gordon. *"I love you. Don't let the bad guys get you down. Take care of Nikki."*

Take care of Nikki? Diane rushed to the phone and called Nikki, who answered, crying.

"Gordon's in the hospital."

Diane gasped and dropped her phone. Leaning over to pick it up, the head rush got her dizzy and she fell to the floor, hitting her head on her bedside table.

"I'm sorry, I'm sorry, Nikki, I dropped the phone!" Retrieving it, she decided it was wiser to take the call on the floor. "He's in the hospital? Tell me it isn't COVID." But Nikki was sobbing now. "Oh my God, no!"

"He – he came home feeling fine, but the next day he started to get aches and fever, and then he had this cough and sore throat. We tried not to panic, there are colds going around, but then --- then he couldn't breathe. Oh Diane, it was horrible!"

"Tell me. Tell me every moment of what happened."

So, Nikki told her. Seeing Gordon struggle for breath, Nikki had immediately put him in the car and driven like hell to the Emergency Room. There weren't that many other patients there – Colorado still didn't have that many cases yet - But as soon as the staff saw Gordon, they put him on a gurney and started to wheel him down the hall, taking information about him on the way. Nikki tried to follow, but when they got to the pneumatic doors, two orderlies in hazmat suits came out to take the gurney. They looked like astronauts.

"Sorry, this is as far as you can go."

Nikki felt like she was in a sci-fi film. "But he's my husband."

"Sorry, ma'am. Protocol."

Nikki took Gordon's hand. "You're going to be fine."

"I know," he responded between gasps. "The insurance bill is on my desk. I didn't get the chance to -"

"I'll pay it."

"I'll be back soon. Be good."

"And if you can't be good, be careful," rejoined Nikki. Their old joke.

Diane listened to Nikki relate this story, her heart aching with pain and jealousy. "Their old joke." Of course, they would have jokes between them. Nikki will take care of the insurance bill; she will take care of everything that needs to be done to keep Gordon safe. She, Diane, means nothing now. She's the girlfriend on the coast that one no one knows about, the person who loves him more than anyone in the world but can't acknowledge it. Diane wasn't allowed to sob the way Nikki was, not in front of her, but when she hung up, the flood gates opened. She pounded the floor in fury and despair; WHY had she insisted he go home? If he had stayed with her, he might still be safe. She paced the floor desperately; she screamed and threw things. She dialed and redialed Gordon's number, to no avail. She *had* to join Nikki in Colorado. Diane grabbed up her laptop and scheduled the next flight out, then called Orla and told her what was going on, and that she was planning on flying out.

"Diane. Don't."

"Why not?"

"You know why not."

"I have to see him, Orly. If there's a chance I can see him —"

"There isn't. They're not letting anyone in. I know this is hard for you, Di, but imagine what Nikki's going through, and Ray. Leave them alone."

Leave them alone. That was the most painful thing Orla had ever said to her. She agonized about whether to go anyway. It wouldn't look weird. It would look like a great friend had come to join them out of care and concern. Nikki might be grateful to have her there, after all she and Ray weren't getting along all that well. Diane could run errands for them. Pharmacy runs, whatever. It didn't have to be weird. Did it?

Then the decision was taken out of her hands; California became the first state to go into lockdown. Diane took two sleeping pills to knock herself out.

The following evening, the three women had a Zoom call. Nikki looked like she was drained of all vitality. Orla's hair was mussed and her pajamas had stains down the front. Diane could imagine what she herself looked like.

"How is he?" asked Diane.

"They've got him on a ventilator."

"Oh good!" exclaimed Orla. "That'll help, right?"

"I don't know."

There was a silence.

"How do you think he got it? Do you think it was the flight home?" asked Orla.

"I don't know. Could have been in Las Vegas. All those people."

Las Vegas. Diane was tempted to just come clean. If not now, when?

"I guess we'll never know," was what she said instead.

"This is so -- fucked up!" Nikki's words caught in her throat.

"He'll be okay, Nick. He's super strong. The ones who – (Diane was going to say 'die') -- the ones who this hits the hardest are the really old people."

"That's true, Nick," volunteered Orla. "Gordon is only, what? Fifty-eight?"

"He's sixty-three," said Nikki, and there was another silence. "If I could only talk to him."

"Can't you? On the phone?"

"We tried to FaceTime. The nurse held the phone up so I could see him, but really all I could see was the fucking ventilator. He couldn't talk. He could barely breathe. He just gave me a thumbs up."

Orla saw Diane's face twist in pain listening to this. "Let's say a prayer for him right now," she said, and though Nikki and Diane had each given up on religion for their own reasons, all three in their separate cities bowed their heads.

"Loving Creator of us all, we pray that Gordon will be healed with every breath he takes, and freed of all fears. Whatever is broken in his body, may it be mended and all infections cleansed. May healing love pass through his body. May he have wisdom to detach from suffering and be liberated. May all heavenly beings protect him. May he be cured."

"Amen," said the three women.

Gordon died three days later.

2021

The entire next year was to become a blank for Diane, Nikki, and the three million other people who lost loved ones to the pandemic. They didn't get to see the victims, didn't get to ease their pain or make them feel loved or say good-bye to them, didn't get to hold a funeral or a memorial service. They just had to exist in suspended animation, until the horror diminished and the rituals could begin. And by then, it was too late, because nothing felt real anymore.

The Zoom conversations amongst the three women ceased. Diane and Nikki walked around in their separate, private worlds of pain. From time to time one of them would call Orla, but Orla's relentless sunniness did not help in this instance, in fact she seemed so disconnected from the facts on the ground that it was annoying. She was, however, the only conduit for information amongst the three of them. Not that there was much information to share; grief is grief.

In her own effort to distance herself from reality, Diane immersed herself in writing a historical novel about Margaret of Anjou, a queen of England in the 15th Century. The brutality of the time period suited her current mood.

Ray had come back to Colorado during Gordon's illness and, anticipating that state's lockdown, made the decision to stay with Nikki, bringing along their partner Valentine, whose "dead name" was Ryan. Though Nikki was in a perpetual state of confusion about their preferred identities, she was grateful to have them both with her. She started up a subscription with Blue Apron and focused on keeping them well fed. It changed the dynamic of her relationship with Ray, who she realized now she had forced into her version of what a little girl should be. Instead of ballet class, she should have let Ray play softball, the way they had wanted as a child, and she should have stopped constantly urging her to be compliant. She said so to Ray, and was gratified to see the diminishment of the seemingly ever-present tension in their brow. As for the loss of Gordon, they took comfort in being able to grieve together the man whose attention they had never fully had. The pandemic brought them together in a meaningful way that was to last.

Meanwhile in New York, Orla was in a state of shock. Numerous clients and a few of her church friends were in refrigerated trucks on the street, which was simply too frightening to think about. Fear was everywhere. The travel agency was doing no business. She was running out of money. By Zoom, Harvey helped Orla to apply for a government loan, and it did enable her to continue paying rent on the office, but to what end? She couldn't even go there herself. She and Harvey had discussed doing lockdown together at his place, but Orla knew this would be a good way to kill the relationship again. By mutual agreement, they took to their respective apartments and communicated on the phone.

"This pandemic connects us palpably to the past, Orla," Harvey said on the phone one night. "Our situation is essentially identical to that of ancient epidemics. Isn't it remarkable? The only defense, even thousands of years later, is isolation. The fragility of man is timeless."

"Uh-huh," responded Orla, who had decided her best course of action was watching episodes of *Tiger King*. In an odd way, her solitary situation suited her. She had been feeling a flagging of her energy in recent months, and a lack of mental focus. It was a comfort not to have to go through the motions of showering, getting into work clothes, making her way through hordes of people to her place of business and trying to keep her agency afloat. The government was now taking care of that for her; she felt grateful for the rest period. She ordered things on Amazon, had her meals delivered from Café Monaco, took Homer on the briefest of trips to the now-empty sidewalks, and then hastened back to her sanctuary. She tried not to think about what was going on outside her building, the deaths and the refrigerated trucks; it was too ugly for her to process. When her assistant, Trevor, called her, ostensibly to check on her welfare but really to make sure he would continue getting a paycheck, he was surprised to find her sunny and emotionally disconnected.

"Oh, I know, isn't that so sad?" she said in a distant way after he told her of the latest death toll, as if tsk-ing at a tsunami on the other side of the world. "But everything's going to be fine, you wait and see." She rejected *Tiger King* for *Mary Tyler Moore*, and watched that show for many hours. When she got to the last episode of the last season, she cried sentimentally and started over from the beginning. On Sundays, she would watch a Catholic Mass on Zoom, because the Latin gave her the comforting sensation of time travel.

After nine months, Nikki suggested by email that they try another Zoom get-together. Diane hesitated, then agreed, and Orla hosted the call. They were shocked when they saw one another. Diane had stopped coloring her hair, and the gray that was coming in made it look like she was wearing an off-white cap. Orla had put on a great deal of weight. Nikki had overcompensated by dying her hair back to black and wearing a great deal of makeup. It was not a good look on a woman her age.

"Hi!" they all cheerfully exclaimed to one another.

It was a weird call. Nikki chattered non-stop in a kind of upbeat monologue about absolutely everything that was going on at her house, from Blue Apron to the best way to buy masks and testing kits to the minutiae of life with Ray and Valentine. When she paused to take a breath, Orla would say something that seemed like a non-sequitur like, "Remember Cloris Leachman?" and then not follow through on the thought. Diane did a lot of "Uh-huh"-ing and would occasionally throw in something like, "Yeah, I saw that story," but really it was all Nikki all the time. Gordon's name was not mentioned once. It was like it was an invisible barrier that the other two couldn't breech until Nikki did, and she never breeched it. Just when Diane thought, this is ridiculous, we can't not acknowledge him, Nikki said, "Oh my gosh, look at the time! This has been fun but I have to make the kids dinner. Let's do this again! Love you!" And was gone. It was as if she knew the moment to mention Gordon had come.

The pandemic had clearly done strange things to all of them. Diane hung up wanting to feel good about being in the presence of her old friends, but instead felt annoyed at both of them. Annoyed at Nikki for monopolizing the entire conversation, and at Orla for being so off-point all the time. When Orla had talked, it was either about her dog or about some guy who was doing her horoscope and what a genius he was. Diane thought Orla was smarter than that, but hey, whatever floats your boat in a pandemic.

When Nikki hung up, she immediately plunged herself into the world of making dinner for two hungry…whatevers. She was proud that she had managed to comport herself so well on the

Zoom call, when really all she wanted to do was cry her heart out. She also constantly found herself pushing down her rage at Gordon, for having been so cavalier about a crisis that was obviously so dangerous. "You idiot!" she wanted to yell. "They told us not to travel, but *you*, you're different, aren't you? The rules are made for everybody else, right?" It was so monumentally unfair that you can't be furious at a dead man.

Orla hung up and instantly forgot that she had been on a Zoom call with her best friends.

2023

Orla didn't notice the looks that were exchanged among her four employees as she came into the agency. "Hello, all!" she sang, and went into her office to face the mass of papers on her mahogany desk. She loved that desk. She had found it at an estate sale on the east side, and it was totally worth all the trouble it took to have it trucked over to Chelsea and hauled up three flights of stairs. She let Homer out of his carrying case and he made himself comfortable on the couch.

Trevor, her twenty-five-year-old assistant, came into her office with a handful of memos, looking tense.

"Morning, Trevor! Don't you look handsome in that green sweater, is it St. Paddy's Day?"

"Uh, it's May."

"I know, honey, I was joking." She looked down at the memos. "Oh, look, the Carlsons want to book another trip! I told them they would love Jakarta. Remember them? They had lost their dear son, and I told them about the spirituality of Indonesia. I was afraid it was going to break up their marriage, you know the statistics of divorce after the loss of a child are not good. But in Jakarta they found a — what's the word? A simplicity and humble, a humble *thing* of life and death that you just don't find in other places. Understanding! I thought about sending them to Thailand, but I worry about its …you know. So close to Burma."

"Uh-huh.

"I have a couple of good friends, adorable, they teach English to Burmese migrant children in Thailand. Poor things, they escaped the military you know, the *thing*. Not my friends, the children, so they're all kind of you know, traumatized. Junta! That's the word. But this wonderful couple goes every year and - "

"Orla." Trevor cleared his throat. "I hate to bring this up again, but everyone is still waiting for their paychecks."

"Oh, I know! I'm so sorry, please tell everyone I am so sorry, but there was a glitch at payroll services. I straightened it out last night. They're going to receive their checks tomorrow."

"Really?"

"Maybe sooner. Call payroll services, they'll tell you, it was an error on their side."

Trevor's tight features relaxed. "Cool. I just, you know – Things have been kind of different since Isaac left."

"Oh, I know! Can't you just feel the cloud lifting? Between you and me, and I wouldn't say this if he were still here but now that he's gone – Isaac was really mean to me. Really mean."

Trevor looked uncomfortable. "Okay."

"He would belittle me in front of other people, other office staff. Oh, maybe you saw? Even when I first started, I think he was jealous because the clientele liked me so much more than they liked him and I was amazed – amazed! When he asked me to come on as partner, even though I was always the highest booker here. He made fun of me, right from the beginning. Well, you remember!"

"I've…only been here three years.

"I really don't think he liked me, but he realized my value to the agency. Of course, he was good with accounting and all that dry left-brain stuff. But smile from time to time, right? He was so grouchy. I don't think it's necessary to create such a tension-filled you know, in a workplace, people work better when they're happy, right? Atmosphere. Oh, by the way, Trevor, would you put a stamp on this and stick it in the mail?" Orla handed him an unsealed envelope. Trevor looked down at it.

"Texas again. Client?"

"Oh no no no. Dear friend."

Trever held the envelope uneasily. "So, tomorrow afternoon then, huh? At the latest."

Orla crossed her fingers in the air. "Scouts honor."

2025

Diane lingered outside JFK in a rental car, dearly hoping she wasn't going to have to circle another time before Nikki came out. *If all else fails, I can become an Uber driver,* she thought. Just as one of the traffic cops started walking toward her, Nikki came out wheeling her luggage.

"Nikki! Over here!"

Nikki waved and threaded her way toward Diane. As she approached, Diane noticed how thin she still was, and how her straight black hair was now a wavy salt and pepper bob. *I should have gotten my hair styled,* she thought, *and worn something nicer. Why do I always look like I'm on my way to plow the north forty?* She caught a glimpse of the pretty pink pantsuit beneath Nikki's fashionable black wool cocoon coat. *Why did she never did think to buy pink?*

"Diane! It's been too long! You look great!"

"So do you, Nick! Get in, get in! That guy's about to give me a ticket."

Remarkably, they very quickly settled into the familiar musical cadence of the friendship, although they were both somewhat on their guard. It felt much more comfortable once they got to the topic of the task at hand.

"Did you hear from the horoscope guy?"

"No. Kind of weird. That type usually snatches up their prey as fast as they can."

"Maybe he's busy conning someone else."

"I wonder how much money he got from her. People like that should go to jail for life," Nikki pronounced, and Diane silently agreed. They drove for a while. "I can't believe we're driving to a mental facility. For our little Orly."

"Maybe it's just a temporary thing. I've heard of people having psychotic snaps and then coming back."

"Yeah, that's right. Let's stay positive about this."

The intensity of the concrete city fell away and soon they were looking out the window at trees and clapboard houses. Nikki navigated on Google Maps, which delivered them to a large, innocuous-looking brick building in the middle of what seemed to be an industrial park, with "Meadowbrook Retirement" burned into a rustic-looking plank of wood imbedded on the lawn.

"Oh, good, so there's an arts and crafts class," cracked Nikki and Diane laughed. They parked and went into the building.

The environment was one of forced cheer. The wallpaper seemed to imply that rather than being in a rest home they were in the entranceway to a zoo, or a children's hospital. Tigers peeked out playfully from behind palm fronds. Zebras sported in a savannah. Monkeys hung goofily from branches. All the animals looked ecstatically happy.

"Wallpaper by Henri Rousseau," Nikki commented.

"During his LSD period," responded Diane.

At the front desk was a Nordic looking woman who reminded Nikki of Inger Stevens in some TV show she had seen years ago. Inger smiled at them professionally.

"Yes, Orla arrived on Tuesday and is still settling in. She's in the sun room right now. I'm sure she'll be delighted to see you." The nurse pointed. They followed the hallway, the jungle animals cavorting alongside them as they went, and entered what the nurse called the sun room, which must have been someone's little joke. There were very few windows, and no way for sun to get through the dense foliage outside. It was a yellow room (perhaps suggesting sun?) filled with patients, predominantly women, who all looked very much the same - grey or white-haired, semi-recumbent, listless. There were chairs and sofas galore: it could have been a furniture store. Some of the seated occupants looked up eagerly as Diane and Nikki entered, as if waiting for a performance to begin, then their gazes dimmed in mild disappointment. Others took no notice. Diane's eyes scanned the room until they landed on a heavyset dark-haired woman, younger than the others, sitting with a blanket on her lap, picking at it nervously.

"Orla?"

Orla looked up, and the multi-colored eyes confirmed it. "Who is that? I can't see without my glasses." She fumbled, not for her glasses but for the blanket her on lap, which she immediately began to fold as if she had been interrupted in the act of doing laundry.

"It's Diane!" She waited for the age-old rejoinder, "Dianasaur!" But instead, there was silence. "Diane Daly."

"Diane Daly?" Orla echoed blankly. "What are you doing here?"

"We've been searching all over for you."

"Well, you've found me! I'm here!"

"So we see. And look, Nikki's here, too."

Orla received Nikki as if meeting someone new. "Well, hello, Nicky! Don't you look nice today?"

Nikki's face was ashen. "Hi Orly," she whispered. She looked at Diane, shocked.

Orla had gained a lot of weight. It was the same sweet face, set in a totally different body. "Roly-poly" was Diane's first thought. "Morbidly obese" was Nikki's. Her legs dangled uselessly from her chair like Humpty Dumpty. Both women thought of the pixyish sprite that Orla had been as a girl and had a hard time reconciling it with this fleshy lump of a woman.

"I've been in Manhattan trying to find you," said Diane, "but no one seemed to --"

"Manhattan! Silly. I haven't lived in Manhattan in years."

"We were told you were in Roosevelt Hospital just the other day."

"No, no, that must have been someone else. I moved here years ago." Orla slapped her folded blanket back down on her lap. "What do you need? Tell me what you need. I only have a little time."

"We need… to make sure you're okay."

"Well of course I'm okay! Look at me, I'm here, aren't I?"

"And… are you happy?" asked Diane.

"Aren't you a funny person! Let's put you in the funny person section. Are you Chinese?"

"Uh, no."

"You should be Chinese."

"Okay, I'll…consider that," said Diane.

"I'm sorry, ladies, but I can't do anything for you. The phone keeps ringing and ringing, but I can't do anything for anybody."

Nikki found her voice. "Orly, we — we don't need you to do anything for us. We heard you'd had some troubles, and we thought we could --"

"No troubles! Everything's fine. I can't make anything better, so it's fine. These people are fine, they're my roommates, they're lovely."

Diane looked around at the lethargic assemblage of patients. A man in a Where's Waldo-like ski cap sitting in a wheelchair facing the wall; a mummy of a woman with a rope of spittle dangling suspensefully from her mouth; a woman in a hospital gown with the flap open in the back showing her wrinkled ass, pacing nervously; a clutch of people watching a TV game show with the sound turned off.

"Is there anything we can do? To make things better?" asked Diane.

"Do? No. No one can do anything. I'm losing my mind, so that's just what's happening!" Orla said, beaming at them brightly.

"Are you?"

"Am I what?"

"Losing your mind?"

"This is exactly where I am. I am nowhere else."

Diane cast about for a response, then thought of Orla's little pooch. "How about Homer? Does someone have him?"

"Homer? Oh, I miss Homer very much, sweet little boy."

"Where is he?"

"Back home. He's fine. He's living in the apartment."

"Living there. Alone?"

"Of course. He's a big boy; he knows the city."

Diane and Nikki exchanged a look. Neither could think of a response to this. Orla jerked her head from side to side, annoyed.

"Answer that, will you? I can't understand why no one answers that phone."

"I don't hear a —" started Diane, but Nikki suddenly grabbed her phone out of her jacket.

"Hello?... Sorry, wrong number." She put her phone back in her pocket.

"Thank you," said Orla. "But you were rude to let it ring so long."

"I'm sorry."

"You two really have to go now."

"Oh, not yet, Orly. We thought maybe we could take you for a walk, or —"

"YOU HAVE TO GO!" Orla was suddenly agitated. "I can't do anything for you. Stop asking me!"

"Orla, we're not —"

"GOOD-BYE NOW! GOOD-BYE!" Orla waved at the two of them as if they were on a ship disembarking from port. "GOOD-BYEEE!"

They turned and stumbled out of the "sun room," Nikki in tears.

"It's horrible, horrible! How did this happen? They must be giving her drugs to make her act this way."

"You think?"

"Yes! That's not Orla. They've turned her into – I don't know what! And my God, she's so fat! What are they feeding her?"

"She's only been here three days."

As they were passing through reception, Inger Stevens stopped them. "Ladies. Do you happen to know anything about the plans they have for Ms. Nevins?"

"Plans?"

"Her relatives have told me she has severely depleted funds, and I'm afraid there is a rather large payment due soon."

"But – Orla owns a business," replied Nikki. "Or anyway, she used to, and I happen to know she has a healthy retirement fund. How can her funds be depleted?"

"I'm just going by what her relatives told me."

"These relatives. Who are they?"

"Her cousins, I believe."

"Do they have her dog?" asked Diane.

"Her dog? I really don't know."

"Is there some way we can get in touch with them?" Diane pressed. "I left my number at her apartment, but no one has called me."

"I can't give you that information, but I can give them a message from you, if you want."

"Tell them we are interested in assisting with the cost of Orla's care," offered Nikki, and Diane masked her surprise at this. She didn't want to tell Nikki that, at this point in her life, she was not in a position to do such a thing, but she knew Gordon had left Nikki quite a bit of money, and was glad Nikki said this. Perhaps it might prompt a call from the cousins.

They rode in stunned silence on the ride back. Finally, Nikki spoke.

"Is it… dementia?"

"I think it must be."

"Harvey told me once that people who can't process the shock of grief go mad."

"When did he say that?"

"When I lost the baby." There was another silence.

"Harvey wasn't such a bad guy."

"No. He was okay."

"I have to return the rental car, then we can take the train to the hotel. It's the Empire, near Lincoln Center. Not very fancy —"

"Oh, let's not return the car. We can park in the city. I'll pay."

In the old days, Diane would have been jealous at the imbalance of wealth between herself and Nikki. Now, she was just grateful.

"I got us one room to share. Sorry, I guess I'm just cheap. If you want to get your own room —"

"Oh no, that will be fun. I've been by myself for so long."

They got back to the hotel and Diane showed Nikki up to their room. It was small, with wallpaper that consisted of repeating red circles. The two twin beds each had zebra striped throw pillows on them, and the rug repeated the circle motif beneath their feet. It was pretty terrible, Diane now realized.

"Perfect!" declared Nikki. She threw herself on a bed and Diane followed suit.

"Roomies. Just like the old days," said Diane.

"And look how that turned out."

Diane groaned. "Oh, no, I moved in with Doris, didn't I? What a jerk I was."

"You were, you really were," replied Nikki with a smile. "But then you weren't."

"How was rooming with Orly?"

"Fun. Strange. She told me the craziest stories about her mother."

"Yeah. Janita must have been something." They lay there in silence for a few minutes with their separate thoughts. "These cousins," Nikki finally said. "Think they're on the level?"

"You mean like, are they the reason Orly has no money?"

"Oh wow, I didn't even think of that. I never heard about any cousins."

"Me neither, but we have been out of touch."

"The doorman said they've been coming and taking stuff out of her apartment."

"Trevor, her assistant, said she was the victim of some kind of hoax."

"Maybe they're robbing her even as we speak."

"Jesus! I hope not!" They both stared at the water mark on the ceiling. Each of them thought it looked like a turkey, but neither felt it was the moment to say that.

"We still don't know how Harvey died."

"We should check the obituaries."

"Yeah, good idea."

Diane took out her laptop, opened it to a search engine. Feeling suddenly daunted at the idea of searching obituaries, she wilted. "You know what, I need to wash off Meadowbrook first."

"Understood. Mind if I use that? I need to check email and my phone's dead."

"Help yourself. See what they say on Yelp about Meadowbrook while you're at it."

While Diane showered, she wracked her brain for who else she could call to get to the bottom of this. It seemed impossible that Orla could have no money. Diane knew about her early investments in IBM and Apple, thanks to Orla's stepdad, Jack. There seemed no point in trying to trace that man; he was probably dead by now and anyway, Orla never spoke of him other than the anecdote about the stock tip. Maybe another call to Trevor? This astrologer of hers, what was his name? Swamy something. Could he have taken all her money? This is the kind of thing she would have called Gordon about; he knew about money. But Gordon was gone.

The thought of Gordon ripped at her heart, and she tried to push it away. This was about Orla, no time to grieve. And yet she grieved every day. She grieved not only for the loss of him, but for the life she could have had if she had never met him, a real life that she could acknowledge to others. She screamed at him once in one of their fights, "You took my life away from me!" But the fact was, he gave her a life that was deeper and more meaningful than she felt she deserved. When he was in California, they forgot everything and lived as a couple. They hiked the canyons, ate in little tucked away restaurants, ran on the beach together. They got into heated debates about politics and actually managed to agree to disagree without vilifying the other side, something that seemed impossible these days. Diane had only a few pictures of their life together, because she was terrified something might find its way into the wrong hands, but she didn't need pictures. She remembered it all, and reminded herself of moments often to keep it alive. As a form of comfort, just yesterday she pulled up the last email Gordon ever wrote to her. She supposed it was from the hospital.

"I love you. Don't let the bad guys get you down. Take care of Nikki."

Gordon was always simple and direct. Even in emails it was more like he was texting, but she could read the feeling behind the lines.

Suddenly Diane froze. *Even in emails.*

Nikki was on Diane's laptop right now, checking her email. Which meant she had to log out of Diane's email.

Holy shit. No.

Diane turned off the water, grabbed up a towel and threw the door open, to see Nikki sitting very still, staring at Diane's laptop. Then she turned to look at Diane.

"I can't open it without your password."

"I thought I put the password in."

"No. You didn't." Nikki closed the laptop, put it aside, and lay back again on her bed. "God, I'm exhausted. Long flight."

Diane got dressed, puzzled. She was sure she had unlocked her laptop. Hadn't she started looking for obituaries? Seeing Nikki lying on the bed with her eyes closed, Diane hesitantly lay down on the other bed. Was Nikki going to sleep? Diane could understand it if she was. The drive had been long, the visit with Orla upsetting….and Diane hadn't really gotten over jet-lag herself. Her eyes started to drift closed….

"You didn't speak at Gordon's memorial." Diane's eyes popped back open.

"What?"

"Gordon's memorial. They asked if anyone wanted to say anything, and you just sat there."

"Well, I mean — It wasn't my place. I didn't think I —"

"Didn't think you knew him well enough?"

Diane heard the edge in Nikki's voice, and her heart started to pound. Nikki had seen the email; Diane was sure of it. This was the moment. Diane rolled on her side to face her. "Nikki, I've been trying for so long to find a way —"

Nikki cut her off. "You know, Mimi had this teacher when she was about twelve. She was still Mimi then, so I can call her that, right?"

Diane nodded, unsure about that and mystified at the shift in the conversation.

"Mimi had a lot of anxiety issues at that time and this teacher, Barry — all the kids called the teachers by their first names, a progressive school, you know. Barry took an interest in her. At an

Open House night, we discussed the things that might be holding her back, and Barry felt that she was having identity issues. He was very intuitive, Barry, he recognized the situation way before anyone else did. He was a history teacher, and he was absolutely an encyclopedia of knowledge on the building of America; how it came to be, what it stood for. I'm sure he's horrified at what's going on now. He was actually friends with Howard Zinn, you know Howard Zinn? The American history guy?"

Diane was stymied. Where was Nikki going with this?

"Anyway, we went out to lunch to discuss Mimi further, and I'm just going to cut to the chase here. We had an affair."

"Oh!"

"Gordon and I had been just going through the motions of being married for years, and I was starved for affection, so Barry and I had – well, it was more than an affair. I fell deeply in love with him. Barry was everything I had been looking for in a man; educated, erudite, kind and caring. He had everything that Gordon didn't, except for one thing: Money. He was a teacher, for God's sake, and even at a private school teachers don't make much. He knew I was unhappy; he wanted me to leave Gordon. He wanted to get married, and believe me I thought about it. I thought about it a lot."

She rolled over and looked at Diane intently. "It would have solved a lot of problems, you know?"

Diane felt pinned by her gaze. She nodded.

Nikki rolled onto her back and looked reflectively at the ceiling. "But it just felt so….messy. I could see the complications that lay ahead. A brutal divorce. A traumatized child. Moving. I loved my house, and no way Gordon would have let me keep it -- He built it himself, for God's sake. The disapproval of my parents, that's a big one. I've always been their golden child; they would have been horrified. And I won't lie; I liked my standing in the community. As a couple, we were a big deal in that small city, always on the society page. Leaving Gordon, it just didn't make sense on paper, you know? I stalled for quite some time, trying to make the affair last as long as it could before Barry realized the answer was no. But he was no fool. He saw I was a dead-end street and eventually found someone else. I let this handsome, educated, cultivated man who clearly loved me out of my life, so that I could continue with my empty marriage. I wonder how many women do that?" Nikki rubbed her forehead, as if trying to erase something. "Then my father died, followed by Mother. And then, Gordon." Nikki glanced quickly at Diane, then back at the ceiling. "Ray came back for the pandemic, but they're back in Oregon now. I'm all alone, and the house is too big, and now I wonder, what the hell was I thinking back then? You and Orly used to always say I knew how to pivot. How did I miss the biggest pivot of all? I guess I just lost my nerve."

Diane lay beside Nikki, trying to process this flood of information. Nikki had had someone else, someone she loved. Someone she wanted to leave Gordon for. Diane thought back to the day, long ago, when Orla advised her to stop torturing herself about Gordon.

"Did Orla know about this?"

"Sure. Orla knew everything. Frequently she knew things before I even told her. Funny how she did that, huh?"

Diane tried to imagine the effort it must have been for Orla to keep both of their secrets, and yet somehow hold them all together as friends. She looked at Nikki, staring at the ceiling, lost in her memories. It had been at least ten years since they'd been in one another's company physically. Nikki looked smaller, frailer, and her beautiful hair was now more white than black, but her delicate face was still lovely. Diane could still see the girl within - and that girl was just as screwed up as Diane! How wonderful! Diane felt a sudden rush of love toward her friend.

As if sensing the flood of emotion heading her way, Nikki parried with a change of tone. "Barry is still alive, of course. Married with three children. He looks very happy on Facebook, so that's fabulous."

"I'm so sorry, Nick."

"Not any sorrier than I am. Orla was right, as usual. You should have gotten Gordon."

"What? She didn't say that."

"Diane." Nikki's tone said cut the shit. "She didn't have to."

Now it was out there. The words were said, there was nothing to do but acknowledge it.

Diane swallowed. "So, you've always ...known?"

A kind of laugh escaped Nikki, and Diane felt like it was that moment in a crime drama when the perp realizes they've blown it by saying too much. "Not really. Yes, and no. I thought you maybe had a brief thing, that it was over. I thought there were others. But, it's always been you, hasn't it?"

"I don't know, to be honest. Do you hate me?" Nikki was silent, and Diane's stomach dropped.

"No. Maybe I hated you for a while. Then I thought, you might be the reason Gordon wasn't leaving me. That's right, isn't it? You wouldn't let him?" Almost imperceptibly, Diane nodded. "Very noble, Diane." Nikki's voice had that edge again.

"I wasn't trying to be noble."

"What were you trying to be? A good friend?"

Diane winced. "I think you do hate me."

"Yeah. Maybe I do, a little. Because you know what? Instead of all the moral agonizing I'm sure you indulged yourself in, you should have just said yes, Di. You should have put us both out of our misery."

The thought electrified Diane. She should have said yes? All these years, she thought she was protecting Nikki. *She should have said yes?*

"Nikki, I —"

Her cell phone rang. Diane looked at the readout. "It's a 212 number. Might be Orla's cousin."

"Take it."

"Nikki, this is a big conversation, shouldn't we - "

"Later. Take it. Could be important."

Reluctantly, Diane answered the phone. "Hello?"

"Is this Diane Daly?" asked the woman on the phone. "This is Suzanne Emerson, Orla's cousin."

At Diane's nod, Nikki rose and went into the bathroom. Splashing water on her face, Nikki studied herself in the mirror. So there it was, a confirmation of what she had suspected for so long. Why, in spite of that, did she feel something like surprise? Her first inklings of suspicion had been ignited all those years ago in Italy. The way Diane and Gordon were arguing that night, it just sounded so....marital. But at the time, Nikki had been so lost in her grief about the miscarriage, she hadn't really cared what else was going on. She had felt at the time as if she wasn't really there, like the others were interacting with her avatar. Years later, when she found that text — so that was Diane, too? Nikki almost laughed, remembering how she had called the mystery woman a skank. No wonder Diane was so weird during her visit! At the time, Nikki had suspected Gordon was with someone else, a co-worker maybe. It had seemed unlikely anything was going on with Diane when they lived in different cities.

But then, that time Mimi announced that she was now Ray, and Diane and Gordon said the exact same thing about it, verbatim. Nikki was struck by it at the time, and had strange dreams. She could have confronted Gordon then. She could have confronted Diane, for that matter. Why didn't she?

Easy. Because she didn't want the answer.

She didn't want the proof positive that she had just received on Diane's laptop. The status quo was much more comfortable, not because she was so in love with Gordon, but because she was afraid of what the future would look like without him. She wanted the security of Gordon. She *needed* that security. She had married him out of fear after the AIDS scare, and that fear of the outside world had never really gone away. That's why she hadn't married Barry, she supposed. Fear. It had driven so many of her decisions in her life. Nikki ran her fingers through her hair, tugging at her scalp as if to release tension. Was it possible, at her age, to stop letting fear guide her actions?

Diane was finishing up the call as Nikki emerged from the bathroom. The tone of the room was now completely different; Diane was in business mode. "Okay," she said, hanging up. "She's at

Orla's apartment right now gathering stuff to take back to Meadowbrook."

"Does she sound legit?"

"I think so. She wants to talk with us, but she has to leave soon. Shall we run over there? Or we could grab a cab."

"Don't be silly, it's only a few blocks. Let's hoof it!"

"Nikki. I just want to say --- I love you. You're my best friend, and - "

"Okay, no time for that now. Let's go!"

The two women threw on their jackets and speed-walked the five blocks to Orla's apartment, each of them thinking a) How glad they were to have this finally out in the open, and b) How much easier it used to be to walk that fast.

They arrived in front of Orla's building huffing and puffing, each making the effort to look less winded than she was. Apollo buzzed them into the lobby and Nikki pushed 14 on the elevator, for what they suspected was going to be the very last time.

2024

Orla was in Harvey's apartment one Saturday morning, gazing at the river. It was a warm day for early March, and though she admired the white translucent curtains she had bought to frame the windows, she was longing to open one of them to feel the first inklings of spring, before the inevitable next round of snow plunged them back into winter. The window frame had been painted over many times since the building was first built in the 1890's, and now it required someone with herculean strength to get it open. Why was New York so filled with stuck windows? She remembered Diane's bedroom window in the Heavenly Hellhole; they had never done anything about that, mainly because Diane worried someone would climb up the fire escape and rob her. She thought of her own solitary window. A high rise had gone up next to her building, erasing even the small slice of view she had had, so it never seemed worth it to open that window. This time would be different.

"I'm going to unstick one of these windows!" she exclaimed to Harvey.

"Why?"

"So we can get some fresh air."

"The bathroom window opens fine."

"The bathroom window has a view of the airshaft."

Harvey sighed. "Why must we improve things? Why is mankind not capable of just taking things the way they are and living peacefully with them?"

"Harvey, when they first built this building, the people had windows that opened. I am just trying to undo the damage done by mankind to its original creation."

Harvey shrugged. "Okay. Suit yourself."

She went to a hardware store and, after a very nice chat with the Hispanic salesman whose mother had just had her appendix out and didn't really understand him, purchased some paint remover, a putty knife and some talcum powder.

Lugging it back to the apartment was more difficult than she had anticipated. She had gained quite a bit of weight during the pandemic, and taken little of it off since. By the time she got upstairs with it all, she had to take a nap. When she woke up, she thought at first that she was in her own apartment, but then realized she was at Harvey's and remembered that he was at the library writing a treatise on somebody, who was it again? When she stumbled out into the living room, she saw her purchases and remembered her task.

She worked on it all day Saturday, and it was a messy business. The chemical paint remover had a noxious smell that made her light-headed, and the ensuing messy sludge was a chore to dispose of; she had to drag messy newspapers filled with the stuff into the garbage can in the kitchen. But finally, Orla divested one of the windows of most of its paint and, to her delight, the window opened! Victory!

Harvey came home to find Orla sitting by the open window in a rocker, gazing out happily.

"Harvey! Can you smell the river?"

"All I smell is toxic chemicals. What are all these stains on the floor?"

"They'll go away. Isn't this window beautiful now?"

Harvey shrugged. "Beauty is subjective. It may have been beautiful before. The nature of things in themselves is unknowable to us."

"How is your treatise going?"

Harvey sighed. "I was writing about Kant's effort to draw a distinction between intuition and objective reality and I suddenly thought, why am I bothering with this? A hundred years from now, will anyone care about the human mind's ability to abstract? Will we even be here at all?"

"You're in a gloomy mood."

"I am. Let's go to your place."

But Orla didn't like having people at her place; it was a bit too cluttered since the pandemic. She had thought Harvey would take more delight in the success of her efforts in his apartment, but it was hard to please him lately. He had long ago dropped the sartorial splendor of their reunion and had retreated into his old habit of wearing the same jeans and tee shirt day after day. He was also extremely preoccupied with the implications of Artificial Intelligence. He revived the topic again as they sat on the stained floor eating the dinner Orla had ordered up.

"These technology whiz kids, they aren't ethicists; they're not thinking through the implications of what they are doing."

"What are they doing?" asked Orla, munching fries.

"They're leading us to oblivion. It's like Oppenheimer, only worse."

"Remind me?"

"Oppenheimer. He invented the bomb."

"Oh right, I saw that. He was so cute, those big eyes. I heard he was Irish."

Harvey barely heard. "These people are so enchanted with the cleverness of their own creations, they don't see what it's doing to the human race. We are about to become extraneous, Orla. Walking the planet with no function other than to eat and shit."

"Harvey. Dinner."

"Sorry, but it's true."

"What if AI is actually good? What if it's trying to teach us something about ourselves that we never knew before?'

"AI is not trying to teach us anything. It is completely oblivious to anything but its own needs."

"You don't know that. Maybe there's something beyond all this, our real selves?"

"What do you mean, our real selves?"

"Don't you get the feeling sometimes that none of this is real? That there's a greater reality beyond this picnic on this floor?"

"Orla, your mother gave you too many drugs at Woodstock."

"She didn't go to Woodstock."

"You can't keep blinding yourself with happy homilies. Mankind is in imminent peril."

This became Harvey's clarion cry. He vitally needed people to see the dangers of a technology that was outpacing any moral constraints. He abandoned his treatise on Emanuel Kant and wrote a long article on the subject of the oblivion he anticipated for mankind. He sent it to Philosophy Now, but they claimed to have already printed a similar article. Harvey read the "similar article" and found it far too even-handed, in fact he was deeply suspicious it was written by AI itself. There was no other side of this issue, Harvey was convinced. The way things were going, the future of civilization was not going to be biological.

Harvey bought himself a typewriter, so as not to be invaded by the virus of AI. He protested the introduction of the Ring

Doorbell to the entrance of his building, driving the other tenants mad with his rants. Every time a food delivery vehicle passed him on the sidewalk, he kicked it. He had enjoyed the ability to research facts on his phone, but the minute it said to him, "Did you mean to write A? Didn't you really mean to write B?" Harvey threw his phone away. This made it difficult for Orla to get hold of Harvey to arrange plans, so she started spending more and more time at his place, and the repercussions she feared almost immediately kicked in. Harvey's obsession with the implications of AI, what she considered his paranoia, were far worse than any of his diatribes about philosophers. She couldn't even follow it after a while.

"People will get it under control, Harvey, I know they will."

"It uncontrollable already. It's irreversible. The Singularity is not near, it is here!"

"You have to stop with this, you're giving me a headache."

But he didn't stop. "We are nothing, you and I. Nothing! We are remnants of an earlier civilization, still walking the planet like Zombies."

Finally, Orla could take no more. "Enough! I'm going home. If you want me, send up a smoke signal!"

Orla had her own problems. She had developed a headache ever since the day in March she had spent with those toxic chemicals, and it still hadn't gone away by July. In addition, there were problems at work. Her employees were starting to look at her distrustfully, and she didn't know why. Also, her dog, Homer, was behaving aggressively; when she fed him, he wolfed his food down as if he hadn't been fed in days. Even her doorman, Apollo, seemed wary of her when she tried to engage him in conversation, which was inexplicable as she thought they were friends.

Her one lifeline was Sunjay, who seemed to understand all. Their phone conversations on What's App gave her a great deal of comfort. He sent her reams and reams of astrological forecasts, and thankfully they were almost always positive, reassuring her that she was on the right track if she only stayed true to her dreams. At this point, Orla's dreams were simple. She wanted a happy environment at work and a happy Harvey to enjoy life with. She wanted this headache to go away, and she wanted to get a good night's sleep every once in a while, a commodity that was becoming harder and harder to attain.

Unlike Harvey, Orla enjoyed the internet. She liked finding out things she never knew before, like the fact that some American businessmen were planning on knocking down the Great Wall of China and putting up a hotel, and the distinct possibility that aliens are creating crop circles to communicate with us.

One day, she logged onto her laptop and received some amazing news. She wanted to tell Harvey, but as he was unreachable by phone, she called Sunjay.

"Sunjay, you will never guess what has happened! I've won the lottery!"

"Indeed? That is wonderful news, Miss Orla. How much did you win?"

"Three hundred and sixty-five thousand dollars!"

"Oh, my goodness! That is very exciting!"

"I know! Now the travel agency can go on forever! I don't even remember entering, but then my memory isn't what it used to be."

"How did you find out?"

"I got an email from the officials who run the lottery. They've been searching for me for months, and the expiration date on the claim was just about to run out, and finally they found me. Can you believe my good luck?"

Sunjay could not. "Miss Orla, did you respond to this email?"

"Of course!"

"What did you say?"

"I said, here I am! You've found me!"

"And what did they say?"

"Well, they asked for my phone number, so of course I gave it to them. And they were just lovely people – the woman was very excited for me – and we worked out a way for them to wire me the money right away."

"Oh no. Oh Miss Orla, in what way did you work it out?"

"It was simple, really. I just gave them my bank routing number and my account number and oh yes my password -- "

"Oh no, no, no."

Orla had never heard Sunjay sound this negative before. "What do you mean?"

"How much money do you have in this account?"

"Well, I don't know exactly. It's my business account, so it has the company assets in it. And it's connected to my personal - "

"Miss Orla, I need you to hang up right now and call your bank. Tell them you have been the victim of a scam and tell them to stop any activity on your account."

"Sunjay! I most certainly will not. You didn't talk to these people, I know when people are good."

"No, Miss Orla, you do not. You think I am good."

"You are good!"

"You have been lied to, and you need to do something about it right away! I'm hanging up now, Miss Orla. Promise me you will call your bank immediately!"

Orla hung up feeling extremely confused. Sunjay was usually so sunny and encouraging; why was he being so negative? She lay down on the bed, intending to do a few of the deep breathing exercises she had learned at Esalen to calm her spirit, but instead she fell asleep again. When she awoke, she thought for a minute she was in Greece, because a breeze was blowing in through her window that carried the smell of olive trees, and it was so intoxicating. Then she realized it was actually her olive oil hand lotion, which had spilled onto her bedside table. Still, Greece had been so lovely. That boy with the goat, and the gondoliers who sang… no, wait, that was Venice. And they really sang! The guide book said they wouldn't, but…and, oh, the canals, so mysterious. The room in her pensione looked right over a canal, and the slap of the water was so comforting as she lay in bed at night ….Maybe one of the gondoliers will make that low sound with his voice now, the one that tells the other gondoliers he's nearby, it sounds a little like, "Ahoy!" Is he going to?….Maybe. Maybe not….But no, wait, she wasn't in Venice, how silly, she was in her apartment, her apartment in New York, and something unpleasant had happened. What was it? And why did it make her fall asleep? Was she turning into her mother? This thought struck Orla with great force.

"Oh! Maybe now I understand Mommy!" Orla felt joyous at the notion, because her mother had been so difficult, really, she had to acknowledge that, yet with this sudden sharp insight, Orla felt that she could find her way to forgiveness. Yes! She was just now filled with such love for Janita, her beautiful, beautiful mother. Maybe she should call her now, and tell her about her revelation? Or no, Mommy didn't like being awakened….She should tell Harvey! Harvey would be so interested!

Orla dressed, put a leash on the excited Homer, and led him up through Riverside Park. She enjoyed walking by the wide flowing river; water always gave her the relaxing feeling that everything was going to be all right. But even with her new insight into Janita......What was that insight again? Oh, just a minute.... And the flowing river, so inexorable, like a mantra....Sunjay, what was it he had said? A scam? That couldn't be. The woman on the phone sounded so happy for her. Why would she lie about something like this? Maybe Sunjay was just having a bad day. Yes, that must have been it. Just....let the river flow and all will be well....

Orla turned right and walked east on 83rd street. There seemed to be some kind of police activity happening on Riverside Drive. As she drew nearer, she saw that a crowd had gathered in front of Harvey's building. A woman covered her child's eyes as she rushed him past the yellow tape that the police were putting up. Orla moved closer, and saw a figure on the ground covered with a sheet. Someone in the crowd pointed upward, and Orla looked up to see what he was pointing at.

It was a wide-open window on the top floor of the building. A pretty white diaphanous curtain, the one Orla had recently bought to bring cheer into the room, flapped gently out the window in the breeze.

2025

Suzanne Emerson opened her door to Diane and Nikki. Suzanne was a pleasant looking woman of perhaps fifty who looked nothing like Orla; tallish, with light brown hair and blue eyes that peered out from behind horn-rimmed glasses. She was holding a cardboard box.

"I'm just grabbing up a few things to bring back to Meadowbrook. Come on in, if you can take it. I'll only be a minute." The two women stepped into the apartment.

First, there was the stench: Elizabeth Taylor's White Diamonds meets dog shit. Then there was the chaos: a haphazard array of travel magazines, clothing; appliances, open cans of dog food, unopened QVC boxes, record albums, videos, stacks of horoscope predictions, smeared food plates, bottles of wine, stuffed animals, plastic bags, and books. If they had been clearing the apartment out, it seemed they had barely made a dent.

Suzanne hurriedly rummaged through a chest of drawers. "Ah! Here it is. Her friends at church want Orla to have this picture of her singing in the choir at last year's Christmas concert. They're hoping it might prompt a memory."

Suzanne showed them the picture; Orla, perhaps a few years back, dressed in a spangly black sweater with festive red trim, her mouth open in a joyful 0, singing beside a bunch of other middle-aged men and women. Someone, maybe Orla, had given it a white plastic Christmas tree bordered frame.

"Okay, let's get out of here. Sorry to subject you to all this. Shall we go down to the restaurant and talk?" Speechless, Diane and Nikki followed her to the elevator.

"We were puzzled when she didn't come to our place for Christmas," Suzanne continued as they waited for the elevator. "She had been coming every year, but the pandemic disrupted that, and then when things got back to normal, we still didn't hear from her much. We thought for sure she'd come for Christmas this year, but she didn't. I guess that should have been our first clue."

The elevator finally arrived. The three of them stood in it silently for a moment, trying not to size one another up too obviously.

"How are you related to Orla, Suzanne?" Nikki asked.

"My father was Orla's uncle, although they never knew each other. Janita and my dad were estranged since they were young because Janita was disowned by her parents, but he used to speak fondly of their early years together. I don't know why they never reunited as adults. About twelve years ago we reached out to Orla. She seemed grateful to know us, and we started getting together. She was so amazingly cool and fun. We were all really impressed that she had made good in the Big City."

Diane and Nikki obediently followed Suzanne into Café Monaco as if it were Suzanne's hangout and they hadn't dined at the restaurant themselves scores of times over the years. It had the same name, much the same décor, but all new faces.

"So, you're Diane?" Suzanne asked as they took their table. "You're married to the real estate tycoon?"

"No, that would be me, "said Nikki calmly. "I'm Nikki."

"Nikki, right! The Hollywood writer."

"No, that's me." Diane and Nikki laughed uneasily.

"Sorry! Orla talked about the great times you three had doing – was it "Fiddler on the Roof? And the trips you all took together. It all sounded so great."

"I wish we could say we heard about you, but we didn't think Orly had any relatives," Nikki said.

"Orly. That's a cute nickname. Yes, we live in a little town in Connecticut no one's ever heard of. We'd come into town every now and then, my sister and I, and Orla would take us out to dinner and a Broadway show. It felt so glamorous! But that was five or six years ago now. Then, things changed."

"When did you first know something was wrong?" asked Diane.

"She called me up one day, and she sounded very strange, not like herself. You know, Orla's always been so easy-going and positive, at least in the time we knew her. On the phone that day, she was angry, and fearful. She said there were people who were trying to take things from her. When I asked her what people and what things, she got mysterious about it all. Said I would know when they called me, and not to listen to a word they said. She was very articulate, it's just, she didn't make sense."

"Right."

"I knew something was wrong, so I drove into the city without telling Orla I was coming. She opened her door just a tiny bit, and ladies, she did not look good. Pasty and unhealthy, you know? She told me she couldn't let me in because of the dog. I couldn't hear a dog, but told her I would meet her down here in the restaurant. I came down and waited, and called, and waited. I was about to go up again when she appeared. I can't begin to describe how she looked. Her clothing was stained, her hair looked like she hadn't washed it in weeks. And… I'm sorry, but the smell. She said that she was fine, that she was sorry if she had alarmed me, that everything was okay now and I should go home. Then she got up and left the restaurant." Suzanne pressed her fingers to her lips, shook her head. "I didn't know what to do. Everything was so clearly not fine."

"No."

"We knew very little about Orla. We had only just made her acquaintance twelve years ago, and saw her infrequently. She talked about you two, but she never gave us your full names. I would have called, if I'd known. Because the next thing that happened, she was in a bank demanding money that she didn't have, and I guess she got hysterical and bit a security guard."

"Bit him? Oh my God!"

"The next day Social Services appeared at her door. She was hostile to them, apparently. Violent, according to them. The police finally came and took her to Roosevelt."

Diane and Nikki were stunned. "My God. This feels like you're talking about someone else."

"I think she is someone else now, honestly. They gave her a brain scan. It's full-blown dementia." The three of them lowered their gaze to the tablecloth, as if seeking solace there.

"The nurse at Meadowbrook told us Orla didn't have any money," Nikki finally said. "What happened?"

"She was the victim of fraud."

"That Swamy horoscope guy!"

"He was only the tip of the iceberg. At least she had something to show for the money she sent him, reems and reems of horoscopes. Don't get me wrong, she sent this guy Sunjay hundreds of dollars, maybe thousands. But the big money went to other scams she fell for. She wrote enormous checks to strangers, and gave away her banking information to at least two other con artists."

"Oh, no."

"Why the banks don't notice when this kind of thing is going on and stop it is beyond me. They should have a special unit for elder fraud."

Diane and Nikki looked at each other with the same thought: *We're elders now.*

"We've got to get some of that money back," said Nikki. "Surely, we can track down this Swamy guy."

"My sister Lily did that. His name is Sunjay Deshpande. Came here from India as a 13-year-old with just his father. Mother deceased, apparently. He got his citizenship at 21, but before that he was kicked out of a number of high schools and was on a government list for some vague offense. A few months ago, they found him in a nightclub and deported him."

"Good."

"Nikki! Suzanne said was a citizen."

"Who cares? He was in a nightclub, spending her money. He was a bad guy, deport him with all the other criminals!"

The other two didn't respond to this, but Nikki could feel that she had strayed into controversial territory. She turned to Suzanne. "Did you ever meet her boyfriend, Harvey?"

"Once. He was … interesting. He came for Christmas a couple of years ago. Harvey died recently, did you know that?"

"Yes, we heard. Do you know how it happened?"

"Jumped out a fourth story window."

"Oh my God!" Diane and Nikki said this simultaneously.

"My theory is, that's what triggered Orla's full-scale dementia. Trauma can do that, I'm told. God. Sorry to dump all of this on you."

"No! We wanted to know. We've been looking for the answers, I'm glad you called," said Diane. "And what about her dog, Homer? Where is he?"

"That's a sad story. When Social Services finally paid a visit, the poor thing was almost dead from starvation and dehydration."

"Oh no. They didn't euthanize him, did they?"

"No. Lily took him, but he's got a lot of problems. I'm not sure what we're going to do with him."

"I'll take him," said Diane firmly.

"Really? You should probably see him first. He's very needy."

"That's fine. I'll take him."

"And I want to help financially, if you'll let me," said Nikki. "We can't let Orla get moved to a state facility."

Suzanne put her cup down on her saucer and sighed in relief. "I am so happy to hear you say that. We've been worried to death, Lily and I. We're both school teachers, we just don't have the resources. And with the way the country is going.... I mean, it's all so horrible, what's happening now."

"Tell me about it," replied Nikki. "I can't imagine the idiots who voted for that guy."

Girl still knew how to pivot.

The next day, Diane and Nikki went back to Meadowbrook and had a talk with the Financial Director.

"She's having a pretty good day today," said the woman, once they had taken care of business. "She's in her room right now, if you'd like to talk to her." Diane and Nikki followed the director down the hall until she paused in front of an open door.

Orla was alone in the room, sitting in a chair facing the window, and appeared to be talking to someone either outside the window or within the window itself. The room was very spartan; just a bed, the chair, a small chest of drawers and a bulletin board with some "Get Well" cards posted on it.

"Orla, visitors!" said the director with bright authority.

Orla turned and looked at them. Diane was prepared to introduce herself again.

"Diane! Nikki! What are you doing here?" Orla exclaimed.

Nikki sighed in relief. "We just happened to be in town, and thought we'd drop in," said Diane.

"That is so sweet! Wow. You've both gotten so old!"

Diane and Nikki looked at one another and laughed. "Yes! Yes, we have!" said Nikki. "But you look just the same."

"It's my good genes," said Orla proudly.

"You seem to be doing really well today, Orly!"

"I am, I am!" Orla turned to include her window friend in the conversation. "These are my friends Nikki and Diane. They have come to get me, and I'll tell you what..." She turned back to her two friends with a conspiratorial wink. "I am ready for my Great Escape."

Diane looked down at the little red pill in her hand. She'd been carrying that capsule around with her like a talisman ever since she found it behind the Renoir print, like a spy who might need to swallow it if captured by the enemy. Diane wasn't sure who the enemy was now. Time, probably. She walked to her window, still holding the pill, and gazed out at a tall row of palm trees momentarily standing at attention in the still afternoon air, awaiting the next breeze to ruffle their fronds.

Ten days ago, the loneliness of Diane's life had gotten her to the point where she saw no reason to continue. Gordon being gone rendered Diane unable to write, since nothing written could be read aloud to him. She would never hear his laugh again, or see him shake his head and say, "How do you come up with this stuff?" Anyway, the most important parts of her life could never be written about, so what was the point? It had seemed like a fitting way to end it all, this little pill, like Anna Karenina, cast to the edges of society, throwing herself in front of the train to atone for her sins.

True, the parallels between Diane and Anna weren't exactly airtight. This wasn't nineteenth century Russia; no one had cast her out and, unlike Vronski, Gordon had loved her to the end. Remarkably, almost weirdly, she and Nikki were still friends, and she had not been punished for her sins. In fact, against all odds she had gotten an email this morning; a major publisher wanted to publish her Queen Margaret book. It seemed wrong; it went against everything Diane had read in western literature about what happens to "fallen women" and adulterers.

Of course, most of those stories were written by men.

Ten days ago, Diane had been on the verge of swallowing the pill when the alert had sounded to evacuate her home. Suddenly, her final act had a new scene written into it, which took the wind out of her sails a bit. While she waited it out in a motel, the fires did incredible, breathtaking damage. People died; lives were changed forever. It could have been her own moment of karmic punishment and yet, once again, it wasn't. Her home was safe - what obscene luck. Now she felt like Chekhov's Uncle Vanya, who couldn't even kill himself successfully.

Diane stared down at the capsule. Who knows? It might have lost all its properties after all this time. The person who sold it to her mother might have just given her a Tylenol; that's what it looked like. A crazy little part of Diane was tempted to swallow it, like a pill version of Russian roulette, to see what would happen, but there was always the chance she would survive as a blithering idiot with half a brain and be a drain on all society. That would be a little too ironic for her.

Anyway, there was currently a little white Maltese pup sitting on her lap, looking up at her with quivering anxiety. No; the time for drastic measures had passed. She went to the bathroom and flushed the pill down the toilet.

Nikki had made arrangements with Orla's cousins and the people at Meadowbrook to have her moved to one of Gordon's senior living centers. "Gotta take care of our golden princess, right?" Nikki had declared, and Diane had readily agreed. She and Nikki did a little research and chose the one in Santa Barbara. Nikki decided to fund the conversion of one of its wings into a memory care unit. It wasn't quite finished yet, but would be soon, and at that point Nikki would fly out with Orla for her final (or perhaps penultimate would be a better word) Great Escape. Diane planned to meet the flight, so the three of them could drive up together.

"Santa Barbara is beautiful," Nikki had said on the phone. "I think I might buy a place there myself. I'm pretty much over Colorado."

"You know what, Nick? I may join you."

"Diane, that's a great idea! Just what Santa Barbara needs, right? Three more widows."

Diane's breath caught; Nikki had just called her a widow. She was deeply moved, but knew how Nikki hated sentimentalism, so she made an effort to match her tone.

"Yeah, little known fact: Tevye's daughters ended up in a rest home in Santa Barbara."

"Is that so? You know, I think I read that somewhere." Without missing a beat, Nikki started to sing the tune to "Anatevka."

"Santa Bar-bra, Santa Bar-bra."

So quick on the uptake; this is why Diane loved Nikki. She joined in.

"Underworked, Overfed Santa Bar-bra." And they laughed. Because if there's one thing they learned from being in "Fiddler on the Roof:" You laugh, so as not to cry.

They still weren't letting people into the fire zone, but you could go down to the beach on a brief stretch of the Pacific Coast Highway. Diane visited the beach far too seldom, considering how close it was. She decided it was time to do that now.

It was getting on for sunset, and a few powdery clouds appeared to be arranging themselves nicely before the sun for a golden display. Diane parked and carried Homer, who was too skittish for a leash but desperate for female comfort, down the long boardwalk to the waterfront.

The tide was going down. The sand gleamed with the late afternoon refractions of golden light. Diane tucked Homer beneath her sweatshirt against her skin, and he relaxed instantly. Sitting on a bench at the end of the boardwalk, she awaited the show that was about to begin.

A woman was sitting on a bath towel in the sand about thirty feet diagonally in front of Diane. She had a backpack beside her and, gazing out at the horizon with the wind whipping her honey-colored hair here and there, she appeared to be deep in thought. Diane recognized the sweater she had on, rose colored with embroidered flowers at the neckline. It looked nice on her. Diane intended to go over to the woman and find out how she was doing, ask after her daughter, maybe even offer her a place to stay.

But that would be later. For the moment, all she wanted to do was watch the sun go down.

EPILOGUE

"Miss Orla! Did you read the horoscope I sent?"

"I did, Sunjay, it was amazing! It predicted everything that was going to happen to me this week, just the way it happened. You really are a marvel!"

"Thank you, Miss Orla, you are very sweet. I, uh… I think I'm falling in love with you."

"Oh, isn't that nice? But the voice is the organ of the soul, Sunjay, and though your voice is very beautiful, I can tell you are not falling in love. You do, however, deeply need to be loved yourself, so I suggest you get out of your house and meet someone. Go to a night club."

"A nightclub? I don't go to those places."

"Why not? It could change your life! Or travel! You might meet your grand passion!"

"I'll think about it."

"Do! Get out of Mumbai and see the world."

"I am in Houston, Miss Orla."

"I have to go now. This has been so wonderful. Good-bye!"

Photo by Daniel Reichert

Catherine Butterfield began her career as an actress in regional theatre. Her first play, "Joined at the Head," launched her as a New York playwright and led to the writing of nine other published and produced plays. Her first novel, "The Serpent and the Rose," is a work of historical fiction about Marguerite de Valois and her lifelong battle with her mother, Catherine de Medici..

Catherine has written and produced for TV and film and has a YouTube channel with her many short films on it. She and her husband divide their time between California and Ireland.

ACKNOWLEDGMENTS

I would like to thank the girlfriends and sisters in my life over the years who have inspired the writing of this book. You know who you are; and if you don't, that's okay. My friends become more valuable to me with every passing year.

Special thanks to Jed Seidel and Gilbert Cole for their great notes and enthusiastic support, attention to detail and wonderfully specific notes. Thanks also to my early readers Shelia Zahm, Laura Ekstrand, Mikaela Kafka, Deborah Strang, Ellen Dolan, and Carolyn Mignini for valuable feedback. Thanks to Liz Georges, with whom I experienced a missing friend incident that inspired this book, and to Lori Zelkind for expert cover consultation. Love and gratitude to my sister, Beth Butterfield, for her smarts, support, and often a great new idea.

As always, to my husband, Ron West, for his indulgence, constant love, good advice, and the provision of a laugh or two just when I need it.

And lastly, to Niall Williams, who has said many wise things, but the one that was my guiding light with this book is the reminder that action must always spring from character.